Devil in Our Hearts

A STEAMY HISTORICAL ROMANCE

LIZZIE JENKS

WHEEL HORSE PRESS

Copyright © 2023 by Lizzie Jenks

All rights reserved.

No part of this publication may be reproduced, distributed, or transmitted in any form or by any means, including photocopying, recording, or other electronic or mechanical methods, without the prior written permission of the publisher, except as permitted by U.S. copyright law.

The story, all names, characters, and incidents portrayed in this production are fictitious. No identification with actual persons (living or deceased), places, buildings, and products is intended or should be inferred.

ISBN eBook: 978-1-960402-00-4
ISBN Print: 978-1-960402-01-1

Wheel Horse Press

Book Cover by Emily's World of Design

Editing by Falcon Faerie Fiction

First edition 2023

LizzieJenks.com

Acknowledgements

The first draft of this novel was written in the Romance Writers of America Pen 2 Paper program, for which I am eternally grateful, and I could never have gotten it finished without the wonderful ladies of the FLFLS, including a super-insightful beta read by Andrée Cusson.

The lovely cover was designed by the talented Emily of Emily's World of Design. Editing was done by Falcon Faerie Fiction, and I would also like to thank Sally Hamer for her generous support on the first chapter.

1

Penobscot Territory, Coastal Maine, July 1679

"Leave my hand be. It is none of your affair," Matthias said.

Ruth Turner grabbed her brother's wrist, digging her fingers into his flesh so he couldn't pull it away. "It is my affair if you die." She turned the crusted back of his hand toward his face. "Do you smell the rotting flesh? That could kill you." He was lucky it hadn't already.

Matthias shifted his arse on his stone doorstep, glaring down at her in the waning light. "I'm not a fool. I've been following the doctor's word like it was gospel." He was big as a bear and, with his ruffled dark hair, could easily be mistaken for one at a distance.

"It hasn't healed in six months. How do you not see that what you have been doing to care for it isn't working?" The bone had set, but months of planting and tending his crops had made the skin continue to fester. She smeared a thick garlic plaster over the rank, red crust. His hand had caught a glancing ball right out of the muzzle of a musket. It wasn't even an enemy musket. A neighbor fired too close to him in the panic of the raids after the war, and the shot had broken the bone and ripped open the flesh. On top of that, the muzzle flash had charred the surrounding skin.

They shouldn't have been fighting at all because the war was more than two years over, but Boston hadn't exactly treated the Penobscot with charity when King Philip and his allies were defeated in the rest of New England. The Penobscot had been winning in the north, and the settlements in Maine had paid the price for Boston's arrogance.

The pointless fighting after the war had made her a widow, and she would be voluntarily damned to hell before she let it take her brother.

"That stinks." Matthias tried to yank his hand away again, but she held tight. She might be a quarter his size, but she had a strong grip.

The heavy summer air hung around them, dampening the humming and buzzing of the evening insects.

She grabbed a leaf from her basket with her free hand, placed it over top of the healing plaster to contain the oozing mess, and then wrapped a strip of linen around it all, holding the plaster and leaf in place. "It smells bad, but it does good. Accept your lot with patience this once."

Matthias wrinkled his nose like the sulfurous brimstone of hell wafted up from his hand. "This is not how Anne and Goody Francis dressed it, and it isn't what Dr. Kingsman directed, either." He shook his head, brows knit together. "Why must you go against your elders?"

She wiped the excess plaster on the grass to get it off her hand before she got it on her skirts and reeked of garlic herself for a week, then tucked a lock of her dark hair that had escaped its pins behind her ear. "Because they are all wrong."

He lowered his brows at her like a stern minister. Even sitting, he was a head taller than her. "Do not stir up trouble. This is not the time, and it is not your place to contradict them. I know you."

Any fool knew it was no time to make trouble. But she knew remedies his wife, the midwife, and even the doctor did not, and she was trying to save his hand, not wreak chaos and upset the social order. Besides, Matthias had been telling her not to stir up trouble more or less every day since she was old enough to remember.

She drew in a breath to answer him, but then a flock of birds flew up out of a tree at the edge of the woods.

Her pulse pounded in her ears, and her muscles went taught.

Before she could process a thought, she was on her feet, grabbing her brother's powder horn as he grabbed his musket. The musket was always loaded, and she would be ready to help reload.

She snatched the mold where he had a few new balls of shot still sitting, then she whirled back around to see Matthias already a few paces in front of the doorstep, methodically scanning each section of the woods for any movement or flash of anything out of place. The cool lead of the shot was heavy in her hand.

Nothing moved.

They waited. A small rivulet of sweat trickled down the channel of her spine.

Anyone with half a wit would have known the birds gave them away, so they had to out-wait whoever was lurking there. At least the open fields behind the house were too open to be inviting to Penobscot raiders. Or French ones.

Ruth's heart banged against her ribs as she stood ready. After two years of war, plus the years of raids that followed, she could load a musket with her eyes bandaged shut if necessary.

The humid air muffled everything just slightly.

A faint rustle? The blood rushing past her ears made it hard to tell.

She stared into the inky shadows at the edge of the trees, and Matthias aimed his musket at the spot where she heard the noise.

Nothing.

The air was thick in her lungs.

Then movement under the elderberry.

Ruth flinched with such force she almost dropped the shot, and then she nearly choked on an unexpected laugh as her body shook from the released tension.

Matthias' tabby-striped mouser strutted out of the woods with a fat, juicy chipmunk in her feline jaws. She yowled to raise to the dead without dropping her dinner.

Matthias grunted and lowered his musket. "That beast is surely in league with the Devil," he said, shaking his head.

Ruth put the shot back in its place by the door and took two tries to hang the strap of the powder horn over its peg.

Matthias leaned the musket against the door frame and wiped his forehead with his bandaged hand.

Her heart still beat too fast as she grabbed his hand and adjusted the bandage he had just knocked out of place before he could pull away.

"Ouch."

If he had let her dress his wounds sooner, he would have been healed by now, and he would have been better able to defend himself. She pressed the bandage to make sure the plaster was still against his skin and not sticking just to the bandage.

He winced, and she pressed just a little harder before letting his hand free.

He rolled his eyes at her, and she blew him a kiss in the fading light.

There had to be a way to get through his thick head that if he didn't follow her instructions, his hand might kill him. For all that the garlic stank, it was better than the stench of the wound itself, and that was not good. He needed to heal. The whole settlement needed to heal.

"You cannot return home now. It's dark. It is too dangerous," Matthias said.

"It was your cat." She sat back down on the doorstep, looking out at the woods she could barely make out in the gloaming. Unfortunately, he was right. It was too dangerous.

She settled her back against the hard oak doorframe and tried to relax her muscles. "I hear a family from Lee wants to buy the Sinclair farm."

He grunted and lowered himself back down next to her, keeping his injured hand protected against his chest to avoid giving her an excuse to adjust his bandage again. "It's odd anyone wants to move here with the French stirring trouble with the Penobscot."

"If we stopped going around treating the Penobscot like we are not on their land, they might not be so eager to give the French a hearing."

"We are not on Penobscot land. We are on land we purchased."

"Not according to the Penobscot."

"Stop speaking out of turn. We don't need new folks stirring up trouble, nor you." He grabbed a stick with his good hand, and it sounded like he was tracing figures in the dirt at his feet, but it was too dark to make them out. "I don't know what we've done for evil to be allowed to run amongst us and take so many, but we need to be very careful."

"You sound as if you think Sinclair might sell his farm to Satan himself. Or worse, to a French family." She rolled her shoulders to loosen them. "Whoever they are, we need them. The militia ranks are quite thin at this point."

"Don't make light." He poked her with his stick, no doubt penance for her extra squeeze of his injured hand. "We let questionable folks in before the war and look what heaven loosed upon us."

She plucked a tall stalk of grass that brushed against her arm. One formerly Catholic family didn't seem likely to have caused the war. They had seen their error and converted long before they arrived, so they hadn't brought evil with them. Besides, when the selectmen sent them packing, the evil kept coming, and the raids lasted for years after the war. The accusations weren't fair.

Many in town claimed the wife was too forward with her opinions, and that was the true root of their objections. She twirled the grass stem in her fingers. They said it was evidence of witchcraft.

Ruth shivered in the warm evening air. The woman was no more a witch than she was, not that it mattered to her accusers.

Matthias went back to drawing in the dirt. "Now Cook has returned." He sighed. "At least that is one more man in our ranks."

Ruth's jaw locked down tight, and the muscles in her temples ached from the effort of not opening her mouth to say what she was thinking. Cook was a careless, hypocritical menace, and not someone to whom she trusted her safety. She didn't understand how his wife had born him getting her with child without emulating Jael and driving a tent peg through his head.

"I hear you grinding your teeth," Matthias said. "Stop. He is a godly man, helping us rebuild order."

Letting his hogs run wild and eat their way through an old widow's garden and livelihood was not order. She glanced sideways at her brother and could barely make out his features now that the sun had sunk below the horizon. It was too dark to see more than a faint silhouette. She started tearing the grass into pieces.

"He is back not a month, and already he has suffered from the evil in our town," he said. "But at least he is doing something about it."

She almost snorted. Any evil the man suffered, he brought on himself. "And what, pray tell me, is Goodman Cook doing to root out evil and restore order?"

She heard him inhale sharply. He hated when she spoke ill of those who deserved it.

He turned toward her, and she could feel him scowling in the dark. "He is helping Daniel Kendrick root out witches."

She had to work to draw her next breath. "And how is he doing this?"

"His hogs are ill, and he has brought charges against the witch responsible for it. And for cursing him and causing his scythe to break."

The world slowed, and cold shivers crept down her spine. The grass dropped from her hand. "And who does he say has done this?"

"I assume I need not point out that our family will stay out of this?"

Her pulse took off like a bolting horse. "Who, Matthias?"

He let out a grumbly breath, probably wishing he hadn't brought up the subject. "Goody Carter witched his hogs and cursed him, and you," he poked her again with the stick he still held in his good hand, "will stay out of this."

She shot to her feet so fast she knocked the stick right out of his hand. Goody Carter had been their mother's best friend and a dear friend to them after their mother's death.

"Sit down."

"How can you let that go unchallenged?" She glared at him in the dark. Goodman Cook blaming Goody Carter for his own troubles was unconscionable. If they hanged Goody Carter for Cook's carelessness, they would all deserve whatever evil providence saw fit to loose on them.

Matthias stood and leaned into her space, the nighttime dark gathering close around them both.

"The town elected Daniel Kendrick warden, and it is for him, and not you, to sort out the moral conduct of this settlement and its inhabitants." He took a firm hold of her arm. "You will not drag our family into this."

She wrenched her arm free.

Her heart ached in her chest. Blast Daniel Kendrick and his blasted witch hunting, even if it was part of his new job as warden.

She stood still for a moment, feet grounded on the warm earth, and tried to slow her breathing and calm her thoughts. At least Daniel was rational and took fairness seriously enough to listen to reason. Unlike certain people she was related to.

In fact, as warden, Daniel Kendrick was *obliged* to listen to reason.

The band of tension around her chest loosened just a little. She grabbed for her basket, missed it in the dark, and then found the handle. She felt around for the pot of garlic plaster and then thrust it at Matthias. "I will be back to put this on you again tomorrow, and then Anne needs to apply it every day for a week when she returns. Do you understand? It will burn the skin, but it will stop the infection."

"You are not leaving." Matthias loomed in the dark.

She didn't take the time to argue. The moon wasn't up yet, but she couldn't wait for it. She turned and marched down the path that her feet knew so well.

"Only those in league with the Devil roam the woods alone at night," he called to her. "You are too forward."

Her heart tripped, but her steps didn't.

"Ruth, you don't know what's out there," he yelled after her, concern creeping into his voice.

She hesitated at the edge of the trees, gripping the handle of her basket like it might try to free itself from her grasp. He was right. Even if she feared no supernatural dangers, she was wise enough to fear the very natural dangers of traveling the woods at night.

And of arriving unannounced at a garrison house after dark.

But Goody Carter stood unjustly accused of a capital crime, and if Matthias would not do anything about it, she would.

Sweat stung Daniel Kendrick's eyes as he climbed the ladder to the second level of his house one-handed, steadying the keg of black powder balanced on his shoulder with the other hand. The lock of his hair that swung in front of his eyes was so wet with sweat it was almost as black as the powder. He tried to keep his breathing even so he didn't inhale the powder's scent too deeply. Its charcoal and piss smell stirred images from the past few years that he would prefer to forget. But he couldn't afford to forget because it would only take one fool to rekindle the whole deadly mess.

He reached the upper level, and the heat stifled his breathing for a moment. Even without a candle up here to illuminate the dark, it was like breathing in a smith's furnace. The air would be even worse with half the town up here. Anyone attacking could just set up a perimeter and wait them out while the heat did their violence for them. Winters here were long and brutal, but summers had deadly hot stretches.

He bent over and set down the powder next to an outer wall, and sweat dripped off the tip of his nose and splashed onto the keg. He straightened as far as he could before his head came in contact with the roof. Cursing his height, he rubbed his shoulder where the edge of the keg's bottom had dug into his flesh, then he peeled his shirt away from his chest to allow a little air against his skin. The stars shone in the night sky out the small window, but he didn't have time to appreciate them this evening.

They needed shot now since powder without shot was about as helpful as a handle with no axe head. They would have to get the townsfolk to pool some resources until Boston sent money to buy shot or lead to make their own. Neither his garrison house nor Aldrich's had been fully restocked since the second treaty, and with the French stirring trouble, they didn't dare wait on shot.

Voices from downstairs rumbled up through the floor. If people would just let him focus, he could bring some order, but they couldn't seem to help themselves. Even the other two selectmen of the town. No doubt Jacob Turner had tweaked Mr. Aldrich's nose over something. It wasn't wise to tweak the nose of the only man in upper Maine with enough money to warrant the title 'Mister,' but Jacob was the sort who sometimes couldn't resist. Daniel and Jacob had each been elected in their fathers' respective places as selectmen in the last year, and Aldrich, the remaining selectman from their fathers' generation, was still adjusting to the change.

Daniel rubbed his stinging eyes and tried not to think about the dark smudges he knew were just below them. He needed sleep as desperately as they needed shot. And he wouldn't get that until he found and convicted the witch.

He tugged at his sweat-soaked shirt for one last bit of air against his body and then swung onto the ladder and descended into the argument that had broken out in his front room.

"How did Cook get away with leaving in the first place?" Jacob pounded his meaty fist on Daniel's table, making the candlestick jump and the flame gutter.

Daniel's heart lurched. Leave it to the Devil to cause a fire to start in the warden's own home. But Jacob steadied the candle before it could topple, and Daniel's heart resumed its normal rhythm. Jacob was shorter and stockier than Daniel and could move quickly when he wanted to. Thank heavens he had just now.

Mr. Aldrich stared at Jacob from under his stern, gray brows. "He was fined for leaving. And now he has prayed on his error and is returned a newly devout man."

The militia needed warm bodies, and even if Cook had broken the law to scamper off to safety in Boston during the raids last winter, his body still counted. It was a shame his wife had perished during the war. She had been a moderating influence on him.

Aldrich turned toward Daniel. "And now Goodman Cook has been visited by a witch." Aldrich's brows hovered low over his bulbous nose, and he appeared to think Daniel should already have sorted that out.

Jacob turned toward Daniel, too, then grinned and slapped a hand on Daniel's shoulder. "You look like shite."

Of course he looked like shite. He barely slept. Daniel ignored him, turned to Aldrich, and pasted on a smile. "When does Goody Francis think your wife will be delivered of her child?"

A genuine smile spread across Aldrich's fleshy cheeks. "Any moment now." His young, second wife was due to produce the man's seventeenth child.

Jacob rolled his eyes heavenward, no doubt as horrified at the thought as Daniel was. Being fruitful and multiplying was one thing, but he had ten living sons, and how on earth could he give each son enough land to marry and support a family of his own? Daniel had just inherited his own father's land at thirty-one, and he at least had no brothers. And Jacob had only half his father's land because his older brother had gotten the other half. The larger half. And that was now owned by Jacob's widowed sister-in-law. This had become the lot of almost every man in their generation. Available land was scarce, and removing to Maine had only marginally improved the problem.

Aldrich raised an eyebrow at him, no doubt remembering Daniel's unmarried status as if it was Daniel's fault he couldn't afford to find a wife until now. Aldrich opened his mouth to speak.

Jacob headed Aldrich off. "He knows a warden can't very well enforce the moral behavior of the community when he himself is not fulfilling his godly duties by marrying." He was grinning like an idiot. "I've written to my wife's unmarried cousins in Wells to solve that."

Daniel tried not to groan. Heaven preserve him from Jacob's cousins-in-law. He had had no time to think of prospective brides, but he had met Jacob's cousins, and he would rather jam a stick in his eye. And he had other problems he had to resolve first.

Then a yawn crept up on him, and he couldn't smother it. He needed sleep more urgently than anything else, but he wouldn't get that tonight, either. The witch wouldn't let him.

Jacob laughed. "Very well, we will continue our business after you have questioned Goody Carter."

Aldrich shook his head, grabbed his musket from the small collection of them by the door, and waited for Jacob to check his own musket and be sure his flint hadn't slipped.

They stepped outside into the sticky night and listened for sounds in the woods as their eyes adjusted to the dark. Crickets chirped, accompanied by the occasional hooting owl. Only once they had gained their night vision and satisfied themselves that no one was lying in wait did they pass through the gate in the palisade and set out together.

Daniel latched the heavy oak door behind them. He leaned against the thick, squared-off logs that made up the fortified outer wall of his home. With this garrison house, he had inherited the responsibility of keeping his neighbors safe. Half of them, anyway. Aldrich's house would protect the other half.

Another yawn almost detached his jaw from his head. But he had more work to do before he bedded down for the night. Not that the witch would permit him to sleep even then. She, or perhaps they, usually chose the moment he drifted off to torment him with visions.

He rubbed his face hard with both hands to wake himself up, then pulled Goodman Cook's scythe from the corner of the room and sat down at his table to examine it in the candlelight for signs of the Devil's work.

He squinted at the handle of the scythe. It was cracked and worn, though Cook said it was only a few years old. The blade had broken off clean at its base.

Candle smoke hung in the humid air, and he rubbed his burning eyes.

A crow squawked its displeasure outside, and Daniel was on his feet before the sound died. Crows were only awake at night if something woke them.

Or if the crow was a witch's familiar.

His blood slammed through his veins, and he ran to the door and grabbed one of the two loaded muskets still leaning against the wall. He checked the flint and readied the pan.

Then he pressed his ear next to the small gun port in the wall and listened, careful not to let his head block the candlelight and cast a shadow.

The gate creaked, and then the grass rustled in the quick, steady rhythm of human legs brushing through it, walking with purpose. His heart pounded to the same rhythm, though perhaps not as steadily.

Only someone up to the Devil's work would be out alone at this hour. If he was lucky, it was Goody Carter, and he might catch her in the act and finally have enough evidence to convict her at trial and put an end to their troubles. An end to years of the Devil's work in their settlement. Once they stopped allowing a witch to do the Devil's bidding in their town, providence would end their punishment and stop sending the French and their native allies after them. The fighting would well and truly be over.

If he wasn't lucky, at least he was in a garrison house, and hopefully Jacob and Aldrich would hear an alarm shot. His muscles tensed.

He rested his fingers on the door latch, waiting, and sweat slid down the ladder of his ribs.

Something scuffed against his doorstep. His heart lurched.

He wrenched open the door and jammed his musket right into the breast of...Ruth Turner, Jacob's widowed sister-in-law.

She froze, her lips parted in a startled little oh. They were full, like a bee had stung them.

He stared.

Those lips stirred sensations in parts of his body he should not be conscious of in the presence of a woman he was not married to. Which meant any woman. But his errant cock was bedeviled and wouldn't listen to propriety. Witches would be the death of him.

He forced a deep breath and yanked his gaze from her lips, where his gaze didn't belong. Her small, delicate hands caught his searching eye, and they held an empty basket. What had she been doing alone in the dark? His sleep-deprived brain was having trouble focusing, but he needed to figure this out.

He drew a fortifying breath. "To what do I owe the pleasure of your visit, Goody Turner?"

She glanced down at his musket, still jammed into her soft flesh. Her hand grasped the muzzle and shoved it aside. She brushed a smear of black powder off the rough, brown wool over her breast. Her breast that he shouldn't be looking at. Then her eyes rose to his and waited, one brow raised in question as though she thought he was the one in the wrong.

He let her stand for another moment, not letting his eyes drift to the smudge on her chest, and then he stepped back and gestured her into the house. It was too dark to tell if anything was amiss behind her in the dooryard. He closed and latched the door.

Then he studied her small form for a moment in the quiet of the room, breathing slowly and trying to gather the reins on his bolting thoughts. She appeared to be studying him in return.

He stood up straighter. He had such a height advantage she had to tip her head back to look him in the face, even though she stood a few paces away. She was so tiny she was positively elfin.

Her dark eyes reflected the candlelight, and a parade of calculations shone behind the reflected flame. He ran his finger along the stock of the musket he still held. She was capable of the mental machinations to do the Devil's work if she so chose.

"I am here to discuss the absurd charge Goodman Cook has leveled against Goody Carter." The way she said "Goodman" made it clear she did not think Cook a good man. Good judgment? Or motive? He wasn't fool enough to think Goody Carter was the only possible witch.

She pointed at Cook's scythe on his table. "He is too lazy to clear his fields and likely broke that on a rock." Her eyes narrowed on him. "And he let his hogs run into her garden, and they destroyed several rows before she could chase them off. She was angry, which she now repents, but she didn't curse him."

She held her hands together in front of herself like she needed to restrain them from acting against her will. She was agitated. He needed to press her to figure out why.

"And how do you account for the two sick hogs?"

She heaved a big breath, which pushed her chest out toward him. He dragged his eyes back to the scowl on her face. This was too important for him to lose the thread of his inquiry.

"They were foraging in her garden and who knows how many other people's. They no doubt ate what they ought not." Her hands flew up in disgust. "Again, his negligence caused himself harm." She paused a moment, regarding him. "It caused her harm, too."

These were the usual defenses. He would sort through them with great care, of course. He would root evil out of the community, and convicting innocent people did nothing to achieve that end. "Goody Carter stands accused, not convicted. Indeed, she is not yet even deposed."

Then she smiled, and his chest relaxed. He gave himself a mental shake. His duties as warden were to uphold the moral behavior of the settlement, and that also made him a target of those who did the Devil's work. The Devil's minions would distract him from his work.

"I know you are fair-minded, and that is why I have come to talk with you before this goes further." Her voice dropped in pitch and seemed to vibrate in his chest. "Goody Carter cannot afford to be tried and jailed, especially now Cook's hogs have eaten so much of her produce."

He forced himself to process her words, which underscored a serious issue. Goody Carter's husband had died, and she had no sons. No one was legally responsible for her or for her debts to the constable for her upkeep if he arrested her. She was a problem. As was Ruth.

"Please, let me help you see her innocence." Ruth's wide eyes pleaded with unnatural power.

Her face drew him to her. Her body drew him to her. Her entire presence drew him to her, and he couldn't force his eyes away from her.

She was bewitching.

His lungs sucked in the hot air. He and others in the community had been targets of the Devil's work for years, and what little evidence he had all indicated that Goody Carter was the witch.

But perhaps Ruth was right.

Perhaps he'd been investigating the wrong woman.

2

Ruth walked along the rough path to Goody Carter's home. The sun was already well up, and it was getting warm.

Her head still ached from attempting to talk logic with Daniel Kendrick the evening before, or from trying to get him to talk much at all. He had insisted on walking her home to protect her after dark, which was annoying but wise. She'd been a fool to go off alone in the night. But he hadn't said a word the entire time. He had kept studying her as if he were trying to figure out which category of evil she belonged to.

She stopped to pick some wild blueberries. The sun-warmed berries burst in her mouth when she chewed them, and she closed her eyes for a moment to enjoy the sensation. Few things tasted as sweet as the first blueberries of the summer. She opened her eyes and grabbed another handful, then started filling her basket with them. There was no reason to let Goodman Cook's marauding hogs get these, too.

Basket full, she continued down the path, stopping to detach her skirts from wild briars that grabbed at her as she passed.

She rounded the last bend and drew up short when she was confronted by Goody Carter's minuscule backside.

Instead of standing to see who had arrived, from her position doubled over in her garden, Goody Carter grabbed up the hem of her skirts and peeked out under them at ground level, the top of her gray head almost brushing the ground.

She presented a ridiculous picture and was also totally defenseless.

"What if I had been a French raiding party?" Ruth said.

Goody Carter harrumphed. "My bony old arse would have frightened them back to Ville-Marie."

Ruth tried not to laugh, but good heavens, so of course, her laughter escaped as a snort, which set the older woman to fits of giggles, and Ruth surrendered to uncontrollable belly-laughs. She doubled over, barely able to breathe, and the older woman laughed so hard she almost toppled forward into her onion patch. Ruth reached for her arm and helped her right herself as they both burst out in another fit of hilarity.

Ruth's head swam a little as she swiped at the tears running down her cheeks. That might have been the first time she laughed that hard since the war.

She took a deep breath and surveyed the garden. The view sucked the levity their laughter had brought right out of her. It was a mess. Goody Carter had tidied up what she could, but there was no remedying the damage the hogs had done.

Ruth swatted at a fly.

This wasn't right.

"You need to counter-sue Goodman Cook. He probably only accused you to put you on the defensive, so you didn't think of suing him first."

Goody Carter looked up at her, and her eyes flashed with several emotions in succession, but Ruth couldn't read them fast enough.

"I don't have the time or desire to sue him, and there would be no point." The older woman shrugged her shoulders in her too-loose dress.

"He ruined your property, and you should not be the one to suffer from the law here."

Goody Carter gave a kindly smile for an answer.

"Why is it so wrong for you to ask the court for rightful compensation when Goodman Cook can go storming in and claim you cursed him, and that is why he broke his scythe and has two vomiting hogs?" The man was negligent, and he should be the one suffering for it, not Goody Carter.

"My avenging angel." Goody Carter patted her on the arm. "Are those blueberries?" She took Ruth by the arm and dragged her toward her house. The old woman was stronger than she appeared.

Ruth followed along with no resistance, in part because she wanted to give the berries to Goody Carter and in part to be relieved from the agony of her grip. The woman could literally squeeze the stomach contents out of a hog. Not that she would say that in front of Daniel Kendrick, in case he took that as evidence against Goody Carter.

Once inside Goody Carter's tiny house, the woman reached for a stack of baskets on a tall shelf. Ruth rubbed her arm as soon as the woman turned her back, trying to rub out the dents her friend's fingers had made, and then she reached for a stool to help with the baskets. Neither of them topped five feet, and the shelf was too high.

Goody Carter gave a little jump, unbalanced the basket stack, and caught it just as it tumbled onto her head. She gave Ruth a toothy grin, then grabbed the basket she wanted. "You can put the rest back." She shoved the stack at Ruth.

Ruth stretched up on the stool and replaced the stack of baskets, then turned to see Goody Carter emptying the blueberries into her own basket, a wide, low one that would allow air circulation. The woman patted the worn bench next to the table. "Sit."

Ruth sat, and Goody Carter shoved the berries in front of her.

"Eat."

Ruth took a few blueberries in her hand and popped one in her mouth. They sat for a few minutes, eating berries in comfortable silence.

"I spoke with Daniel Kendrick last night."

Goody Carter almost choked on a berry. "What were you thinking? Never mind," she held up her hand, "I know what you were thinking, but you shouldn't have."

"They have unjustly accused you."

"How many times has your brother called you a witch?"

"What?" Ruth couldn't keep up.

Goody Carter laid her bony hand over Ruth's own and gave it a gentle squeeze. "You meant well."

Ruth's chin came up. Of course, she meant well. She was trying to avoid a tragedy here. "What has my ill-begotten brother to do with this?"

Goody Carter turned on the bench next to her so that she was looking her in the eye. "What do you think it would take for Goodman Cook, or Daniel Kendrick, to take your brother's words to heart?"

Ruth's breath caught for a moment. No one would listen to her brother being a, well, a brother.

She stood, unable to be still any longer. She paced the few steps there was space for in the room, then turned back. "Daniel Kendrick may have a massive stick up his arse about witchcraft right now, but he has always been clear-minded and fair, and that is why I went to reason with him." And there was no reason she shouldn't have.

"Hmm."

"Hmm?"

"Daniel Kendrick is unmarried."

Ruth's head spun from the changes of subject. "You marry him."

Goody Carter laughed so hard that the bench wobbled and threatened to topple backwards. "I might if he'd have me." Her eyes glinted with more than laughter as her face flushed.

The older woman was impossible. Just because Daniel was tall and well-muscled and had a promising air of confidence about him did not make his marital status relevant. Her cheeks heated and were no doubt redder than a beetroot in the stuffy little room. "That isn't worth shackling yourself to another for." No matter how the idea of it warmed her nether parts.

Goody Carter's face sobered up. "You should have told me your dear departed husband wasn't up to the task. The Penobscot say that cone flower—"

"Stop." Now, her face was on fire. This was not what she was here to discuss. "He was perfectly competent—"

"Competent?" Goody Carter clucked her tongue. "You deserve better. I bet Daniel Kendrick is better."

Ruth turned on her. "Goodman Cook has accused you of witchcraft and has taken the accusation to the warden. This isn't gossip. This is an accusation of a capital crime." She clenched her fists at her sides so she didn't knock anything over. "I don't think I was able to talk Daniel out of questioning you." She gave up and let her arms flail. "We need to figure out how to handle this."

Goody Carter smiled at her again, though perhaps not so indulgently as before. "I appreciate your concern. Always helping others and never letting others help you. You are a better friend to me than you are to yourself." She stood. "Now, how have you planned your harvest? Did you ask Jacob for his help?"

Bile rose in the back of Ruth's throat. She had almost lost her freedom the one time she had asked for Jacob's help, and she would never make that mistake again.

Goody Carter clucked her tongue and shook her head. "Were you at least able to hire Goodman Brower's son to help you with your corn?"

Ruth's stomach sank a bit. "No, my brother-in-law had just hired him when I asked." But she would harvest the corn herself if she had to. It wasn't like they had gotten much planted in the spring, while Esau had slowly died from a festering wound around a lead ball in his back. "But that is not as important as you being hauled to answer to the court."

Goody Carter glanced around her sparse little room. "Winters are much longer without corn." She looked at Ruth. "You will sort everything out. But it would be easier if you were willing to ask for help." She raised her eyebrow, and Ruth glanced away.

"I am not here to discuss my corn harvest. We need to figure out how to make them see your innocence." She didn't need help, but Goody Carter did. And while Goodman Cook wouldn't see past his own snout if it didn't benefit him, Daniel Kendrick was smarter and more reasonable. "We need to make Daniel see the reality of the situation."

Goody Carter gave her that overly indulgent smile again. "Just make them see the truth. I love your faith." The older woman took another handful of berries and rolled them around in her palm without eating them.

Of course, she had faith in the truth. Goody Carter didn't curse Goodman Cook's hogs, so they couldn't hang her.

The town had no space on its leger for another lost soul.

Daniel walked along the path to Goody Carter's house, followed by Goodman Cook, who was searching for blueberries and raining judgment on whoever had been before him and picked the bushes clean. Daniel tried to stay upwind of him as they walked. No one would ever doubt Cook kept hogs.

Cook's hound ran ahead and dove into some bushes, flushing an angry songbird. Then it disappeared down the trail.

They rounded a last bend, and there was the little house with its cracked, weather-worn clapboards. The door stood open. She must be at home.

A small flock of chickens roamed the dooryard, pecking around for their lunch while eyeing Cook's hound. The dog was already sniffing and lifted its leg on three different shrubs in succession before trotting around the side of the house and disappearing.

Between Daniel and the house was a large garden. Parts of the garden were in pristine condition, the vines and stalks heavy with late summer produce, but other sections had clearly been ripped up and not by human hands.

Daniel glanced over his shoulder at Cook, who stared at the house and showed no signs he had even noticed the garden. The man removed his hat and ran his hands through what remained of his greasy brown hair, then stuffed the crumpled hat back down on his head. The stout little man was filthy. He probably hadn't bathed since his wife died.

Daniel shook his head and turned back to the aged little house. The roof sagged a bit, but there were no gaps and no weeds around the doorstep. Goody Carter maintained it as well as her meager means allowed. Everything was quiet except for the occasional clucking of the hens and the general hum of late-summer insects and birds.

"Why do you hesitate to perform your righteous office?" Cook said from behind him, almost pushing him toward the house.

Daniel stood for a moment. "All in good time, Goodman Cook." He made no move to go to the door. After a moment, Cook sighed and stopped shifting from one foot to the other. Only then did Daniel step toward the house. Goodman Cook charging in and trying to take over the proceedings would not improve his odds of a productive interview. It was too bad he had to let the man come along at all. Had he not been the aggrieved party, Daniel would have forbidden his presence, but the man had puking hogs and a broken scythe, and he wanted justice.

The destruction in the garden drew Daniel's eye again. It was extensive. He shook his head, stepped up to the open door, and knocked on the frame. He ducked his head inside, and as his eyes adjusted to the dim light, they fell on not just Goody Carter but also Goody Turner.

Goody Carter sat at the table with a large basket of blueberries in front of her, and he was hit with an unbidden sense of relief that the older woman had gotten to the berries before Cook had.

Goody Turner stood just behind her and was glaring at them with those big brown eyes. If either was surprised to see him, they hid it well.

"To what do we owe the pleasure of your visit?" Goody Turner gave him his own words back from the night before, and she sounded no less sarcastic than he had. If Goody Carter had been home alone, it would have made for a simple interrogation. Goody Turner could complicate that.

"She is training an apprentice in the Devil's work," Cook said from over Daniel's shoulder.

Goody Turner's delicate face turned to stone at the sound of the man's voice.

Yes, she was definitely a complication.

She studied them for a moment longer and then launched herself in their direction.

Cook flinched.

"Ruth, wait." Goody Carter tried to stop her, though she would have had as much luck trying to stop water rushing through a burst dam.

Goody Turner drew alongside Daniel, and he braced himself for whatever verbal assault she might direct at him, but she grabbed his arm and spun him toward the outdoors.

"Look at that." She pointed at the destroyed rows of the garden where the hens were now searching for grubs. "Goodman Cook's hogs did that. He owes her compensation."

Cook snorted behind them. "She cursed my hogs, and I don't owe the Devil's minion anything."

Ruth Turner turned on Goodman Cook, and her slight frame seemed to grow large, like a bear rising up and about to charge someone who had been fool enough to poke at her.

Daniel fought off a sigh and stepped in between them before she could take a swing at Cook or do whatever her next impulse drove her to. "One charge at a time." He turned to Goody Turner. "It is not your place to make that accusation since this is not your property. And we are here to depose Goody Carter, so that is what we shall do today."

Cook puffed his chest out at her like he had just won the argument. Daniel caught his eye and tried to silently warn him to be quiet. Goody Turner had a point, after all. But Cook was unable or unwilling to heed the warning.

"Know your place, woman," said Cook.

Her eyes grew wide, and she took a step toward Cook. Tiny though she was, Daniel had no doubt she could cause Cook some damage if she went after the man.

"Enough." Daniel put a hand on Cook's chest and pushed him back, and he used his body to block Ruth Turner from getting at Cook. "Goodman Cook, as there is not much space in the house, you will kindly sit yourself on the doorstep." He could keep the man's hog stench outside while also keeping order.

Cook opened his mouth to protest, but Daniel was done suffering fools for the day.

"You can hear perfectly well from there and take part if needed, but as you can see," he gestured around the tiny room with his arm, "there is limited seating."

The man hesitated a moment, then sat himself down, crossed his arms, and leaned his back against the door frame. He glared at Daniel with his eyebrows lowered, and his chin shoved forward in a pout.

Daniel ignored him and turned toward Goody Turner. "If you are staying, would you take a seat?"

Ruth Turner pulled her shoulders back, turned like the queen, and lowered herself down next to Goody Carter on the bench that appeared to be the only intact seating in the house. There was a cracked chair in the corner, but if he sat on it, both it and he would likely end up in pieces on the dirt floor. No matter. He could stand.

He took a slow breath and ran quickly through the line of questions he had worked out after Goody Turner had invaded his home last night.

"You are aware, I believe, of Goodman Cook's charges against you?" He watched Goody Carter's face.

She kept it demurely downcast. "I am heartily sorry I lost my temper with Goodman Cook when his hogs destroyed my garden. But I promise I never cursed him, and I have spoken with Reverend Maitland about my unseemly anger at the destruction. I have asked him to pray with me to help bend my will to the Lord's."

He glanced at Goody Turner. She stared at Goody Carter, her jaw tight, and if he didn't mistake himself, she was annoyed.

"Did you curse his hogs?"

She shook her head so hard that a few strands of hair escaped the confines of their pins. "I would never wish ill on an animal, even if it did just eat my winter income."

Daniel almost chuckled at the barb.

"I am just a widow, and I know better than to curse the will of fate." She glanced up at him, then dropped her gaze to her lap again. "As I have said, I have asked the reverend for his help in mending my temper."

That would be easy enough to check. He would already have asked the reverend's opinion of Goody Carter, but the man had spent the last few days visiting his sister in Wells and had just returned this morning.

"Do you practice malefice?"

Her head popped up, and her eyes went wide. "I have never in my life practiced any witchcraft, for ill or good. I am a churchwoman." She then recited the Lord's Prayer as proof.

Satan was wily, and Daniel had never quite trusted that those in his sway could not recite the Lord's prayer, but he believed Goody Carter.

"She witched my hogs," Cook said as he bolted to his feet. He wasn't such a fool that he couldn't figure out this wasn't going the way he wanted. A hen that had been pecking around near his feet squawked her displeasure at his sudden movement.

An ungodly baying came from outside the house. The hen wasn't the only one startled by Cook's sudden movement. The dog bounded toward its master, heedless of anything in its path, including the rest of the chickens, which flapped their wings in a fury and scattered in every direction, including toward the door. Two flew right up in Goodman Cook's face, and he batted at them to keep them at bay.

Goody Carter and Ruth were on their feet as one, and they tried to catch the panicked birds filling the room with feathers and chaotic squawks. Ruth then bolted past Cook and out the door. "Let go," she yelled at the hound.

Startled, the dog opened its mouth and let its feathered prey go. The chicken batted at the dog with its wings as it struggled in the ungainly way of chickens to get airborne. It must have startled the hound, which whined and cowered.

Cook charged at Ruth and grabbed her by the arm, then whipped his head toward Daniel. "She sent her familiars after me and my hound. You witnessed it, Warden Kendrick."

Daniel's mind locked like a jammed millstone for an instant, then lurched back into action.

As warden, he couldn't ignore the accusation, and as a selectman, he couldn't crack the man's head against the doorjamb.

3

"Greetings, sister." Jacob's voice boomed across the field that separated them.

Ruth cut a sprig of mugwort before sitting back on her heels and looking up at her brother-in-law approaching with his characteristic short, quick strides, his chin jutting forward. She tucked the mugwort in the front of her dress, and the swarm of gnats thinned. If only mugwort worked as well on uninvited visitors.

She rose to her feet. It wasn't fair to think of Jacob like that, and it wasn't his fault that he had hired the only lad she had a chance of affording before she had gotten to it. The fault for that lay squarely at her own feet for not being quicker about it.

The sun beat down on her as she glanced around her expansive garden and then out at her sparsely planted cornfield. So much to do. She hadn't even finished weeding a quarter of the garden yet, let alone started sorting out the corn harvest. The weight of it was heavy on her shoulders. With Esau dead, and dead before they had children to share the load, the work was all hers.

She brushed the dirt from her skirts where her knees had pressed the fabric into the soil. The choices were also hers, and she answered to no one. And that she would not give up. She smiled as Jacob drew closer.

His face was a younger version of her husband's. They could almost have been twins. He waved and returned her smile as he approached. "I came to check in and see how you are doing." He looked around her garden, then out to the field. The field brought a frown. "You two got almost nothing planted this spring, but even so, you can't get that all in by yourself."

She bit her lip to keep words on the tip of her tongue from escaping. She was in no mood to have her competency questioned, no matter that she had been thinking the same thought mere moments before.

But it wouldn't serve to tell him what she thought of his assessment of her ability. "How is William's stomach doing? Do you need some peppermint to take back?" Of course, if the child would stop putting everything nasty he could find in his mouth, his stomach would fare far better. "Would you like some chamomile for him so that you can all get a little sleep?"

Jacob rubbed his hand across the stubble on his chin as he concentrated on her corn. "I don't know if you have enough corn there to get yourself through the winter." He turned toward her, and her gut sank. "Why don't you move in with us? We can take care of you and farm your fields."

Her heart thudded in her breast. Jacob's offer was kind, as it had been every time he made it since Esau died, and when he tried to buy the property from Esau when it was clear Esau would not make it, but she could not bear to set herself up for that. She had seen how it crushed her mother.

"I'll be just fine."

He eyed her.

She watched him right back and forced her chin to remain modestly lowered, even though it wanted to jut right out at him and defy him to contradict her.

"This is too much for one man, let alone a woman."

Her vision went red. She clasped her hands together behind her back so that she didn't take a swing at him.

He meant to be kind. He failed spectacularly, but that didn't change his intent. She counted to ten. She forced a smile. "Yes, it is a lot, but I am very much capable of it."

He shook his head like he was dismissing a suggestion one of his children had made about how to run Parliament. Then he looked down at her.

"I was there that day."

She went cold. "As were many others. I know what happened." She turned away from him and knelt down where she had left off weeding. Jacob's alarm, which proved an error in the end, had started the entire disaster. Then she grasped a giant handful of weeds and yanked them up so hard they sent a shower of soil across her lap. She grabbed another handful and yanked again.

"Daniel was there, too, of course."

Everyone in the militia was there. It changed nothing.

She tipped her head back to look at him. "It is past, Jacob." She reached for some mint and plucked a handful of leaves. She stood and set them in his hand for little Willy, then knelt back down and resumed her violence against the weeds. Not that yanking them out by the root made her feel one bit less alone.

He squatted down next to her. "Daniel lost his father as a result of that day."

She yanked another handful of weeds up and almost ripped up an onion. She threw the weeds aside, pushed the onion down, and firmed the soil back down around it. For just a moment, she leaned her weight on her hands in the soil and dropped her head. Every able-bodied man in the town had been there. There was no point in bringing this up again.

"He is certain it was witchcraft."

She groaned. "If he is so certain his father's death was witchcraft, why is he harassing Goody Carter for Goodman Cook's negligence? Doesn't he have more important witches to hunt?" Daniel Kendrick's problems were the last thing she was going to spend energy on today. She tossed aside more weeds and just missed Jacob's knee. He was interfering with her work.

Jacob studied her with his head tilted to the side like he was pondering something. She stood and shifted to the next row before kneeling again. She glanced at the sky and wanted to growl. Too much of the day was already gone, and she still needed to gather some meadowsweet.

"Not just his father's death."

"You are keeping me from getting my work done." She tried to soften her tone. "I have no time for riddles. I need to finish weeding, gather meadowsweet, and sort out a plan for my harvest—"

"You don't have time to be taking care of the likes of Goody Carter right now."

Her head snapped up. She would help whomever she wanted. Her time was hers, and she was not his ward. He needed to stop acting like she was.

"I have a neighbor in need, and it is my choice to aid her." If he would not leave off, she would hurl the next fistful of weeds right at his mouth.

Jacob was on his feet and grabbed her wrist, pulling her to her feet, too. She stared at his hand encasing her wrist like a manacle and did not trust herself to say anything.

She trembled.

"You aren't listening to me," he said. Her eyes snapped to his face. He stared back at her. "Daniel thinks everything that happened that day, and since, is the result of witchcraft. Others think he is right."

The hair on the back of her neck prickled. If Daniel thought multiple deaths were a result of systematic witchcraft, that shed a different light on his investigation of a petty accusation like Cook's. She searched Jacob's face. He released her wrist. "You need to come and stay with my family. You are much safer as a ward."

Absolutely not. Well, yes, of course, she would be safer, but she would not do it. She would be no one's ward, even if it saved her from hellfire itself. Indeed, wardship was rather how she envisioned hell if pushed to describe it.

She blinked. Then she surveyed her land. It was her autonomy. And she would not let herself be sucked in by Jacob's fears.

"I am sure Daniel Kendrick will be like a wolf on a scent as he tries to hunt down a witchcraft conspiracy so large that it is causing everything that has happened since we arrived, but that does not affect me."

He rested his hands on his hips and looked at her like she was being obstinate. Which she was and intended to continue being.

"Cook accused you. I believe you were right there when he did."

She let a breath escape. Of course, he already had heard about that. But it was a stupid accusation, and Daniel wasn't fool enough to ignore the evidence of his own eyes. Cook startled the chicken and then worried the hound with his own reaction, and that caused the whole chain of reactions. This was absurd. She had things to do. "He will not start a formal investigation of me because Goodman Cook is afraid of chickens."

This conversation needed to be over now. She turned to go to the house, and Jacob could feel as insulted as he liked by it.

"Are you certain?"

Something in his voice made her turn back to him, and over his shoulder, she could see Daniel, his long legs striding toward her. Her heart stopped for a moment. She glanced around to see what else might befall her in the next moments. Perhaps a millstone falling out of the sky onto her head?

Her blood pounded in her ears, and she marched past Jacob and out to meet Daniel. "Are you seriously here to question me about something you witnessed with your own eyes?" She pointed a finger at him, and her whole body burned like the blaze from her hearth. She shook with anger.

"No."

She was still for a moment. She searched his face and found no trace of humor.

Why on earth was he here then?

Jacob shook his head. A warning perhaps, but he was wrong. Daniel was not here to question her. And she was done with being ordered around.

"I am here to order you to the meetinghouse tomorrow at noon to answer formal charges in front of the selectmen and the town."

Her bile rose, and her pulse took off like a bolting horse, and she tried to make sense of what he had said. She wasn't being granted an initial interview. She already stood officially accused of a capital crime.

The burly constable escorted a bent man in rags from the meetinghouse, where they had set up court for the day. It pained Daniel to see the man so hard up, but it was the duty of the selectmen to keep outsiders from becoming a public charge the town could ill afford. He was one of the selectmen, one more thing he had inherited when his father died. And it was his first court day since being elected warden.

He spun the pot of ink on the table. On the tenth rotation or so, he stopped.

Jacob glanced at him sideways, and Daniel ignored him. Daniel was the one who had spent countless hours into the night preparing for court today, not Jacob. Jacob and the other selectman had families, so the duty had fallen on Daniel. His pulse quickened. He relished the opportunity to begin weeding out the evil that had cost him and the community so much over the past few years.

The oiled linen windows glowed from the sun outside but didn't let all that much light into the cavernous building, so a lamp sat on the table so they could see well enough to record the proceedings. Thank goodness it was summer, so they could leave the doors wide open. That let in the most light. It also let in flies and a dog that seemed to have come with the hope of finding food scraps that people dropped. Not unlike the man who had just been escorted out.

Jacob sat down next to Daniel while they waited for the constable to bring in a family that wanted to take up residence on a farm they intended to purchase from Goodman Sinclair, who wanted to move his family back to Boston. The frontier had taken too much toll on the man. Another stabilizing influence gone.

Daniel looked toward the door and all the muskets stacked there, where men had left them when they entered the meetinghouse. Maybe the new family would put down roots and become part of their tiny bulwark against the French and their allies.

"You going to head to Boston to look for a bride now that you finally can afford one?" Jacob's voice startled him, and he glanced around the assembled crowd to be sure no one else had heard. It was none of anyone's affair. He knew his duty, and he would fulfill it, but he wasn't leaving town right now to do it. He had other duties, too. Caring for his ailing father and then seeing to his affairs hadn't put him in a romantic frame of mind, nor had being the target of witchcraft himself.

"We don't need any more clueless city folk up here." He would figure out a bride on his own when he had time, and he didn't want to discuss it in the meetinghouse, where half the town would share their opinions on what course he should take.

Then Mr. Aldrich chimed in. "Yes, look for someone with a little more backbone in order that she can support you in your duties up here." The man smiled, and Daniel's gut dropped. "She will need to be sturdy for the likes of you." Daniel's cheeks burned out of proportion to the temperature of the room.

"With a wife in your bed, maybe the witches will give up hope of having their way with you and leave you alone at night, or perhaps your wife will get jealous and run them off for you." Jacob laughed so hard at his own jest that the crowd all looked up at the dais. But then they all looked back at the door as the constable entered, leading the family petitioning to become citizens of the town.

Daniel sat up straight on his seat on the dais, and Jacob managed to bring his mirth more or less under control. Daniel shot him a glance. Jacob held up his hands in surrender and forced a sober expression. Daniel's responsibility to the community weighed heavy, and he was in no mood to have his first chance to make some progress marred by his friend, making him look a fool.

He turned his focus back to the new family. They appeared sober and strong if dusty from travel. Perhaps they would be a good fit. As long as the man of the family could handle a musket and swore to serve in the militia, they could stay. The town couldn't afford to further weaken their defenses. Of course, just having extra bodies didn't always mean anything good if they didn't follow the chain of command, as he had learned.

The man of the family stepped forward to address Daniel. "I thank thee for hearing our petition."

Daniel almost groaned out loud, and the minister and several others gasped. Daniel and the other selectmen exchanged glances. Only Quakers clung to antiquated thees and thous.

They might as well have shown up dressed as Macbeth's witches, and as warden, the town's moral standing was his purview. Quakers were the worst kind of heretic, and only two decades before, Mary Dyer had been hanged in Boston for trying to spread her Quaker beliefs.

He held up his hand to stop the man. There was no point in letting him waste anyone's time. But he could at least begin with a simpler question than their relationship with the Devil.

He watched the man's face. "Let us save time and address a critical issue. Will you serve in the militia?"

The man shifted and glanced at his wife. She lay a comforting hand on his arm, which seemed to give him strength. He returned his gaze to Daniel. "As thee has surmised, we believe thou shalt not kill applies to all situations, and therefore, I cannot serve in the militia." Daniel opened his mouth to speak, but the wife jumped in.

"He is a skilled mason and builder. We can help build defenses to keep people safe." She met Daniel's gaze. "We won't kill. That does not mean we wish to die or wish to see our neighbors dead. We will do all in our power to help keep the town safe, short of breaking God's law. Surely, thee cannot ask us to go against God to stay in this town."

They needed a mason. Desperately. But the woman spoke out of turn. And her husband didn't appear to be the least bit concerned about her speaking for him. Even if she were not a witch, this lack of deference was exactly what brought disorder, and disorder was dangerous. Indeed, it was deadly.

It seemed he would have to be more direct.

"Have you been run out of your previous home for witchcraft?" Daniel asked.

That brought a sharp intake of breath from the woman, and now even Jacob leaned in, watching her face.

The husband stepped in front of her, blocking their view. "I will not have thee malign my wife in front of the good people of this community. If we are not welcome, tell us. We will take our skills and trade somewhere else." He held his chin high as he still shielded his wife from them. He had the instincts needed to be an excellent militiaman if only he hadn't allowed himself to be led by the Devil. He was no coward.

But Daniel could not risk the lives of the community if the man would not serve. It was against the law. And with the Devil already among them, he could not risk allowing Quakers to stay.

"I see you have not denied the charge," said Daniel.

"How can we when we are accused the moment we open our mouths?" the wife asked, stepping out from behind her husband. "If people assume a connection between our faith and witchcraft, we are accused for merely trying to go about our lives."

The two of them stood there, side by side, shoulders squared, facing what they had to know was expulsion. And not for the first time, it appeared. But he had to discharge his duty.

"I am sorry, but we cannot allow you to become part of our community."

They squeezed each other's hands but otherwise did not react. No matter how much they had hoped, it was clear this was what they had expected. As well they should.

For all that he knew not to trust outward appearance, especially in times like these, they seemed a decent pair. He considered suggesting they try New York. He glanced around the meetinghouse and saw all eyes upon him.

"We wish you should be on your way today."

The constable came and escorted them from the meetinghouse, and Reverend Maitland uttered a prayer asking the Lord to preserve them from Quakers in their midst and any lingering heretical contagion they might trail in their wake. Cook muttered something about Satan's work from the front row.

Daniel had fended off two destabilizing forces from the community today, and he should feel better about that than he did. He stood to stretch his aching muscles and walked a few paces to loosen them further, then he turned back to the dais and saw Jacob watching him. Jacob was probably judging his work with the cases so far, or he might be anticipating the final one of the day since that one touched close to home for Jacob.

Daniel rubbed at his aching back.

Since he would not bring formal charges against Goody Carter after his interview with her, he needed to get on with charging Goody Turner. He needed to show some results, so he had skipped questioning her before he brought her in front of the court. With luck, he wouldn't regret that.

He glanced out to the road and saw the Penobscot Sagamore and a few of his men approach in an orderly formation. The Sagamore was easy to spot, with his graying hair carefully pulled back from his face, his shoulders at least as broad as any other warrior's, English or Penobscot, covered in a beaded collar that denoted his high rank. Daniel glanced at Jacob and Aldrich. They weren't scheduled to meet with the Sagamore, so perhaps he was just in town to trade the furs. He looked back out the door.

The Sagamore strode right for the meetinghouse, and Daniel's pulse picked up again. Everyone on the dais sat up straighter, and the sound of quiet voices from the crowd created a hum that grew in intensity as the Penobscots reached the building. Since Daniel was the only selectman on his feet, he went to the door to greet the Penobscot headman.

The Sagamore's face might as well have been carved out of the local granite. Something had angered him. He looked to Daniel and then to the other selectmen and then took in the crowd. "I am here to make sure the headman in Boston told you that every family in this town owes my people one bushel of corn as soon as it is harvested."

The governor had told them no such thing, at least not that Jacob and Aldrich mentioned. Daniel turned to the other selectmen to see if they knew what he was talking about, and both had their jaws set in defiance. Neither appeared confused.

A chill crept up Daniel's neck, raising one hair at a time.

His head swiveled back to the Sagamore.

"This man is surprised." The Sagamore stabbed his finger into Daniel's chest. "Be sure no one else is." And he turned and left, with his men following close behind.

Daniel's chest might as well have been stabbed with a knife rather than a finger. After two years of war and two more years of raids, a bushel of corn was a purse of His Majesty's own gold.

And if they didn't pay it, they would pay in lives.

Again.

4

Ruth marched along the road to the meetinghouse. She should not have to be answering to the selectmen based on Goodman Cook's charges, especially when Daniel Kendrick had been right there to witness the whole ridiculous affair.

She might lose her mind and knock their heads together if they didn't listen to reason. If she had to pay for a misdeed, it might as well be one she had the satisfaction of committing.

She passed the Penobscot Sagamore and his men and smiled, then bowed her head, not making eye contact. No need to be rude to them. They, at least, had done nothing to earn her ire.

When she reached the meetinghouse, she stopped. A cloud drifted across the sun. She closed her eyes and took a few slow breaths.

Then she opened her eyes and marched into the gloom of the meetinghouse.

It was crowded and in turmoil.

"I never agreed to the treaty conditions. If people in Boston want to pay a quitrent to the Penobscot, they can go right ahead and do that, but no one even consulted us, so why should they get to say we have to pay to live on our own land?"

Ruth couldn't see who was talking in the dark interior of the building. At least they were not arguing about her.

She stood just inside the door as her eyes adjusted to the dim light. Were her neighbors all here to see her questioned? They must have more pressing work to do somewhere else.

Daniel banged his fist on the table, making an ink pot bounce and almost topple. He grabbed at it just in time to keep it from obliterating his notes. "Enough." The crowd went silent. He glared at the mob. "We will discuss this in the next town meeting. Today is court day, and we have important business on the docket to contend with."

He caught her eye and hesitated. Heat spread up her neck and across her cheeks. She was the important business.

Every set of eyes in the room followed Daniel's gaze to land on her. The meetinghouse hummed as neighbor elbowed neighbor, and they whispered back and forth. Her breathing was steady, but it sounded loud in her ears. She heard "witch," "forward," and "familiar." She almost grunted. If she were to take up witchcraft, she would have better taste than to pick a chicken as a familiar.

Daniel motioned for her to come forward. She couldn't read his expression in the dim light from where she was, and the constable didn't give her time to stare as he took her arm and pulled her forward. He wasn't as big as her brother, but he was almost as strong. They walked up to the center of the building, and the heat of every pair of eyes burned her skin.

She forced her own eyes to stay locked on Daniel's rather than let them stray to the faces of her neighbors. She didn't even look at the other selectmen. Not even Jacob, her brother-in-law. Daniel had to understand these proceedings were nonsensical.

She reached the dais, and the constable let go of her arm. The sensation of fingers lingered, but she resisted the urge to rub it away. She would not let them know how much his grip pained her soul if not her arm.

Daniel leaned forward, and Jacob leaned back slightly as if he was not part of what was coming.

"Goodwife Turner," Daniel said, "we are here to determine if you should be officially indicted for witchcraft." His voice seemed to bounce around the rafters in the ceiling, coming back to her over and over, and the cold formality of his using full term 'Goodwife' froze the blood in her veins. "I trust you understand the seriousness of the proceeding?"

She did, and she should not be in this position. She wanted to yell at him for the absurdity of it all. But, as he said, this was deadly serious.

She nodded her head once, not risking opening her mouth.

"Goodman Cook has accused you of setting your familiars upon him at Goodwife Carter's home. Did you do this?"

She took a slow breath before answering. "You know I did not." She kept her eyes on him. How dare he.

"She—"

Daniel held up a hand in Goodman Cook's direction, his eyes never leaving hers. He said nothing. Her ears felt as though they had burst into flame. He gestured for her to continue.

She took a deep breath that verged on a sigh, which was a mistake because Cook stank of his hogs even on court day, and she had just drawn it deep into her lungs.

"He flapped his hands at one of Goodwife Carter's chickens that strayed close to him," she said, trying not to gag on Cook's stench, "and he startled it, causing it and the others to fly up in his face in their effort to escape, and he panicked and caused the hound to come running, and it grabbed one of the chickens." She heard a few chuckles from the crowd, and if it weren't possible for her to be hanged for this, she would laugh, too. "The hound grabbed one of the chickens, and I had to save the chicken from its jaws because Goody Carter cannot afford to lose yet more of her winter food supply to Goodman Cook and his errant livestock."

"Did you command the bird to attack him?"

Her jaw hung slack for a moment. "You know I did not. You were there."

"Because I did not hear it does not mean it did not happen." His voice was level as if he cared not a whit for her logic or for the logic of his own eyes. "Goodman Cook claims you have a history of witchcraft, and in these times, we cannot ignore that."

Her spine straightened, and she might as well have been slapped across the face.

Cook's voice piped up. "Her mother was a witch, and I've even heard her own brother call her a witch, and...," he trailed off, looking at the dais. Jacob shook his head, and Daniel glared at Cook for speaking out of turn.

Her mother was most certainly not a witch, and Ruth felt tears sting her eyes for the first time. "My mother spoke her mind, and she stood up for justice." And she taught Ruth to do the same. A sob almost escaped Ruth's mouth. Her mother had paid a high price for her outspokenness. But she had been in the right.

Ruth raised her chin and looked Daniel in the eye. "Once again, this town appears to treat widows with a distinct lack of godly charity. Unless you have evidence against me, you have no business hauling me before the court like this."

The audience inhaled sharply, almost as one, and then went silent. All eyes rested on Daniel. He appeared unmoved.

He looked to Cook. "Is her brother's accusation the only evidence you have of past witchcraft?"

"Apart from the Lord, who knows a person better than family?" Cook looked to Jacob and then back to Daniel and then glanced around at the crowd. "I am not the only one who has heard this."

She should have taken Goody Carter's warning more seriously.

Except this was ridiculous. Because her brother had not the wits or patience to accept her did not mean his favorite insult for her should be used as legal evidence against her.

Her eyes searched the meeting house. Familiar faces gazed back at her with expressions varying from curiosity to sympathy to open hostility.

There. Matthias had buried himself at the back of the crowd. She looked him in the face, and he shifted his weight from one foot to the other, not meeting her eye.

"Matthias Derwin, what evidence do you have that your sister is a witch?"

Matthias stared at his feet as everyone else stared at him.

Daniel rephrased the question. "Why have you called your sister a witch?"

Matthias' shoulders rose and sank like he had taken a deep breath of resignation. Finally, he directed his eyes to the dais. "She is too forward."

The skin on Ruth's body rose like gooseflesh. Daniel's eyes swung her way. She should perhaps not have barged into his home to defend Goody Carter.

But someone had to stand for justice, and it was clear that would not be any of the men in the community.

Daniel turned back to Matthias. "Most of us have family who try us. Is that all the evidence you have against her?"

"She does not take direction and insists on supporting herself gadding about as a doctoress." Matthias' words were flat, and he gave the impression he wanted the floorboards to swallow him.

Her last surviving blood relative was ashamed to be publicly associated with her.

She glanced at Goody Francis, the local midwife. She was plump, and her tight knot of chestnut hair didn't shift at all as she jerked her face from Matthias' to the dais. She was the only other woman in the meetinghouse. Ruth was not part of the community of women who assisted childbirth since she had not yet had children, but she did not infringe on the midwife's work. She only came in with medicine sometimes when a new mother was in a particularly poor way long after she should be back to her life. The midwife turned and glared at her. It wasn't Ruth's fault that she had learned remedies the midwife didn't know.

Midwives had some legal standing in these matters, which was no doubt why she was present today, but it was obvious the woman was not coming to her defense. Ruth was not part of the midwife's network, and that was that.

Daniel cleared his throat, and all eyes swung back to him. Ruth's chest tightened. None of what was said was sufficient evidence to indict her. Her mother had had much more evidence against her and had not been formally charged. Acid rose in her throat.

She studied Daniel's face. He had dark smudges beneath his eyes, and his lower lip jutted out like he was working something over in his mind. As the newly elected warden, he was obliged to hold the hearing. But he was still rational. He had to let her go.

Daniel's shoulders sagged. "We will adjourn this hearing until I can question Matthias Derwin and any other witnesses that might come forward today."

Her eyes snapped to her brother, who stood like an oak, mute and unmoving. Even from where she stood, she could see his hand was healing. He might be ashamed of her doctoring, but it saved him from losing his hand. Or worse.

He kept his eyes on Daniel, no doubt to avoid risking eye contact with her.

Her chest tightened as if by an unseen rope.

Daniel leaned toward Jacob and whispered something to him. Jacob nodded. Surely, he would send her home now.

Daniel stood. "You will remain in the household of your husband's brother until we reconvene this hearing."

The entire dais seemed to waver. She grasped the constable's arm for support, and panic grasped her throat.

The next morning, Daniel sat by himself in the meetinghouse, waiting for Jacob and Matthias to join him. No other witnesses had been willing to come forward, but if Matthias could provide him with better evidence than Cook, Daniel would at last have a witch to put on trial so he could do what the town selected him to do as warden.

And none too soon.

Of course, if he had taken the time to depose everyone before bringing Ruth before the court, he wouldn't have embarrassed himself by having to delay the proceedings publicly. Humbling lesson learned about rushing the judicial process. If he weren't so sleep-deprived, he might have recognized his poor judgement before it smacked him in the face.

He rubbed his eyes and stifled a yawn. He had been afflicted again last night with images of the disaster in Jacob's woods. The day Ruth's husband was fatally injured.

Perhaps she held him responsible? Perhaps she held the entire town responsible.

He stood and stretched, then rubbed his hands through his hair to stimulate his mind. He needed to better understand how a witch might rationalize her behavior.

The door opened.

Daniel spun around, his heart pounding out of his chest. His eyes strained to see who was silhouetted in the morning sunlight that blazed outside.

It was Jacob Turner.

Daniel let out his breath. He never used to startle so easily, and the strain of it was not helping him think straight.

Jacob's laughter bounced around the rafters of the big room. "You looked as though you expected Satan himself." He entered and approached Daniel. "Sorry to disappoint." He thumped Daniel on the back, then sat himself down on the pew they had placed to serve as a bench for the selectmen.

Daniel avoided his gaze and instead looked around the dark, empty meetinghouse. Empty, but not empty. He could almost see the dead sitting in the rafters, looking down and waiting for him to end the evil. Judging him for how long it was taking.

A shiver crawled up his spine. He had to shake off the affliction that was planting these visions in his mind.

In walked Matthias. At last.

Daniel went to him and clapped him on the shoulder, ready to get started. Aldrich's wife had begun her labors overnight, so it was just the three of them.

Daniel opened his mouth to speak, but Jacob spoke over him.

"Brother, you are very welcome." Jacob stood and joined them in the middle of the room. Jacob and Matthias took each other's measure.

This had to be awkward for them as the accused was the sister of one and the sister-in-law of the other.

Sweat beaded on Matthias' brow despite the early hour. He turned to Daniel. "Are we really to pay the Sagamore a bushel of corn from each family?"

The corn. Daniel had meant to ask Jacob about that after the meeting yesterday but had been so focused on finding a witness with some hard evidence that he clean forgot about it.

The corn would be a big deal if that was true. But this was not the time. He had a witch to catch before he collapsed from lack of sleep. He looked to Jacob.

"We did not negotiate that," said Jacob, "nor were we consulted, so no. Boston has taxed us to death, and they cannot now have us pay taxes to the Penobscot, too. The war is over."

That sounded simple. Perhaps too simple. "When did this come to pass?" Daniel asked.

Jacob waved him off. "While you were nursing your father and then attending to his affairs. We didn't bother you with it because there are no grounds for us to pay it."

He should remember to get more details later to be sure that logic was sound, but it was time to get to the business at hand.

"Let us sit." He gestured to the pew in front of the dais. Matthias sat. Daniel and Jacob moved to the pew on the dais and sat. Matthias fidgeted as he looked up at them, but they had to maintain the dignity of their roles.

Daniel leaned forward a bit, but it wouldn't do to loom. Few people responded well to that.

"As you know, your sister Ruth stands accused of witchcraft by Goodman Cook."

Matthias nodded.

"He says you have also accused her of witchcraft." The muscles in Matthias's temple twitched as Daniel spoke. "Is this true?"

Matthias looked from Daniel to Jacob and back to Daniel. He let out a long breath, and his eyes dropped to the floor. "I have called her that, though I did not realize it was within others' hearing."

Daniel's pulse quickened. "On what grounds?"

Matthias shifted his bulk awkwardly on his pew. "She goes about as a doctoress."

"That is quite forward of her." But it was not hard evidence, which Matthias knew. Daniel waited.

Matthias shifted, not meeting his eyes. "She scoffs at the idea of witchcraft."

Daniel could see Jacob shake his head out of the corner of his eye, but Jacob's pen continued to scratch against the paper, recording the proceedings. Daniel kept his eyes on Matthias. Patience was more than a virtue. It was a useful tool.

Matthias sat, inspecting the healing wound on his hand, perhaps searching it for the right words.

Daniel waited.

Matthias' face grew more strained as the silence lengthened.

Daniel resisted the urge to scratch an itch on his left ear. He stayed still, eyes on Matthias.

At last, Matthias' head drooped a little further as if the weight of it was too much to keep holding up. "You know my other reasons."

Jacob's pen stopped. "We need you to state your case for the records."

"I don't have a 'case'," Matthias said, "I just have the same knowledge everyone else has." Now, he was looking hard at Jacob like he was trying to suss him out.

"Then state that knowledge," said Jacob.

Daniel didn't remind Jacob that, as warden, it was for Daniel to direct the interview. It let him study Matthias more closely when the man's attention was on Jacob.

Matthias flung his hands up in frustration. "My mother. Obviously."

Daniel's skin prickled. All of this was important and could help secure a conviction, and he needed just one new piece of hard evidence against Ruth to start the formal process for a trial. He needed Matthias to just spit out what he knew.

"Your mother was accused but not convicted," Daniel said.

"You have no idea what it is like to live with that," Matthias said.

"Did she teach your sister malefice?"

Matthias went pale at the word. "How would I know?"

"You lived with them," said Jacob. Jacob inhaled to say more.

This time, Daniel raised a hand for Jacob to stop.

Jacob flashed him a glance but then inclined his head in Daniel's direction, ceding the floor.

Daniel turned back to Matthias. "You are right that your sister has shown strong indications that she is a witch, but do you have hard evidence?"

Matthias looked at him. "Only what I have told you." He looked at Jacob, then back at Daniel. "She needs to be brought to heel before she causes real trouble."

Jacob broke in. "Just last week, she was deriding the remedy of Doctor Kingsman for a malignant eye. Goody Randolf didn't know whose advice to follow, and now her son can't see. Goody Randolf hadn't even called her to the sickbed. She just showed up uninvited and countermanding Doctor Kingsman's treatment."

Daniel sat up straighter and turned to Matthias. "Did Goody Randolf use your sister's remedy instead?"

"No, she used Doctor Kingsman's."

"But she hesitated and debated, and that could have made a difference," Jacob said, voice subdued.

Daniel felt the air go out of himself like a deflated goatskin bladder.

Still no hard evidence. He should have done more investigation before calling a formal hearing. He'd been too rash in his hopes to finally put this to rest.

"Everyone knows your sister is a doctoress, but have you hard evidence of witchcraft?"

"I have told you all I have. I don't know with any certainty that she practices witchcraft." Matthias crossed his arms in front of his chest.

Daniel's hands fisted, and he stopped himself from flinging the ink pot off the table.

He needed to find the witch or witches at work, but accusing someone of witchcraft and finding the genuine witch were not the same thing.

Focusing his attention where there was no evidence could distract him from his calling.

"We have nothing," Daniel said.

Matthias stood. "She needs to be brought in line so she doesn't bring further disorder."

He was right. Daniel rubbed his hands over his face. Even without evidence to bring her to trial for witchcraft, she was sewing trouble.

But there was no definitive evidence she was the underlying cause of the pervasive evil, and he needed to focus on the larger aim. And he should have known better than to pin his hopes on Matthias having miraculous evidence that would wrap up the issue with a tidy bow. Evil was wilier than that. What a fool.

Jacob placed a hand on his shoulder. "I have faith in you." He squeezed. "And in the meantime, she can remain as my ward, and I will take responsibility for her."

"No," Matthias said, the abruptness of his reply making Daniel jump. "She needs to remarry and become a productive member of the community."

Daniel wasn't sure it mattered which way she was brought under someone's legal restraint. Both would put her under authority that could keep her from causing further trouble, so either would serve his purposes and let him get back to work on righting the course of the community. Just because she wasn't demonstrably a witch didn't mean that her behavior didn't draw evil to them.

The unknown sucked eggs.

"I can help keep her lands productive," said Jacob, "and if she wants to remarry later, she can, and her land will bring more to her marriage, giving her better choices."

Matthias stood. "And you would choose who she could marry," he said, voice cold. "Or not allow her to marry."

The air between them grew brittle.

Daniel's eyes bounced from one man to the other. Now, the witches were setting neighbor against neighbor. And it was his job to stop them.

5

Ruth grabbed some jars of various salves and a small bottle of her meadowsweet tincture and shoved them into her basket alongside the splinting materials already there. She didn't know if Goodman Smith had actually broken his leg, but she would not take a chance that he didn't have the supplies she needed or make him wait while she ran back home to fetch them.

She stepped out her door and rammed face-first into her brother-in-law's chest.

"Oof."

He was unfazed. If she were taller, she would have some more heft to her body, and at least he would have oofed, too. Instead, he caught her basket before she dropped it and then set it down on the doorstep.

She glared up at him. "I am in a rush to help Goodman Smith. He fell from his loft." She tried to step around him, but he moved to block her path.

"Let his wife tend him."

"She doesn't know how to set a bone."

He looked down at her. "Has he broken a bone?"

"We won't know until I get here, will we?" She tried to shove past him, but he wouldn't budge. "Unless you have a serious feud with Goodman Smith that I am unaware of, let me go to him so I can ease his pain."

He placed one hand on each of her arms and steered her bodily back into her house.

"If Goody Francis can't handle it, they can call for Doctor Kingsman."

She yanked free of his grip. "He's not giving birth, and Goody Francis is with Mistress Aldrich, who is. And I can help him faster than Doctor Kingsman."

"Let's focus on your ability to feed yourself through the winter."

Winter was later, and Goodman Smith was hurt now. This was beyond Goody Francis' scope, and Doctor Kingsman was fifty miles away in Wells, assuming he was even at home.

She tried to push through to the door again.

"Being charged isn't enough? You need to be indicted, too?"

She stopped trying to bull her way past him and stared hard at his face.

"You need to be careful." He was looking at her like she was a small child playing near the hearth.

Good to know what he thought of her judgement.

"What do you have to eat this winter?" he asked.

"Enough." With luck. And it wasn't like Matthias would let her starve if it came to that.

He turned her in the doorway so that she was facing out toward her nearest field. It wasn't much, but she estimated it was enough to get her through the winter with seed for next year if she ate sparingly. She would be alright.

"How are you going to get that in before winter by yourself?"

Her lungs deflated. She had helped Esau bring in the harvest, but she helped—she followed directions—she didn't know what to do when. There was so little, and she still might not be able to get it in. Esau had barely gotten half the field planted, then she had been too distracted tending to him as he lay dying and hadn't had time or energy to tend to what he had gotten planted. Now, the fields were patchy, with bare gaps where some of the corn had been strangled by weeds and died.

She glanced at Jacob's face. He was looking at her like he could see into her head and watch her work through the question.

But she could figure it out. If a fool like Goodman Cook could do it, she certainly could.

"Such a waste of productive land." Jacob shook his head.

She shoved herself away from him, and her mouth hung open for a moment before she could get words out. "For having a lead ball lodged in his back, he did a pretty impressive job of getting as much planted as he did." Her eyes stung at the memory of her husband dragging himself out to the field to plant, shaking with fever, and gore oozing through his clothes. He knew he would not live through the spring, but he did what he could to feed her through the winter. He'd been a good man. One she could have grown to love.

Jacob's eyes had gone wide. "I didn't mean...." He turned away.

Maybe it wasn't fair of her to lash out at him.

Of course, it wasn't fair of her to lash out at him. Esau had been his brother. She inhaled, then exhaled in a rush.

She gave him a hard look through narrowed eyes. When she had gone to Jacob for help when Esau was dying, his answer had been to try to buy the farm right out from under her and to have her live in his house as little more than a servant. He would have had the legal right to keep her in an endless indenture and forbid her from practicing healing, and he would have done it. He didn't approve of her skills.

If she hadn't interrupted them, Esau would have sold the land. His idea of help was her idea of hell.

"I'm sorry, but I need to get to Goodman Smith." Enough brooding over the past. The present was where she could be useful. She grabbed her basket from the doorstep, but he grabbed it too. She stopped pulling before the handle broke. "What?" She glared at him.

"He fell from his loft."

"I believe I already said that."

He took a slow breath. "He has climbed in and out of the loft a thousand times if he has done it once."

She resisted the urge to roll her eyes. "Yes, and on the thousand and first time, he misstepped and fell. And he is in agony, with no one there to tend his injuries."

His eyes narrowed slightly like she was the slow one and was trying his patience. "Or a witch sent a specter to push him."

For the love of heaven and all that was holy, he was going to drive her to distraction. "Well then, I had better get there to help him lest anyone think I had anything to do with his fall. Surely a witch wouldn't mend an injury she caused?" She pulled her basket out of his hands before he realized what she was doing and turned and trotted down the path.

"Do you want to show an unseemly interest in his injuries?"

Stopped and whirled around to face him. "Unseemly? I am trying to help the man." She wanted to shake her fist at him. "I have the skills to help him, and he can't afford to pay to have Dr. Kingsman come all the way from Wells. In case you hadn't noticed, the past few years have been hard on everyone, not just us."

"Can't you see I am trying to protect you?"

She pulled in a long breath that quavered, and then she had to pull in another one before she could speak. He and Matthias were as close as she had left to protectors. But even though Jacob was now a selectman, a position he had more or less inherited from his father, since Esau had had no interest in politics, there was only so much he could do if she was indicted. She closed her eyes, then opened them. This was what had happened to her mother, and her mother hadn't survived. It would not happen to her.

"They have agreed for you to be my ward. If you behave, we can have an end to the charges."

He might as well have tossed a bucket of ice-cold water in her face. "If I behave?"

Under no circumstances would she become anyone's ward. Ever. She would have even less autonomy than in marriage and none of the benefits of marriage. "I am a grown woman with assets and skills, and I do not need a guardian to tell me what I can and cannot do."

She spun away so he couldn't see her lip trembling. Tears of anger rolled down her cheeks, and no way was he going to have a chance to misinterpret them.

"Ruth, stop."

She ignored him and kept walking, her limbs shaking. She would not hand over the entire direction of her life to him after finally breathing freely for the past few months.

"How do you expect me to protect you if this becomes evidence against you?"

She spun back once more. "If my aiding a neighbor can be used as evidence against me, and my not aiding him can be used as evidence against me, then I may as well go to him and tend his injuries so that I can at least live with my own conscience." Her voice echoed back from the trees behind her house, sending its vibrations right back through her body.

Fine, let the heavens hear her. "If anyone is so illogical as to not see the absurdity of such 'evidence' that cannot be disproved, then perhaps it is the people hearing the evidence who are in league with the Devil."

Her breath came hard and fast like she had been running. She watched his face turn to stone.

They were both silent as the air crackled between them like right before a lightning strike.

She had perhaps overstepped, but someone had to point out the truth.

"You need to stop acting out and let me help you, before you swing from the town oak and your lands are forfeit to Cook as your accuser."

Her blood grew cold for a moment.

She would not be the first widow to hang unjustly. But those were in panics, and that happened years ago in Connecticut, not here. The selectmen were not fools, nor were they easily brought to panic.

And Jacob was one of them. Which meant he already had a terrible amount of power over her right now. And he wanted her to agree to be his ward.

She might just as well swing from the oak.

Her mind felt detached from her body like she was watching herself debate her actions as a disinterested spectator. She waited to see if she would make a sensible decision.

"You are doing what you can to bring healing to our town," she said, "and so am I." The community had been through enough, and she would not let fools like Cook, who had scampered off to Andover when the raids started, infect the town with absurd notions of witchcraft whenever things didn't go their way, and she wasn't going to let her neighbor suffer from a fall from his loft while she could do something about it. "I am going to help Goodman Smith now."

"Your own brother has testified against you. Please, listen to me and let me help."

Everyone knew Matthias didn't have evidence against her. They wouldn't force her into guardianship for helping a neighbor.

Of course, that was probably what her mother had thought.

Daniel's eyes scanned the empty meetinghouse. He was spending rather more time here than he had expected he would. He sighed, but the humid air felt like breathing underwater. Even the bench felt warm beneath him and already damp with his sweat.

He hadn't been able to dig up any more evidence against Ruth Turner, but she still needed to be dealt with legally. Just because there wasn't enough hard evidence to put her on trial for a capital offense didn't mean there was no evidence. Her attitude alone could have her in gaol in some jurisdictions.

Jacob entered the meetinghouse. "Matthias is bringing her."

He seemed his usual smiling self today, so he must not be concerned about serving as her guardian, which was well. At least someone Daniel trusted would keep her out of trouble or, at the very least, would share evidence against her if it came to that.

"Good," said Daniel. "I am ready to move on from this." Everyone had to get ready to bring in crops, and he had other cases to investigate. Summers were short up here.

Jacob sat down on the bench next to him, then he looked around the empty meetinghouse and back at Daniel.

"Where is Aldrich?" Jacob asked. "Don't tell me his wife is still in labor. Poor woman."

"She died last night, along with the baby."

"Oh."

They were both quiet, and Daniel said a silent prayer for Mrs. Aldrich. He didn't know her well since she was from Boston, and Aldrich had married her during the war. It hadn't been a great time for social calls and get-to-know-yous. And since Aldrich owned the other garrison house in the settlement, it wasn't like they were one of the families piled into Daniel's house, cheek by jowl, whenever the alarm was raised.

The close air was stifling in the meetinghouse, but there wasn't much he could do about it, so he just sat.

At least no one had suggested Mrs. Aldrich's travails were anything beyond it being her time. Ruth Turner had been tending Goodman Smith, so hopefully, there was no connection to witchcraft.

"Now we have two unmarried selectmen. That won't do." Jacob elbowed Daniel in the ribs. "And now you are going to have to compete with Aldrich for a bride. He likes them young, and he has a lot more money than you, so you need to move fast."

Daniel saw Jacob smiling from the corner of his eye but didn't turn to meet the man's gaze. Mrs. Aldrich wasn't even in her grave yet. This was no time for jokes about Aldrich. And he didn't exactly have time to go searching for a woman to court with all the turmoil, so Jacob could keep his stupid jests to himself.

A shadow crossed the doorway, and both Daniel and Jacob stood as Matthias led Ruth into the meetinghouse.

Her cheeks were in high color, no doubt from the heat.

The temperature in the meeting house seemed to go up ten degrees.

She raised her chin defiantly as she caught sight of them. Matthias' face was grim.

Ruth stepped out in front of her brother. Matthias crossed his arms over his chest and met their eyes over her head.

"You asked me to bring her, and I have," he said. "I hope you have thought on my words."

Ruth snapped her head around to look at him. Or perhaps glare at him would be more accurate. Matthias clearly knew his sister better than to meet her gaze, but the look she gave him must have left burn marks on his skin.

Time to rescue the man.

"Ruth Turner."

She swung her gaze back toward him, and now he felt the fire. She certainly had to be contained.

He tugged at his collar before he caught himself and dropped his hand to his side. Sweat be damned.

"I have decided not to try you for witchcraft right now."

Her pert mouth took on the shape of a smile. She tilted her head at him as if to say, 'Of course not.'

His pulse kicked up. "I am not finished."

Now she crossed her arms over her chest, a tiny mirror of her burly brother behind her. Massive as Matthias was, she might be the more intimidating of the two. At least in the meetinghouse, it should be harder for her to use her spells on them, if the books were accurate.

"Since you have no husband to take responsibility for you, we will appoint you a guardian."

Her face went white and then livid red in the span of less than a breath. She appeared to grow taller as she stretched to her full height and opened her mouth to speak.

He held up a hand to stop her. "Jacob has agreed to be your guardian."

"Well, I don't agree to that." She practically spat at them.

Daniel stood up straighter.

"I beg your pardon?" he asked.

"I would sooner hang."

She turned her blazing eyes on Jacob, and Daniel looked at him, too. His jaw hung slack for an instant, and then he snapped it shut.

Daniel glanced at Matthias, who was the only one in the room who did not look surprised. Daniel looked back at Ruth.

Clearly, he was missing something. "Would you prefer for your brother to be your guardian?"

"No!" She was agitated now, and glancing from one to another of them, like she didn't quite understand what was happening.

Jacob stood. "Then you shall be my ward." He took a step toward her. "I will help you survive and tend your lands. Don't worry." He put his hand on her shoulder, and she threw it off with such force it was a miracle she didn't wrench Jacob's arm from its socket. Instead, Jacob stepped in toward her. But before either of them could say anything, Matthias shoved his way between them.

"She should marry." Matthias was glaring at Jacob, which made no sense. Why should Matthias be opposed to Jacob becoming her guardian until she found a husband in her own time?

Jacob moved in until his face was just inches from Matthias'. "Shirker."

Ruth was practically climbing over Matthias to get between them. Even when she wedged herself between their bodies, she was so tiny he feared she might be smothered between their chests. Then she stomped on Jacob's foot so hard he yelped and jumped back a pace.

"I will never be anyone's ward. Not yours," she poked Jacob in the chest with her finger, "not yours," she pointed at her brother, "not anyone's. Ever."

Her face held the wild look of an animal hemmed in on the edge of a cliff, contemplating jumping to its own death rather than being taken.

"Your only other choice is marriage," Daniel said. Surely, that would help her see wardship would give her more options in the long term.

"I will not be a ward." She was shaking from head to foot.

She backed up a step and crashed into the bulk of Matthias behind her. He caught her before she lost her balance, but she ripped free of his grip.

He raised both hands as if to show he meant no harm. "Who would you marry?" he asked, his voice gentler than Daniel expected. As ward or wife, she would lose control of her land but gain protection, and someone would become legally responsible for her.

Her mouth opened, then closed again. She went through that cycle two more times, and still no words came.

"Cook is in need of a wife," said Jacob.

That loosed her tongue. "Have you lost your senses?" She glared at Jacob, whose lip turned up at the corner. Clearly, he didn't think anyone would accept that idea, which was good, because Daniel would have never approved that match, even if Cook would have her, which was unlikely since he brought the charges of witchcraft against her. The man couldn't control his own hogs. He didn't have a prayer with Ruth Turner.

Jacob's eyes narrowed. "Are you holding out against guardianship because you want to marry Aldrich?"

Her jaw dropped. "How can you even say that when Mrs. Aldrich right now still labors to bear his child?" Her chest was heaving with her breath, straining against the fabric of her bodice.

She hadn't heard.

Daniel stepped toward her and almost reached out to her but stopped himself. "Mrs. Aldrich died last night."

Her face tightened as though she were in physical pain, then she dropped her head and breathed for a moment.

"Poor Mrs. Aldrich. She deserved better." She raised her head then, looking up at the rafters and blinking fast. Then she turned on Jacob. "How can you be so disrespectful as to suggest I would marry her lecherous old husband before she is even cold in the ground?" She shuddered.

Daniel said, "If you don't wish to marry, I will have to appoint you a guardian." Her eyes snapped up to his as if she had almost forgotten for a moment why they were discussing the Aldriches. The haunted look returned.

"I will not be a ward." Her voice was flat for all the emotions fighting for preeminence on her delicate face.

"Well then," Jacob's voice boomed in the quiet building, "Daniel it is." He smacked Daniel on the back and grinned.

Daniel looked from Jacob to Ruth. Ruth's face mirrored the shock that must be written on his own.

He looked at Matthias, who studied him, then gave an almost imperceptible nod like he had just given consent.

To what? Daniel looked at Jacob, who was still smiling at him, almost daring him to refuse.

Shite.

He looked at Ruth again.

At least he would be able to gather evidence against her if she persisted in her ways, since she could hardly escape him if they lived under the same roof.

He forced himself to breathe. Perhaps it was her diminutive size that made her look like a lost child.

His heart pounded loudly in his ears.

If she wasn't a witch, she wasn't such a terrible choice for a wife. He had to marry, and she was already part of the community. If he hadn't been so busy, he might have thought of the idea himself.

"It's Daniel's wife or my ward," said Jacob, clearly assuming she would see reason and agree to be his ward.

She looked into Daniel's eyes, her expression almost pleading. But what did she want him to do? Agree? Not agree?

The humid air hung heavy over their heads as they all stared at each other.

The idea of being Jacob's ward had provoked the most obvious panic.

He breathed in the thick air.

"I am willing if you are," he said.

She glanced at Jacob, whose jaw had gone slack with surprise, then back at Daniel and gave one small nod of her head.

Jacob blinked a few times, and then his brows lowered as he realized he had not gotten the result he expected. That clearly displeased him. "Since we are conveniently in the meeting house. I shall post the banns on the door right now," he said, louder than necessary. Jacob stared at Daniel like he expected him to realize his error and back down.

Daniel squared his shoulders and looked back at Jacob. The man had at least solved the problem of finding a wife.

Jacob stared a moment longer, then snorted and grabbed his pen.

They all listened as Jacob's pen scratched against paper, and the magnitude of what had just happened sank in.

Daniel's eyes found their way back to Ruth's face again. It had become a grim mask.

But he had done the only logical thing. Logical if he ignored the possibility that she might still prove a witch. Or just kill him in his sleep.

6

"Felicitations to the happy couple!" said Jacob to their friends, gesturing to Daniel and Ruth.

Daniel smiled and nodded to him, then glanced at Ruth. She didn't look happy, but at least she didn't look miserable. Just...thoughtful. It was the same expression she had worn when they arrived at the magistrate's this afternoon, through the quick wedding formalities, and then back to his house.

Their house, now.

He stole another glance at her. Sharing this house with her was going to be an adjustment for him. And for her, too, of course. There had to be some way to make that easier. He was going to make this work.

Matthias' wife, Anne, interrupted his thoughts, bringing out a platter of roasted venison, and the rich, fatty aroma made his mouth water. He wasn't alone. The din in the room grew even louder as everyone gravitated toward the table and crowded in for their share of the feast she had orchestrated. Luckily, she was a large, stout woman who could carry the overburdened tray and still make her way good-naturedly through the hungry crowd.

Anne and Matthias had stood in for Ruth's parents, and Matthias had gone out hunting and, after two days in the woods, returned with a massive ten-point buck. They had all agreed it made sense to hold the wedding feast at the garrison house since it had more room than Matthias' house, and seeing everyone gather comfortably in the large main room, it was the right decision.

Hopefully, the occasion for it was, too. For Ruth and for the town.

A warm, soft sensation radiated out from Daniel's chest as his eyes took in the gathering. It was nice to have everyone gathered for a merry occasion again.

"More beer," Jacob said as he brought the pitcher and refilled Daniel's cup and then circulated through the crowd, filling every cup offered. At this rate, Daniel would have to ration his beer through the winter or recruit a new brewer to the town soon.

Matthias' children burst into laughter in the corner of the room, and soon, the surrounding adults joined in. Even Ruth smiled when she turned to watch Matthias' youngest daughter wearing a napkin on her head like a turban and grinning at her audience.

A laugh bubbled up from Daniel's chest and startled him. When was the last time he laughed? When was the last time most of the adults in the house had let loose with genuine belly laughs?

"You've done a good thing." Mr. Aldrich appeared behind him and rested a hand on his shoulder. "People needed this. No more death if we can avoid it."

Ruth must have heard what he said, and her body went almost imperceptibly stiff.

Who knew if Aldrich was referring to her not hanging or to his own wife's death or to the collective death toll of the past five years, but he was right whichever way. Daniel smiled up at him and laid his own hand on top of the older man's for a moment.

Aldrich squeezed his shoulder. "Your father would be proud of you. You are restoring divine order. Stability." He gazed up at the ceiling like he could see right through the roof to the heavens. "You remind me of him." He gave his shoulder a last pat and turned to go talk with Jacob.

"He has her handkerchief tucked in his pocket," said Ruth.

Daniel almost jumped. She hadn't spoken to him since the guests had arrived, and even before then, their conversation had just been practical logistics. Now, she sounded a little wistful, like Aldrich's tiny gesture toward his late wife moved her.

He smiled. He should probably say something, but he might say the wrong thing and make her tense up again. Better she get to relax.

She gave him a little smile in return and then looked back at her niece's antics. Her nephew had now joined in with his own napkin, and they appeared to be reenacting something they had no doubt seen in town.

"Auntie Ruth!" the littlest called, "Come show me how to fold a kerchief!"

She went to her and sat the little girl on her knee.

Jacob sat down on the bench where Ruth had been sitting. "We are not giving the Penobscot a bushel each of our crops. I worked hard for my corn, and it is mine, no matter what Boston says." The corners of his mouth were drawn down in a frown, and his chin jutted out.

"Are you talking taxes to me at my wedding feast?"

Jacob considered him for a moment, and then his face broke into a wide grin. "Are we a little nervous to be making our debut with a seasoned performer tonight?" He thumped Daniel on the back so hard he almost dropped the mug of beer he had just been lifting to his lips.

Heat burned Daniel's cheeks as his beer sloshed.

He set down his mug and then smacked Jacob on the arm. "She is a widow, not a professional, you arse."

Jacob laughed so loud that others turned to see what was so funny. But he was the one person in town who always laughed, so they soon turned back to their own conversations and the children's antics in the corner.

"Afraid your cock won't rise to the occasion?"

Quite the reverse, not that he was going to say a bloody word about it to Jacob. He had had to go sit in the icy water of the creek more than once over the past three weeks since the banns were first read.

"Your father was a good man," said Jacob, "but his longevity was not good for the state of your stones."

Daniel's chest constricted a little at the thought of his father. Jacob's choice of conversion topics this evening was obnoxious, even for him.

Daniel would figure out what agent of Satan had been the cause of his father's death in the militia disaster in Jacob's woods during raids, along with all the other evil, including whoever was planting the visions in his sleep. Too many had died in the war, and even more had died in the raids after the war, at each other's hands in confusion and panic, which could only be a sign of the Devil's work.

He let out a slow breath. At least the image of his dead father eased the constriction in his trousers.

"Don't worry," said Jacob, "for all that she speaks her mind, I doubt she will tell you straight out if you don't compare well."

For the love of heaven, Daniel mercifully hadn't thought of that possibility. Until now. He took a sip of beer.

"Of course, we Turners do make an impression, so you might want to put in a little effort tonight." Jacob stood and slapped Daniel on the back. Bastard knew he was safe here and that Daniel wouldn't disturb the peace to knife him in the gut like he deserved.

Jacob crossed the room to his wife and murmured something in her ear that brought a sultry smile to her face.

Yes, he had thought of having Ruth in his bed these past weeks. It had kept him up more nights than the witch had. Assuming they were not one and the same. But even on those tortuous nights, it hadn't dawned on him that others might be thinking about it, too. And laughing.

He might have gotten more sleep if it had. Or at least it would have eliminated the perpetual cockstand that kept him from rolling over in bed. It was too dangerous to go sit in the creek after dark.

He spent the next hours trying to play the convivial host and to not think about lying with his new wife.

The air in the house was hot and close. Between the late August weather and all the people, the humidity made him work to breathe.

Jacob's wife gathered their children, throwing occasional glances Jacob's way and smiling every time they locked eyes. She seemed as eager as he was to get home and into his bed.

Ruth still played with her nieces and nephew. She didn't seem concerned about the last step to formalizing their marriage.

Unless she was trying to distract herself from thinking of it.

He turned his beer mug a few times in his hands.

Jacob was an ox's arse.

Anne gathered what little food was left, with the help of a few other women from the community, and Matthias began to restore order to the furniture. Daniel went to help Matthias.

"Oh, no, you don't," said Matthias. "You need to save your strength for other things." His new brother-in-law smiled at him, but at least his smile wasn't mocking like Jacob's had been. "We'll just get the worst of it cleared up, then leave the two of you to it. We'll come back and finish clearing up in the morning."

Daniel's cheeks flushed again. He was an oblivious fool not to have realized that everyone else would be as focused on his wedding night as he was. It was the event of the year. They really needed other things to occupy their minds.

Matthias smiled at someone over Daniel's shoulder. Daniel turned to look. Anne was escorting Ruth from the room.

It had grown quiet. At some point, most of the guests had left. They had just slipped out, probably figuring Daniel had other things on his mind than saying goodnight to them.

"Keep her out of trouble." All trace of a smile had vanished from Matthias' face. "Make her too busy raising children to cause mayhem. Keep her safe."

Matthias set the final trestle by the wall, then turned again to face Daniel. "Best keep her well distracted until the first child arrives." He still wasn't smiling. "She might witch something you value."

With that, Matthias joined Anne and their children at the door, grabbed his musket, and they left for their own home.

Daniel was alone in the cavernous room. His ears strained for any sound but were met with silence. He had a sudden urge to call Matthias and his family back.

Instead, he went to the door and latched it. There was nothing else to do but put out the lights, so he went to each candle and snuffed the flame out. The house was put right for the night.

He looked around in the darkness. The only light left was a soft glow coming from under the door to the other room.

She was waiting.

Ruth sat on the edge of the narrow bed in just her shift. The shutters were closed against insects and any larger intruders, and the air clung close and heavy. She fiddled with the hem of her sleeve, then forced herself to let it go and pulled the pins from her hair to let the soft length of it slide down her neck as it came free.

The bed creaked when she leaned over to place the pins on the small table holding the candle. It was the only sound she heard. The conversation and laughter of the guests were gone.

Maybe Daniel left with the guests.

She fiddled with the hem of her sleeve again.

No, his trousers had clearly been strained much of the evening, so he was probably desperate for relief by now. Not that his body's eagerness was speeding his progress to his bed.

The poor man had put up with quite a bit of goading this evening, so he was likely doing battle with his nerves out in the main room. Marital relations were the one thing all his friends knew more about than him.

She ran her fingers through her thick hair and started to plait it for the night, then stopped. It was prettier loose. Her cheeks heated, but they were married. That little vanity wouldn't send her to the Devil.

He might disagree. She gathered it in sections again.

No. She deserved to feel pretty on her wedding night.

She combed through it again with her fingers and lay back on the mattress, arranging her loose waves to the side. Her heart raced. She did not know what to expect from him.

The door latch gave a barely audible click in the silence. The door didn't open.

Her breath caught. But that was silly.

She tugged the fabric of her shift away from her body a few times like a bellows to cool her skin and then shifted again on the unfamiliar bed.

At last, the door opened, and he entered the room, and before she could enjoy the little addition of fresher air, Daniel closed the door behind him. He stood with his back to the closed door and watched her watching him. His gaze set off an unexpected shiver up and down her entire body, and it settled in her core.

But she had no unrealistic wedding night expectations this time around. Men were pretty hopeless the first time. And the second.

He still stood by the door, watching her. The stress of the day hadn't affected his readiness to consummate their marriage, judging by the bulge still evident in his trousers. At least he didn't need any of Goody Carter's cone flowers to make their marriage official.

He moved to the other side of the room and began to unbutton his waistcoat. He fumbled the last button before freeing it, then slid the waistcoat off his arms and hung it from a peg on the wall.

She looked up at the ceiling and studied the shadows dancing among the beams in the faint light of the candle. No need to make him any more self-conscious by staring at him while he undressed in front of her for the first time.

His empty shoes sounded hollow when they hit the floor, and she kept her eyes to the ceiling.

Her heart beat a little faster in her chest as she waited.

Silence.

He must be breathing, but her own breath was all she could hear.

She should probably say something to help him overcome his uncertainty, but what? They barely knew each other. Saying the wrong thing might make this even more awkward.

Then fabric rustled against fabric. Presumably, his trousers sliding down against his drawers as he removed them.

She closed her eyes against the urge to see his body.

Finally, the sound of him removing his drawers made her steal a glance, but his shirt hung down to mid-thigh.

She turned her head to look at him full-on. She couldn't help herself.

He stood, looking back at her, feet unmoving. His entire body was as stiff and strained as his cock, which jutted against the linen of his shirt. He seemed to have become rooted to the floor.

After a moment, she reached her hand out to him, and that got his feet moving.

His body appeared to exhale some tension as he crossed to the bedside. He gave her a hesitant smile. She smiled back at him, and her own muscles relaxed a fraction, too. When he got to the edge of the bed, he hesitated, then reached for the candle and snuffed it.

The room went black as pitch.

Then, the bed shifted a little under his weight when he lowered himself onto it. Her hand reached out again and felt his knee in the dark. He must be sitting with one leg on the bed so that he could face her while still keeping the other leg grounded on the floor.

Her eyes began to adjust to the dark, and a faint silhouette of his body emerged over her, darker against the dark of the room.

He took a quick, raspy breath. Silence.

He took another breath. "I know—"

She stopped his words with her fingers over his lips. If he started talking, he might not stop. She reached out and gave his shoulders a little tug to pull him down so he was lying next to her. In that moment, his body by her side was oddly comforting.

His cock twitched against her thigh. She shifted her leg, so it rubbed against his heat, making his cock jump again with more force.

His breathing got louder. So did hers.

They lay like that for a long moment.

Then his hand reached out and felt down her leg until he found the hem of her shift. He drew it up and almost lost his hold when it caught on her knee. She straightened her leg to make it easier for the hem to pass over it. The rough linen skittered across her skin as he raised it higher, making her flesh rise up in excited bumps. She shifted her hips to free the fabric from underneath her and gave it a tug with her own hand to bring it to her waist.

He let the hem go and brought his hand to her side. She lay still and waited.

Then he lifted his hand and placed it on her breast, which he kneaded through her shift. He probably didn't even realize his hips were driving against her leg in rhythm with his kneading. Panting breaths made his chest rise and fall, pressing against her other breast with each inhale.

A quiet gasp escaped her mouth and startled her. She pushed into his pressure. It had been a long time since she had a man's hand on her body.

He crushed her breast methodically against her ribcage. Despite his unpracticed efforts, her center grew warmer, and her hips rocked toward him.

Then, still kneading, he shifted his body on top of hers, his shoulder just under her chin. The alignment pushed her head up at an awkward angle. Apparently, in his eagerness, he forgot he was more than a head taller than her, and now he was humping her knees.

His fumbling movements broke her heart open a little, and she reached under his arms and pulled him up higher, her breath coming quicker as his body dragged along hers, sparking sensations she hadn't felt in an eternity. Then she bent her legs to cradle him between them.

His cock poked at her leg, where it joined her body. He shifted a little and poked at her again. He grunted.

If he had any clue what he was doing, she would think he was teasing her, but he was too inexperienced to understand the various consequences of drawing things out.

She reached down to guide him before he injured himself.

He gasped at the contact of her hand, and the sound sent heat down to her toes, and then it burned right back up into her lower belly.

His actions lacked finesse, but that didn't stop her body from being ready for him. She placed his head against her damp center, and his hips seemed to take over on pure instinct. A moan erupted from her throat.

He thrust into her with such force the bed banged against the wall. He didn't seem to notice as he thrust again.

His chest crushed down on top of her, and she had to turn her head sideways to breathe. His chest hair rasped against her cheek, and his breath sawed in and out somewhere above her head. He pounded into her with focused abandon. The sheer animal enthusiasm of his actions set off a spiraling warmth in her chest that spread down to her belly.

Who would have guessed that upright Daniel Kendrick could let go of control of himself like this?

She reached around and massaged his muscular thighs, stretching and reaching her hand until she felt his bollocks.

His body reacted as if he'd been struck by a lightning bolt, and he slammed into her so hard her twisted neck ached. But she kept her grasp on his stones and massaged them as the sweaty skin of their thighs and bellies slapped together, drew apart, and slapped together again.

His breath grew even more erratic like he couldn't coordinate his muscles to draw in enough air to supply his lungs. Then an anguished groan ripped from his chest as his entire body went rigid, and he spilled himself into her.

She could feel his balls pulsing in her hand as his hips continued to thrust, clearly beyond his control, and wave after wave of his seed pumped into her. His release went on and on until he finally collapsed his head down above hers.

Her head was light, and while he had no idea how to draw the same response from her body yet, her world had shifted just slightly.

After a few long moments, his breathing slowed, and his muscles melted into relaxation. His weight pressed even more heavily on her chest and face, and breathing became more difficult.

She held him a moment longer, then, of pure necessity, nudged him to roll off of her.

He quickly rolled away, like he hadn't even realized he was lying his full weight on top of her. Something made her reach out and catch him with her arm and pull him back toward her.

She curled up, and her back pressed back against him of its own accord. After a moment, he wrapped himself around her and pulled her close.

She stared at the wall on the other side of the room. Eventually, his breathing evened out behind her. A while after that, light snores vibrated through her hair, tickling the top of her head.

Slowly, the sound lulled her out of her own head and into sleep. She dreamed she felt his cock pressing against her from behind, and she ground her hips back against him.

She woke and reached back for him and felt only the cool mattress ticking.

She was alone.

7

Ruth bent over to move the scrubby branches of the undergrowth out of her line of vision. No mushrooms. Just bugs.

She let the branches spring back.

A lonely hawk called in the distance.

She kicked aside another low-growing set of branches but only unearthed more bugs and a toad, who did not appreciate the intrusion. The toad hopped back further into the undergrowth as she straightened.

Daniel had not been in the house when she woke. She hadn't seen him since last night.

The early morning sun reached through an open spot in the tree canopy and shone down on a small patch of grass ahead of her. A round, white fungus as big as a loaf of bread grew in the center of the mini-clearing. She went and picked it and placed it in her basket. Nothing medicinal, but a good way for Goody Carter to stretch her bread supply.

She stood back up and rubbed her back. It did not appreciate doubling over, looking under bushes for the fruits of the woods. It was going to be even less happy breaking ground at Daniels' house—her house—to get her fall plantings into a new garden. A few things would transplant, but she would be traipsing back and forth between gardens into the spring.

If Daniel hadn't vanished last night, she would have gotten started on that first thing this morning, but who knew if he cared where it went, and she wasn't going to clear the ground only to have to re-do it in a different spot if he disapproved of the first location.

Who left their marriage bed in the middle of the night without so much as a by-your-leave?

She kicked a branch. It made a satisfying crack when it hit the trunk of a sugar maple and broke into pieces.

One piece of the stick landed next to a cluster of mushrooms. She bent over them. Poisonous. She went to straighten and felt the hair on the back of her neck stand up.

She froze. Someone was watching her.

She forced her muscles to relax. No musket. She hadn't wanted to just grab one from the garrison house, and it was broad daylight. She shouldn't need one. Shite.

Her knife weighed heavy in her pocket, so she made to brush her hand against her skirt to brush off some dirt and casually slipped her hand into her pocket.

Her fingers grasped the handle, and she took a slow breath.

One, two, three.

She pulled out the knife and whirled around to see who was there.

She froze again, heart pounding out of her chest.

Two dark eyes peered back at her from the undergrowth. There were long whiskers and two tawny ears. Its muzzle was almost white. It had to be the largest catamount she had ever seen.

The vibration of its growl traveled through the ground, up her legs, and right into the core of being.

The birds had gone silent. She couldn't hear the big cat breathe. Her own heartbeat would drown it right now out, even if it were possible.

Stand. She had to stand upright and make herself look big. Not easy at her height, but she wasn't going to sit there and let it pounce. As smoothly as possible, she straightened to her full height, knife clutched in her right hand.

Its whiskers twitched.

She screamed for all she was worth and waved her hands and the cat.

It flicked its ears and growled, clearly debating whether to attack or flee.

Why couldn't she have been as tall as her big oaf of a brother?

Sweat streamed down the channel of her spine.

She screamed again and waved her arms at it.

It lowered its tail, and the muscles in its hindquarters flexed and coiled back to spring. Just as it lunged, a blood-curdling screech came from behind her.

Time slowed.

The cat's eyes appeared to widen as it twisted its body midair and changed course to its left, landed, and ran off into the trees.

Ruth whirled around, knife out, heart pounding even faster than it was before.

A Penobscot woman was running right at her, her own much larger knife in hand.

Ruth braced herself.

The woman slid to a stop just out of arm's reach.

They each stood panting, and Ruth's hand trembled from the nerves of the moment. She swallowed. The woman had to be a full head taller than her. She was as tall as Daniel.

The woman held out her left hand as though to keep Ruth at a distance, then, gradually, she lowered her knife-hand. Without breaking eye contact, she gestured to Ruth's knife with her chin.

The catamount had been about to attack, had already started, and this woman had distracted it. If she meant to kill Ruth, she wouldn't have stopped, leaving skid marks in the leaf mold a rod long.

Ruth forced her right arm down, letting her knife hand retreat to her side.

The woman slid her knife into a sheath belted over her calf-length dress and then held both hands out like she wanted to convey that she meant no harm. "You are safe?"

"Yes," said Ruth, "thank you."

The woman nodded her head once, braided hair swinging freely, apparently approving of her answer.

"It tracked you. You need to be more careful."

That stung. If her new husband hadn't decided to be a man of mystery, she would never have been so distracted.

No. It was her own doing. She was a fool to let herself be caught so off guard in the woods. Beyond a fool, and she knew better.

Heat burned her cheeks.

"You are usually more careful," the woman said.

"Excuse me?"

"Usually, you take better care."

Ruth's eyes felt like they had gone as wide as saucers. "Have you tracked me?"

The woman laughed. "No. I just collect the same things you do, so I have seen you. You and your old lady friend. She is not careful." She shook her head disapprovingly, her long black hair swinging and amplifying her opinion of Goody Carter.

Furs. She had come with the headman trading furs. "I have seen you." Ruth straightened up as tall as she could, still not reaching the other woman's chin. "I am Ruth Tur—, Ruth Kendrick."

The other woman gave her a warm smile. "I am Marie."

Ruth's eyebrows must have risen so high they got lost in her own hairline.

The other woman laughed and waved her hand like she was batting at a fly. "You people cannot say my real name. The French call me Marie. You call me that."

"The French?" Ruth's hand edged toward her knife again.

"The French, the Portuguese fishermen, the English, all of your people." She was still relaxed and didn't reach for her own knife. "Your people are bad at languages. So we learn yours."

Ruth needed to shut her mouth. She was staring, slack-jawed.

Marie looked into Ruth's basket. "You missed the meadowsweet." She shook her head. "You don't have your head on right today."

Ruth's cheeks were burning again.

Marie reached into her own basket and put some meadowsweet in Ruth's. "You walked by it first." She smiled.

A musket shot cracked, and Ruth and Marie both flinched and searched with their eyes for the source.

The sound echoed off the trees and vibrated the leaves, but it had originated off to the north. Voices reached them.

They weren't speaking English, but it didn't sound French, either. Ruth reached for her knife yet again. Marie cocked her head and focused all her attention toward the voices. Then she gave a quick nod, almost to herself.

"Their early waking has been worth it. My town will feast on a deer like yours did."

She felt the corners of her mouth sink. They had indeed feasted, and Ruth should get back and get to work on cleaning up what Matthias and Anne had had to leave last night. Maybe her errant husband was back.

Marie tilted her head to the side. "You frown."

Ruth forced her face into a smile. "No, I just should be going home. The feast was at my house, and the mess waits for me."

"It was a celebration?"

"Yes."

Marie waited.

"My wedding feast."

Marie's face almost split in two, she smiled so broadly. "Now I understand your carelessness this morning." She clapped her hands together. "You go to your man. Make him help clean. It's a fair trade." She laughed, which drew a chuckle from Ruth. "He will learn."

Her own smile faded. He couldn't very well learn anything if he kept vanishing.

She took a deep breath of the piney-scented air. And looked back up at Marie.

"Thank you," she said, "for the catamount."

"You would do the same?"

"Absolutely!"

"Then we are friends." Marie hesitated, then reached her hand out.

Ruth stared at it a moment, then shoved her own hand out. They gave each other an awkward shake and then let go.

Marie turned, waved, and walked off toward the hunters.

Ruth glanced around. No one was in sight.

She picked her basket up and headed back to the garrison house at a brisk pace. Hopefully, no one else was out in the woods to have seen her talking with Marie. Half the town thought the Penobscot were in league with the Devil already, and she was in no mood to explain it all to Daniel.

Shrieks echoed through the woods, and Daniel fought the underbrush to reach his father. Every step seemed to draw his father further away instead of closer, but he could see blood flowing from the hole in his father's chest.

He yelled to his father, who shook his head, brows lowered. The gunfire and screams were deafening, but his father's voice came through clearly as if he were standing in the front room. "You failed."

Daniel shot upright, and his eyes darted around, searching for where the sounds were coming from.

The only sound that reached his ears now was the faint rustling of the mouser prowling through the hay in the loft next to him, hunting for her breakfast.

Stands of hay clung to the sweat on his cheek, and his his lungs still worked as if he had been running to save his life.

He closed his eyes and could still see the fading image of his father, bleeding and disappointed.

But it wasn't real. The witch had put the image there, as always, taunting him for his inability to put an end to the Devil's work.

The sun was already fully up. It was late, and he needed to start his day. His muscles quivered, barely able to hold his weight as he swung himself onto the ladder, descended to the ground level of the barn, and headed for the house.

Time to face his wife.

He paused on the doorstep, then he grabbed the latch and pushed the door open. His nerves buzzed.

Maybe she had put the visions in his head. Or maybe someone else had. Either way, he didn't need her to witness him flailing and kicking and screaming in his sleep.

The main room was empty. That should not have been a relief.

He went to the bedroom. The bed was tidy, but the room was empty. There was no sign of Ruth.

He went to the ladder to the second floor and climbed. He poked his head above the floor level, but that room, too, was empty.

The increased rate of his heartbeat was more than just from the climb. Where was she?

He hastened back down the ladder and made one last check around the main room, looking below the stacked trestles. Of course she wasn't hiding under the trestles, but she had to be somewhere.

Had she returned to her old house? Maybe to her garden?

He stopped short, with his hand halfway to the door latch. The quiet of the house weighed on him. Did she think he abandoned her? He had been so wrapped up in how she was affecting him that he hadn't even considered how his own actions might have affected her. A husband for less than one full day, and already his performance was lacking.

His hand grabbed for the door latch, and his legs propelled him out the door. His feet aimed for the path to her old house.

"Daniel."

He turned, and in his sleep-deprived state, he almost overbalanced.

Matthias had spoken, and Jacob was with him. Jacob laughed, and Daniel snapped his jaw shut before any unproductively honest words escaped. He should be grateful the two seemed to have come to a truce.

"We would have come earlier," said Jacob, "but we didn't want to interrupt you two lovebirds in case you were still trying to figure out how to join your giblets."

Matthias glared at Jacob. "That is my sister you are talking about. And unless your brother was utterly incompetent, I am certain she could give Daniel basic directions."

"True," said Jacob. "She doesn't suffer fools."

Daniel's face burned hotter than if he had stuck his head in the fireplace. She had given him directions, if not verbal ones, and the experience had far exceeded his expectations. And it had had thirty-one years of expectations to live up to. His cock swelled at the memory.

"Good gad, he has a log in his trousers just thinking about it." Jacob was almost doubled over, and he laughed so hard he wheezed.

"We just came to finish clearing up from last night," said Matthias, "and collect our trestles." The man attempted an innocent smile as he gestured toward Daniel's groin. "Is this a bad time?"

He would have to arrest himself if he cursed them. Beating them was not a socially acceptable option, either. And they were family now, too, so he was stuck with them. What a lucky man he was.

Daniel kept his jaw locked down tight, returned to the door, opened it, and glared at them.

Grinning unapologetically, Jacob walked past him into the house, with Matthias following a few paces behind.

"Where is Goodwife Kendrick?" Jacob peered around under the trestles like she might be hiding. That just made Daniel's face blaze hotter because he had searched in the same stupid place just moments before and because he had no idea where she was.

At least the idiots had made quick work of deflating his cockstand.

They seemed to figure out he wasn't going to answer and went to the stacked wooden table supports. Matthias pulled out the first two, then handed the next to Jacob as he sorted out which belonged to whom. They worked silently for a short while.

Daniel really should help them. Instead, he bent to pick up one of the logs they had used as a stool last night and carried it out back to his woodpile. He set it with the other logs that still needed to be split.

He returned to the door.

"Corn is going to be short again this year." It was Jacob's voice.

Daniel stepped across the threshold. It was going to be short for everyone after years of war and raids. The Devil would see to that. He wouldn't have as much to take to market with another mouth to feed. But she had corn, too. Which he would have to harvest. He rubbed his hand over his face. His list of tasks was growing longer than he was tall.

Matthias shoved another log toward Daniel, then turned back to Jacob.

"Daniel?" It was Ruth's voice.

Daniel spun, and she hesitated in the doorway like she didn't know if she could just enter without permission.

His eyes took her in while his brain processed how odd it was for a female voice to call him by his Christian name. Except, of course, it wasn't odd. She was his wife now.

She stood there waiting for him to say something.

"Where have you been?" was what came out of his mouth. It was not really what he should have led with, but it was what he really wanted to know. Relief made his knees a little weak.

Her eyes narrowed, and she stood up taller.

"Hah, he did misplace her!" said Jacob, chest puffed out like a cock crowing on a dunghill.

This was their first real discussion as man and wife, and he would be damned before they were going to have it in front of an audience. Especially this audience.

He took her arm and pulled her out the door with him.

As soon as they were out of sight of the men inside, she yanked her arm out of his grip and glared up at him. "Since you were nowhere to be found, I saw no reason not to get started with my day. Where were you?"

In the hayloft, itching. In more ways than one. But she didn't need to know that.

He hedged. "I had to get out to the back field to check on the mare."

She raised one little eyebrow. At least she didn't tap her foot.

He looked at her overflowing basket. "What is that?"

It was a moment before she answered. "A giant puffball for Goody Carter and various other plants for medicines."

"You were out in the woods alone?"

She didn't have time to answer before Matthias and Jacob emerged from the doorway, each carrying a stack of lumber. They stacked it in the cart they had arrived in. Jacob's horse started, but Daniel turned and steadied it, stroking its neck. He adjusted the traces, which Jacob had twisted, and checked the brake was set. It was second nature.

Jacob's horse, his own horse. They were reminders that this had been an unusually prosperous community before the war. If they had to purchase draft animals now, they would be lucky to afford a yoke of oxen between them.

"My horse doesn't need you to whisper to him, oh great horse-master. You need to keep your whispers for your wife now," said Jacob.

"Don't let us interrupt," said Matthias, shaking his head at Jacob.

Matthias went back inside, but Jacob lingered. "Good morning, sister. It surprised me to see you not at home when we arrived." He was smiling benignly.

Ruth glanced at Daniel. He gave a slight shake of his head, which she seemed to understand. She remained silent and just glared at her brother-in-law. Did Jacob still count as her brother-in-law now that she had married Daniel? That was too big a puzzle for today.

With both of them just staring at him, Jacob chuckled and turned to help Matthias.

Since they were not going to have a moment's peace until Jacob and Matthias were gone, Daniel followed them into the house to grab the next load and speed their work. Ruth's footsteps followed, but he kept his eyes on the two men.

Daniel grabbed an armful of lumber, then he turned and almost whacked Ruth with the boards. She dodged the boards, went to the hearth, and began unloading her basket.

"Heard firing in the woods to the west earlier," said Matthias. "Might just be the Penobscot hunting, but someone should probably scout for signs of the French."

Jacob stopped in his tracks. "The French?"

They needed to keep moving and get out of his house.

"It was the Penobscot."

Everyone turned to look at Ruth.

"What? I was in the woods, and I could hear them. You think I don't know French when I hear it?" She glanced up at them for a moment, then went back to unpacking her large basket and wrapping something up in a cloth.

Jacob sent Matthias a meaningful look. Matthias just shrugged.

Ruth put her cloth-wrapped bundle into a smaller basket and stood. "I'm off to deliver this to Goody Carter," she smiled at him, and his heart gave an extra hard beat. "I'll be back before mid-day."

"Ruth," Daniel said.

"I won't be late," she said and went out the door.

He stared after her.

"You are supposed to be keeping her out of harm's way," Matthias growled in Daniel's ear, "not letting her go gallivanting around with an accused witch or running about in the woods with the Penobscot."

Daniel turned on him, but Jacob interrupted. "You know your sister is hard to govern. Give the novice time to get his feet under him." Jacob turned to Daniel. "Can't expect him to figure too much out the first few days when all the blood in his head has rushed down to his drawers."

Daniel pointed to the door. "Out. Now."

8

Ruth hustled down the path that led to Goody Carter's house. Yes, she should have stayed and talked things through with Daniel, but who knew how long Matthias and Jacob would linger, and her well of patience was not bottomless. Especially not today.

The trail passed into the woods, where a few of the trees were already starting to show their fall colors. A squirrel darted across the path in front of her with both cheeks stuffed with acorns for winter. As she rushed by, it stopped and stared at her. It had to have at least three acorns in each cheek. It would not go hungry this winter if it could help it.

And she would likely not go hungry this winter either. Marriage to Daniel did at least have that benefit.

She spied another giant puffball and picked it for Goody Carter. Goody Carter, too, would eat through the winter if Ruth had any say in the matter.

Her feet crunched on the twigs that littered the path, and she walked on at a more relaxed pace. If Daniel had planned to come after, he would have caught her up by now.

She came to a small clump of maples and stopped. The orangey-red leaves at the tops of the trees twitched in the breeze and looked like thousands of agitated little birds. The air was cooler today and was, like the leaves, a harbinger of the early Maine winter.

An agonized scream ripped the air around her, and she spun toward the sound. It was human, and it continued as if the hounds of hell were after whoever was screaming. And there was furious barking, so perhaps it was the hounds of hell.

North, it was coming from the north. She left the path and ran through the undergrowth in the woods, slowing only when her skirts got so tangled in various branches and thorns that she risked rending her skirts irreparably. As soon as she freed the faded fabric, she was off again.

The screams wound up to a higher pitch, like whoever was making them was not only in pain but panicking.

The voice was male, and man, not boy.

Her feet pounded through the leaf litter on the ground, and her legs were stinging and scratched and probably bleeding, but she didn't slow to check. Her woolen stockings would doubtless take many evenings to repair.

The cries reached a new frenzy as the barking receded into the distance.

She was almost there.

She passed under a large oak, and the acorns bruised her feet. Then she spotted him. The man was rolling on the ground in the undergrowth, and she slid to a stop, the acorns under her feet rolling like marbles and almost upending her. Blood was everywhere, covering the leaves and debris on the ground.

She had to move fast.

The man rolled toward her, and she saw Goodman Cook's face. She froze for an instant. If anyone deserved to be left to that fate, it was him. But she was back in motion without further thought. Even he didn't deserve to die when she could help.

She slammed both hands over the wound, and Cook groaned and went still. Good. Having him unconscious would give her some quiet to think.

She had a needle and some thread in the pouch she carried in her pocket, and she could reach it with one hand. She kept the needle threaded so she might be able to get started sewing him up without removing both hands from the wound, and judging by the puddle of bloody mud Cook lay in, he had already bled too much.

Her eyes searched the area. There were just trees and undergrowth as far as she could see. She listened. Maybe his bellowing had drawn someone else's attention. But the hound, whose baying receded by the moment, would only draw off help, misleading them about where they were needed.

Cook's breathing rasped. Even unconscious, his body was in distress.

There were no footsteps or any sounds of someone approaching through the undergrowth. It was just her and him.

No time to dither.

She pulled the torn edges of skin together and pressed down hard with her left hand. She wiped the blood off of her right as best she could on the ground and then reached for her needle. Pulling it from her pocket wasn't too difficult, but now she had no way to pull it free from the fabric of the ribbon it was embedded in.

She glanced down at Cook's face. It was far too pale. The fool was in serious trouble.

She reached down with her teeth and pulled the needle free. The thread pulled free from the eye of the needle and dropped onto Cook's side. Blast.

Holding the needle in her teeth, she set down the sewing kit and picked up the thread. She tried to thread it one-handed, but the thread kept missing. Sweat dampened her armpits despite the cool breeze.

Her back ached with the strain of being bent over and from pressing as hard as she could on the wound, all while trying to hold still enough to thread the needle.

She tried again. And again.

This wasn't working. She needed both hands.

Her lungs pulled air in deep, held it for a moment, and then let it out.

Her foot. She set the thread down on Cook's side and used her now-freed hand to remove her shoe. Then she bent her leg in tight until she could wedge her foot between herself and Cook and stepped on her own hand.

She paused again, breathing, then carefully slid her hand lengthwise along the wound, keeping the sides of the skin together as best she could while she pressed her stockinged foot down to replace her hand.

Blood oozed out from under her foot, but it wasn't too bad.

She grabbed the thread in one hand, pulled the needle from between her teeth with the other, and got it threaded on the second try.

The cool air in her lungs helped her focus.

Needle clamped back in her teeth, she slapped both hands back over the wound as she removed her foot. She almost toppled sideways because her leg had gotten stiff from the awkward position, but she caught herself.

No time to worry about her own aches. She pulled the edges of the skin back together as evenly as she could, then grabbed the needle from her teeth and made her first stitch. With only one hand to both keep the edges of the skin in line and apply pressure, the bleeding picked up. She got another stitch in and another.

"We can help," said a voice behind her.

She jumped so violently her hand slipped, and the blood flowed freely again. She slapped her hand back on the wound as she cranked her head around to see two Penobscot men, one older and the other younger, both with mostly plucked or shaved heads, wearing long shirts and leather leggings, and looking so alike they must be related, and a skinny, young boy who shared the family resemblance.

Cook groaned, and everyone's eyes went to his face, which went even whiter as he looked at them all, screamed, and passed out again.

The men glanced at each other and then at her. If she ran, Cook would bleed to death, and they would catch her, anyway. And she couldn't leave a patient, so it didn't matter. They said they could help, and she would have to trust them.

"Can you hold the skin together while I stitch?"

The younger of the two men nodded and knelt down to push the skin back into alignment as she removed her own hands. His hands reminded her of Daniel's. Calloused and strong, but agile.

Ruth adjusted his hand, and he held firm in the new position. She began stitching as fast as she could.

"You are skilled," said the older man, holding his musket from swinging forward as he leaned in to watch her work. "Your man is lucky."

"This is not my man." She shuddered. "He is a selfish fool."

The older man grunted and nodded. He seemed to agree with her assessment of Cook.

"Did you injure him?" asked the younger man.

Her hands stopped, and she stared at him a moment. "Of course not." Not that it wouldn't have been tempting.

The boy stared open-mouthed at her.

She calmed herself and smiled at him. "I heal, I don't harm."

The boy narrowed his eyes and kept his distance.

"This man has done me harm and one of my friends, but I am helping him. See?"

The boy stared a moment longer, then gave a quick nod, still not coming closer.

She went back to stitching.

When she reached the final edge of the wound, she tied off the thread. She reached for her basket and pulled the cloth off the puffball she had wrapped for Goody Carter and tried to rip it.

The older man pulled a knife, and she froze.

He narrowed his eyes at her and gestured at her to hand over the cloth. She started breathing again. What a nervous fool she was. He shook his head as she handed over the cloth. But when he held the knife against it, he asked, "here?"

"Yes."

He sliced the fabric in two.

"And cut each half lengthwise, too."

He did as she asked and then handed the four strips back to her.

She tied the ends together and wrapped them around Cook's leg to stop the last of the oozing blood and tied it off.

Now, she had to figure out how to get him back home.

"This man let his hogs eat our crops two years ago," said the younger man. "We almost starved that winter." His voice was flat and sent a little chill down her spine.

She swallowed. "Yes, he did the same to my friend this summer."

"Did your court convict him this time?"

Her gaze fell to her hands. "No."

Both men grunted but said nothing. Their grunts were as expressive as her brother's.

She took in a breath to say something to defend the court and stopped. That same court had forced her to marry yesterday for no crime at all.

"I need to get him back to the village."

They all stood, looking down at Cook, who was blessedly still unconscious. With great good luck, he wouldn't remember waking and seeing them.

Sighing, she bent to reach for his arm. The two men looked at each other, and the older one gently pushed her arm aside. The Penobscot men positioned themselves on either side of Cook, and each took an arm. Carefully, they pulled him up so that each could put one of his arms around their own shoulders, and then they looked her way. "We will follow you. But if he wakes up, we will have to leave you. This man is trouble. We are helping you, not him."

Together, Ruth, the boy, and the two men half carrying, half dragging Cook, made their way to the edge of the woods.

Cook's head lolled, and he snorted and then groaned.

They all looked at each other.

Cooked blinked a few times, eyes not registering anything yet.

Ruth slid her basket handle up to her elbow and took the place of the older man, grabbing Cook's hand to anchor it.

Cook was struggling to get his feet under himself and process where he was and what was happening.

The younger man freed himself from under Cook's other arm, and without looking back, the two men and the boy melted back into the woods.

Ruth staggered under Cook's weight. She was so much shorter than him that his knees almost brushed the ground.

He flailed his legs again to get them under him. Then, his eyes focused on Ruth's face. His face scrunched up like he was about to spit.

"Satan's whore, get your filthy hands off me."

She stared at him.

They were almost back to the village. He would survive waiting here until Daniel could gather some men to come get him.

She let go of his arm, and he collapsed in a screaming heap on the ground.

Daniel's heart stopped for a moment at the sight of Ruth in the doorway, blood on her hands and feet, and her hair sticking out in all directions.

"Goodman Cook is at the edge of the woods. I stitched his wound, but he has declined my further assistance."

Everyone in the garrison house stared at her.

As soon as his feet would move, Daniel crossed to the door. "What happened?"

Mr. Aldrich appeared at their side. He had arrived with selectmen business that couldn't wait.

"I don't know what he did to himself," said Ruth, "but I heard his scream and followed it. I found him writhing on the ground, bleeding next to one of his traps, and then he passed out." Both her voice and her gaze were steady.

"Are you hurt?" said Mr. Aldrich.

She would have said something if she was not alright. But what got Cook?

Unease crawled up Daniel's spine.

"Of course not," said Ruth.

Daniel looked from one to the other. Everything about the set of Ruth's jaw and shoulders said she was annoyed. Aldrich's brows bunched, and he opened his mouth and then closed it again without speaking. At least Daniel wasn't the only one Ruth had that effect on.

The room was silent for a moment.

"Goodman Cook is awaiting someone's assistance." Ruth stepped over the threshold and brushed past them to get to the hearth, where she set her basket down.

"I'll send my man for him," said Aldrich. "Will he need to take the cart?"

Ruth's body relaxed. "Yes, that would be wise." And she explained where to find Cook and what his condition was.

Much of her hair had escaped its knot, and she had a few leaves and twigs stuck in it. Her hands were bloody, and her stockings were tattered and even bloodier. Should he offer to buy some wool so that she could make another pair? Later, perhaps. Without an audience. He was only a day into his husband role and still had no sense of how to interact with her.

He crossed the room, and she looked up, eyebrows raised. His chest tightened. "Are you truly unhurt?" he asked so that no one else could hear.

Her face softened, and the corners of her mouth turned up. "I truly am unhurt." Then, some emotion flashed in her eyes, but he did not know what it meant.

She started to turn, and he took her arm and kept her facing him. He kept his voice low. "What isn't right?"

She took a deep breath. He forced his eyes to stay on her face and not drop to her chest. She was silent for one, two, three heartbeats. At last, she said, "he called me Satan's whore."

Daniel's heart slammed against his ribs. He would sue the man for libel.

But Cook had already accused her of witchcraft, though he used more polite language the first time. And Daniel had begun legal proceedings against her. And she was his wife as a direct result of that accusation.

Neither of them said anything.

"Was Cook attacked by the Penobscot?"

Daniel and Ruth both jumped when Jacob spoke.

"No," said Ruth, then she hesitated.

Daniel's muscles braced against the idea of the impact that would have on them. They had had so many false ends to the war and then raids after the war was over. They couldn't withstand much more. She said it wasn't the Penobscot, but his brain kept jumping to the possibility. If the Penobscot attacked Cook, they were likely starting to ally with the French.

"How do you know?" asked Jacob.

Her back stiffened. "Do you think I dragged the man out of the woods myself?"

No one breathed for a moment, and Ruth snapped her mouth shut like she hadn't meant to let those words loose.

"What are you saying?" said Jacob, so loud that his voice bounced off the ceiling and rattled around the room.

Daniel put his hand up to stop Jacob. "There is no need to raise your voice."

He turned to Ruth, took her arm, and guided her to the table. He gestured for her to sit, and she looked up at him, eyebrows questioning.

Jacob was glaring at him, and Aldrich seemed to study both Daniel and Ruth. Daniel's hand went to Ruth's shoulder. She was warm through the rough wool of her dress.

He sat next to her. "How did you get Cook out of the woods?"

Unease began crawling up his spine again.

"Two Penobscot men and a boy helped me. One of them also helped hold Cook's wound closed while I stitched it." She glared over Daniel's shoulder. "They helped." She hurled that last word at Jacob.

The Penobscot *were* involved.

Jacob flung his hands up in the air. "How very convenient they were there to help." Jacob turned to Aldrich. "You know they don't like him. They might have been giving him a warning and then pretended to help when they realized there was a witness."

Aldrich rubbed his jaw and didn't answer.

Ruth looked from one man to the next. Then, her gaze settled on Daniel. "They *helped*."

He said nothing. Jacob had a point.

She shook her head. "No one in their right mind likes Cook." Aldrich scowled at her, and she ignored him. "But I would never have seen them if they did not come to help. They had no tracks to cover, except with Cook, in which case being seen would not serve."

"If they attacked Cook, that sounds like a breach of the treaty," said Jacob. He stood tall, thrusting his chest out.

Daniel's stomach sank toward the floor. "I don't like the treaty any more than anyone else does." Nor could he figure out how to meet its terms comfortably. "But we can't very well expect the Penobscot to abide by a treaty we don't also abide by."

"It doesn't look like they have abided by it. I am not about to give them any of my corn after this." Jacob sat hard in the chair opposite the table from Ruth and Daniel.

Mr. Aldrich had been listening intently. "We don't know that they have broken the treaty."

"They haven't." Ruth smacked her hand down on the table. "Wasn't anyone listening to me?"

All the men's heads turned to stare at her. She closed her mouth.

"Ruth," said Daniel, "you only know what you saw. You don't know what happened before you arrived."

"And I saw the Penobscot helping me stitch up Cook and then helping me drag him to the edge of the woods." She looked around at all of them, eyes a little wild. "How on earth is that a violation of the treaty?"

"It might not be," Daniel said. But it might be. They would have to talk with Cook before they had a better sense of it. "It is not for you to determine."

A cart rumbled to a stop outside the door.

"Could you have hit one more rut on the way?" Cook's voice boomed from outside.

Everyone jumped up and ran to the door. Aldrich, who had been closest, got there first. Cook lowered his hand. Aldrich would have had him in court if he had taken his hand to Aldrich's servant.

Cook's hound sat beside the cart. It had debris stuck in its coat, and its tongue lolled out as if it had run for miles and was about to drop, but it still growled at them. It must have tried to return to Cook and then followed their scent and found him.

Ruth ignored the dog's protests and pushed past the men to approach the cart, looking at Cook's leg. "Don't thrash around, or you will pull a stitch and start bleeding again."

"Keep her away from me." Cook flailed his hand in Ruth's direction. He seemed almost drunk. Judging by the blood on Ruth's hands and stockings, he was probably delirious from blood loss.

"She saved your life," Daniel said.

Cook gasped and seemed to make a show of glaring at Daniel. Daniel's hands fisted of their own accord. But that wouldn't do. He forced them to unclench.

"She tried to kill me! She signed a compact with Satan and was there with her henchmen. I saw them."

Ruth took a quick step toward Cook. "You ungrateful—"

Daniel grabbed her arm and pushed her behind him. "I'll thank you to be more polite to my wife." The word still felt odd on his tongue.

Cook crossed his arms over his chest and glared at Daniel.

Daniel turned to Ruth. "Go inside. This is selectman business now." Cook would not be of any use while she was still here. "And you need to stay out of the woods until we figure this out."

She stared at him, eyes hard, then turned without a word and went into the house.

Daniel turned back to Cook. "Let's start from the beginning. How did you get injured?"

"I was hunting."

Cook's face grew a bit too pale, and his eyes were going unfocused. "And...?"

"And then...then...." Cook's eyes rolled back into his head, and he collapsed back into the bed of the cart.

It would be rude to poke him to make sure he wasn't play-acting. That didn't mean it wasn't tempting.

Aldrich turned to his man. "Take him to his house and get him into his bed. Then send for Goody Francis to tend him." He turned to Daniel and Jacob. "She should be able to handle his care from here since the stitching is already done, and we can talk with him tomorrow when he has recovered himself a bit."

Daniel lifted the exhausted hound into the cart next to Cook. No need for the poor beast to walk when it could ride, too.

Jacob nodded. Then he smiled, his humor returning as quickly as it had left. "Good luck to Goody Francis." He made a show of brushing his hands against each other in front of himself like he was wiping them free of the situation. "Are we done here? I have corn to harvest."

Aldrich chuckled. "As do I. Let's call it done for today. We'll leave the newlyweds to themselves."

They grabbed their muskets and walked off together since Aldrich's man had taken the cart.

Daniel's nerves wouldn't settle. Yes, the Penobscot might have instigated this, but Ruth could be right, and heaven would not help them if Cook, or even the selectmen, were the ones to unravel the treaty.

9

Ruth hacked at the earth with the hoe. It gave easily. This area had once been Daniel's mother's garden, and a few perennials still struggled through the weeds.

Her fingers gripped the smooth wooden handle that might as well have been custom-made for her. Perhaps Daniel's mother had been a small woman, too.

If she could get the bed prepared this morning—

"Ruth Kendrick?" a small voice said behind her.

Her heart almost leapt out of her mouth as she spun to see who had spoken. It was the boy who had been so uncertain about her when she was sewing up Cook. She put her hand to her chest like that might slow its bellows action.

The boy rocked back on his heels and observed her. If she so much as twitched in his direction, he would be off like a hare.

Her lungs pulled in a deeper, steadying breath.

"Yes?" She hadn't given her name when they first met.

The boy stood up as tall as he could, puffed out his slender chest, and drew his eyebrows down, presumably trying to look stern. Ruth tried to hide her smile now she had recovered from the start he gave her.

"Marie needs your help. Please come with me."

Ruth looked over his shoulder, but he appeared to be alone. Her eyes scanned the edges of the woods, and her cheeks fell. The hairs on the back of her neck stood up. Someone was watching. Somewhere. The past few years had honed that reaction like the blade of a razor.

"Where is she?" Her eyes didn't leave the woods.

"Back in the village," his voice stuck a little on the last syllable. "She is trying to heal my grandfather, but she needs help." He paused. She let her gaze shift away from the woods and come to rest on his face. He forced his shoulders back but couldn't keep his chin from quivering. "I saw how you helped the other man. You can help my grandfather."

She looked around the fields, but Daniel was interviewing Cook, now that Cook was done with his theatrics and willing to talk to the selectmen, and then Daniel intended to take stock of her fields. He would be gone all day.

She looked back at the boy. Then, back around the farm and at the garrison house. Not a soul was in sight to tell him if she defied his instruction to stay out of the woods. Her hands twitched at her sides.

"Tell me what happened so I know what to bring with me."

The boy explained his grandfather's condition, and she went into the house to grab her basket of supplies and a musket.

His solemn face softened when she returned as if he hadn't quite believed she would. Then his eyes went to the musket and back to hers.

"A catamount almost attacked me the other day. I am not letting it have a second chance."

He narrowed his eyes, not fully accepting her explanation. Smart boy. Humans were her primary concern, not animals. Her stomach tightened. Daniel would not thank her for this.

The boy's chin quivered again.

"Lead on."

He hurried ahead of her but kept glancing over his shoulder to make sure she was following. His legs were already longer than hers, despite his young age. Her lungs burned from exertion by the time they reached the wood's edge.

Her feet hesitated of their own accord.

Birds chattered uninterrupted, and squirrels darted about, rustling the leaves as they buried their winter stores. No humans appeared. No shoulders or feet stuck out from behind any tree trunks.

The boy beckoned her with his hand, waving her into action again.

The raids were over, and there was a peace treaty. She was safe. The Penobscot had suffered as much as the English, and they weren't fools.

A Penobscot man emerged from a tree.

Her heart slammed in her chest like it would break her ribs. She raised the musket and aimed it at the center of his body. He had been invisible.

He raised his hands, and they were empty. It was the younger of the two men who helped her with Cook.

"I did not want to frighten you by appearing at your door when you were alone, but I am here to take you to Marie."

She lowered the musket but kept both hands on it. Her breath was still short and quick, and her heart beat too fast.

"Let us go." He turned, put his hand on the boy's shoulder, and hurried ahead of her along the path.

If he was willing to turn his back on a loaded musket, he could mean her no harm.

She rushed to catch up, her feet making more noise than theirs.

When they reached the palisade surrounding the Penobscot village, her lungs were laboring. They had to have covered at least four miles.

The village was as populous as her own but much more compact. There were buildings in every direction, and they appeared to be covered in sheets of bark, with the walls rounded at the top to become the roofs. Smoke drifted out of the center of the roofs of some.

The boy grabbed her hand and started dragging her to a building close to the heart of the village. Now that he was on home soil, he lost his hesitancy. "Come."

He pulled her through a door so low even she had to stoop to enter and into a room lit only by the fire in the center. On the far side of the fire were Marie and two other women, bent over an old man who was writhing on a couple of layers of blankets on the floor while the women fought to keep him still and apply pressure to his leg.

The air was close and stank of sweat despite the cool day. Sweat and blood.

The two women Ruth hadn't seen before both had trails of tears glinting in the firelight. Marie's entire face shone with sweat.

Ruth inched a little closer. The leg was as much raw meat as limb.

"How bad is it?"

Marie's head popped up. "I knew you would come." She gestured toward the man's leg with her chin. "The bone is through the skin, and the main tear is long. Come look."

Ruth edged past the fire, set her basket down, and knelt next to Marie.

Her stomach gave a lurch. Bone was sticking out the middle of the man's thigh, and one gash ran from the top of his thigh down to his knee, and another seemed to run crosswise. Not good.

His eyes were wild, and he kept thrashing around despite one woman sitting on top of him. As he moved, blood kept being squeezed out of the blanket beneath him to puddle at its edge.

Ruth reached for her basket and pulled out some valerian root. The women couldn't move their hands, or his bleeding would get even worse.

"This will help calm him and make it easier to work."

Marie met her gaze and held it.

"It won't hurt him, and he might kill himself thrashing about like that."

Marie's gaze still held Ruth's, then she gave a quick nod. Ruth's heart squeezed for a moment. Please, dear Lord, let her be able to help so she could repay the trust Marie had just shown her.

She swallowed hard and then turned to the old man's head. His eyes bulged, and he tried to wrench himself away from her.

The boy still lingered in the doorway, every muscle tense as he watched her. She waved him over with her hand. His eyes went wide, and then he looked to Marie. She nodded to him.

Ruth placed the tincture in his shaking hand. "Have him swallow this." The boy just stared back at her. "He trusts you, and it is the only way we can help him."

The boy leaned in next to his grandfather and whispered quiet words to him that Ruth couldn't understand. The man's eyes went from the boy to her and then back to the boy. His mouth opened, and the boy gave him the draft.

"We haven't been able to set the bone because we could not keep him still enough. We needed another pair of skilled hands."

The other women darted their narrowed eyes between Ruth and Marie.

The boy spoke for the first time since they entered the house. "I saw her sew up a man."

The women's eyes snapped toward him, and he retreated to the doorway. Perhaps he had overstepped. Ruth caught his eye and flashed him a quick smile.

Marie began speaking to the women, presumably explaining what they had to do to help her set the bone and hold the leg steady so that Ruth could stitch the wounds, and they could then splint the leg.

Ruth glanced toward the old man's face. His eyes had already drooped. With great good luck, they could get in position to set the bone now that he was still, and then he would pass out from the pain. If he didn't, this was going to be a very long afternoon and likely the old man's last.

Ruth pulled out her needle and then cut several lengths of thread. She grabbed one and poked the end through the eye of the needle on the first try.

She nodded to Marie, who said a few words to the other women, looked back at Ruth, then at the old man's face. Then, when she was confident the women had his hip stabilized, she grasped his knee and pulled with all her might.

The old man's shriek echoed off the walls, and it was followed by Marie's grunts of exertion after the man passed out.

This was more of an assembly project than a quick mending.

Starting from the topmost end of the biggest gash, Ruth stuck her needle into his flesh and out the other side of the gash, pulled it tight and tied off the stitch, then she pierced his flesh again and again.

Their collective breathing took on a rhythm. In when she pierced, out when she pulled.

A chorus of shouts erupted outside the building, but she kept going.

A musket fired, and her heart stuttered. Everyone in the room jumped.

The boy grabbed Ruth's musket and took up position to guard the door.

Ruth's fingers kept going. She tied off another stitch and moved to the second gash. She *would* save this man.

Daniel paused. The palisade surrounding the Penobscot village was a good two heads taller than he was, and the logs were sharpened at the top. No doubt it would be just as effective at keeping him in, should they decide not to let him leave, as it would be at keeping him out if he were attacking.

And here he was, entering alone. The other selectmen didn't even know he was here.

He shook his head. That might not have been the wise move it seemed when he left them at Cook's house. But Jacob would have caused a diplomatic incident, and he just wasn't sure where Aldrich stood on the Penobscot. Aldrich had been quick to encourage Cook and ignore Ruth's report.

Daniel needed to hear from the Penobscots themselves to determine what happened to Cook. He couldn't reestablish order by letting people who had already made up their minds interfere with his investigation. So here he was. Alone.

Matthias would have been helpful backup if he had thought of it before he left, but that wasn't much help now he was already here. And it wasn't Matthias' job, anyhow, since he wasn't a selectman.

The palisade loomed. His lungs pulled in a bracing breath, and he pushed on toward the gate.

Several Penobscot men gathered at the gateway, shouting at him. They weren't speaking English, so he didn't understand the details of what they were threatening, just the general tone.

One fired a shot into the air, and Daniel's feet stopped. He swung his musket round to his back and raised both hands toward them. He was here to talk, not fight.

His heart drummed against his breastbone.

He ought to have told Ruth where he was going, just in case his efforts went awry. She might not thank him if he made her a widow a second time and in such short order.

A Penobscot man of medium height approached, hatchet in hand. A deep scar ran down the side of his face from the bare skin above his ear to his mouth, and it pulled the corner of his lip up in a perpetual sneer. With luck, it was a hunting incident and not from the war. This would be easier if he could talk to someone without such a legitimate reason for animosity toward the English.

They were all likely as scarred by the conflict as his own people were, so it probably made little difference if the scars were on the outside or the inside.

"I come to speak with the Sagamore."

The man looked him up and down. "You will leave your musket here." He gestured toward the gateway of the palisade.

The man had planted his feet, and he was clearly ready to enforce his demand. The men behind him were there to back him up, not that they needed to be. Daniel wasn't a fool.

His chest clenched as he stood the musket up against the logs of the great wall. His fingers lingered for a moment on the barrel before sliding away from it. No defense now but his words. He swallowed hard and showed both empty hands to the man with the scar.

The man stared for a moment, then gave a single sharp nod and turned to lead him into the village.

Daniel glanced over his shoulder. The other men followed just a few steps behind, arranged in a crescent formation. They knew their business. A sour taste flooded Daniel's mouth. They each knew their role and didn't appear to have any discipline issues. Would that he had been so fortunate during the raids.

Not a good time to ruminate.

He focused on the building the scarred man was leading him toward. It was larger than the ones surrounding it but was still smaller than the meeting house back home. A wispy rope of smoke twined its way up from the roof into the air above.

The scar-faced man halted at the doorway. "You will wait here." Then he ducked through the low doorway and disappeared into the dark interior.

The hair on the back of Daniel's neck prickled as the semi-circle of men closed in behind him. They didn't speak, but a general buzz came from the surrounding buildings.

A cool breeze sent the smoke from the roof swirling.

The scarred face reappeared. "Come."

Daniel ducked down to enter the room. It smelled of wood smoke and tobacco smoke. His eyes took a moment to adjust to the dim light inside.

The Sagamore sat on the far side of the fire, and light from the flames warmed his dark eyes and sharp cheekbones.

Daniel waited for the Sagamore to speak first.

"What can we do for you, Daniel Kendrick?"

He blinked. They knew who he was. Whether that was a good or bad thing remained to be seen.

The smoke stung his eyes.

"I came to ask who helped my wife tend to Robert Cook's wounds."

The Sagamore studied him for a moment. "Why do you wish to know this?"

To keep any wild guesses and misunderstandings from destroying the peace from the treaty, but that didn't seem to be the wisest way to phrase it. "I need their help in determining how Cook was injured."

The Sagamore was again studying him. He forced his hands to remain still by his sides. Then the Sagamore looked to a man behind Daniel and, with one brisk wave of his hand, called the man forward.

This man was tall and watched Daniel through narrowed eyes. "We found him after your wife was already tending to him."

The man did not appear to feel Daniel needed any more explanation. Daniel looked to the Sagamore, who inclined his head. Hopefully, that was permission to ask another question.

"Could you see how he had gotten injured?"

"I believe he must have tripped a trap and upset the catamount. Or his hound did."

"His own trap?"

The man snorted. "We don't set such clumsy traps."

Cook was very capable of a clumsy trap. But that didn't mean it was his. "Were you out checking traps?"

The man blinked. Daniel was clearly trying his patience. "There is no profit in setting traps near a catamount den. And she has cubs. We stayed well clear of it. We were teaching my son to set fishing nets."

That rang true. And fit Ruth's description of the spot.

Cook was lucky the cat got spooked and didn't come back after him while he was down. So was Ruth. That thought didn't sit well in his gut. At least he had put a stop to her wandering in the woods.

"I thank you for assisting Goodman Cook."

The muscles around the man's eyes tightened. "We helped your wife."

Daniel's back stiffened. "I thank you for assisting my wife." The man ignored his posture.

"She is thanking us for herself." The man's eyes shifted to the doorway. There stood a skinny boy just inside the door. He had a musket slung over his shoulder.

Daniel blinked hard. But the image remained when his eyes opened. His father's musket in the boys' hands. "Where did you get that?" He reached for the boy, but three sets of hands restrained him.

His head whipped back to the boy's father. "Bring her to me."

"She is healing my father. When she is done, we will bring her."

His pulse pounded in his ears, and he yanked his arms free. How was Ruth in the Penobscot village? She had been hoeing the garden when he left for Cook's house. She didn't have the musket with her then. Something made her arm herself.

"We thank you for allowing your wife to come to our aid." The Sagamore's voice was flat and firm. Clearly, he was aware from Daniel's reaction that he had done no such thing.

Daniel drew in a long breath, held it for a moment, and then released it, forcing his muscles to release with it.

"We have no desire to break the peace." The Sagamore's voice had less edge now.

The muscles of Daniel's jaw flexed against his will. If they had taken Ruth against her will, they had broken the peace after all. He breathed. But that might not be what happened.

"We will bring the women when they are done," said the Sagamore. "Sit."

None of the other men were sitting, and a few exchanged glances. The Sagamore had surprised them.

Daniel took a step closer to the fire and then folded his legs and sat. The Sagamore nodded.

"Our men did not harm the man, Cook, even though he has harmed us. We have no desire for more war." Everyone in the room was leaning in, listening to the words of their headman. The man with the scar stared at Daniel. "You will send your corn when you finish your harvest, yes?"

Of course. The treaty worked too well in their favor for them to want to break it. Boston had won no friends among the settlers in Maine with that treaty. But it was legal, and as much as the community would never acknowledge it, it was fair, too, and they had to abide by it. "I will give to Caesar the things that are Caesar's."

A man leaned down and said something to the Sagamore in their language. He nodded and turned back to Daniel. "Good. You quote your holy book. That is good." Then his eyes narrowed a bit. "But what about your fellows?"

"As long as the treaty is unbroken, they are bound by it." Daniel shifted. Leaving Jacob and Mathias home was the right choice, after all. He had to convince them they were bound by the treaty. And he would because it was his job to restore order, and order was Divine will, and then the Devil would stop sending his minions among them. He would make it happen.

Then, every head in the room swiveled toward the doorway.

The air went still.

There was Ruth, hands once again covered in blood. But the Penobscot faces behind her were soft and smiling, as was hers, if not as confidently as the others.

"Your wife has done us a good service. She has saved my wife's father. We thank you."

Ruth's eyes found his and went wide. She had apparently not seen him in the dim light. Or been told he was there at all.

He searched her face as she composed it. She did not appear frightened. At least not of the Penobscot.

A man standing behind her reached out with the musket Daniel had left by the entrance to the village and the musket the boy had been carrying.

Daniel took both muskets. Ruth hesitated just inside the doorway next to a Penobscot woman whose hands were also bloody. They exchanged brief glances.

Daniel forced his eyes from Ruth to the Sagamore, who held up an open hand.

"We believe you will uphold the treaty. We also have every intention of upholding the treaty. You may go in peace."

Daniel nodded. Words weren't necessary at the moment, and most of the words pounding at the gates of his teeth were for Ruth anyhow.

He slung the muskets over his shoulder and grasped Ruth's arm.

They ducked out the low doorway, and he pulled her toward the opening in the palisade. A group of Penobscot men watched them go.

10

Ruth had to jog to keep up with Daniel as he dragged her out of the village and into the woods. His hand gripped so hard that he was close to stopping the flow of blood through her arm.

After they had covered a good half mile, his pace slowed to a more sustainable walk.

"May I have my arm back now?"

His eyes met hers for the first time since they left the Sagamore's fire. "I told you not to go into the woods."

"You told me you were going to Cook's house to interrogate him and then to my fields. Why were you there?" She gestured back the way they had come with her free arm.

They both kept walking, and she studied the trail ahead of them to keep from glancing his way. Had he come to find her? Had they fetched him? Maybe he was there for some unrelated reason, but short of Robert Cook, Daniel was the last person she would have expected to see at the Penobscot village.

He stopped and spun her toward him. "Why did you leave the house when I told you to stay?"

Her spine snapped straight. "I was fetched to help with a medical case. Of course, I went."

His eyes bore into hers. "Did it occur to you it might have been a ruse?"

She stared right back at him. "I am not a fool."

He was silent.

They both breathed in and out.

"The boy who came was there when I stitched up Cook. I know him. And his father carried Cook back. He made sure we were safe."

Daniel's eyes closed for a moment. "And who made sure you were safe from him?"

He clearly thought her dimwitted. "I took a musket, but I know them, and they told me Marie needed my help."

His eyes popped open, and he sucked in a breath. Then, instead of speaking, he took her arm and started walking again.

Their feet beat a rhythm on the dirt of the trail, and leaves rustled in the breeze above their heads. A jay scolded in the distance.

"And who is this French woman, Marie?" His eyes were on the path ahead, not looking at her.

"I am not a traitor. Marie is just the name she goes by because she doesn't like how we mispronounce her Penobscot name."

He glanced her way, one eyebrow raised like he was asking if she was really that gullible.

"They have to interact with the French, just like they have to interact with us." It wasn't like the Penobscot could ignore the French to their north. "And she saved me from a catamount."

He whirled toward her. "What?" His face was a shade paler than it had been.

"I owed her. Not that I would have said no to anyone who needed my skills."

"A catamount?"

She had a sudden urge to soothe his worry. "She ran at it and scared it off before it could hurt me." Just barely before it could hurt her, but he didn't need to know that.

She reached out and put her hand on his arm, feeling its warmth through his sleeve.

He stared at it, and then, after a moment, he placed his own hand over it.

The warmth from his hand spread up her arm to her chest. He wasn't chastising her for being in the catamount's path in the first place. Esau would have. Matthias would have. Jacob certainly would have.

He stood there for a moment, a hundred thoughts flitting across his face.

"Show me where Cook was hurt."

She blinked. "Um, it was down past the giant oak."

"Take me there."

Well, at least he wasn't worried about her anymore. Or grilling her about why she had been in the woods. That was good, anyhow.

She led him through the dappled shadows along the trail for about a mile. They were both silent, except for the crunching of their feet in the leaf litter on the trail. Then, they reached a bend in the trail next to a granite boulder. She led him off the trail and through the undergrowth. Less light penetrated the leaf canopy over them here.

Keeping what sun there was to her left, she passed the large oak, pushed aside some scrubby growth, and arrived at the spot where she had found Cook.

"Here." Not that it wasn't obvious. The blood-stained leaves and ground still gave off a coppery smell, and all of the brush around was broken and in disarray.

Daniel's eyes seemed to search for something, and then he stepped to the far side of the little trampled area and bent over. She joined him.

It appeared to be a sharpened stick that could have been part of a trap. There was blood on it.

"Is this consistent with the wound he had?"

She studied it. He was asking her opinion. Her medical opinion. Her heart gave an extra hard thump.

"His wound was more than what a single jab from that would do." It had been more of a jagged gash than just a puncture.

There was a low, reverberating growl behind them.

They both spun, and Daniel slung one musket off his shoulder and dropped it so that he could swing the other into position.

She grabbed the one on the ground as Daniel stepped between her and the sound.

If she grabbed for the powder horn or flints, she might hamper Daniel if he had to move quickly, so she grasped the musket in her hands like a club. Daniel did the same with the one in his hands.

All the birds had gone silent.

Eyes glinted from the underbrush. A great cat stared right into her eyes and then let loose a cry that sent the birds into flight and Ruth's heart slamming around like she was running for her life.

The cat's teeth were a nauseating yellow and shiny with spittle. She couldn't pull her eyes away from them to see what Daniel was doing.

Then, a tawny paw reached forward, claws digging at the ground.

Her head did a funny bobble.

Those claws were what got Cook. She was certain. They fit the jagged tear in his flesh and wouldn't leave the reciprocal tear of upper and lower jaws. He only had one gash, not two.

Her stomach lurched, and she was lucky it had been a long time since she had eaten, or it would have emptied itself on the ground.

Daniel lifted the musket, waved it, and yelled, stepping toward the big cat.

Ruth flinched. The cat blinked, then decided he was not worth the trouble and withdrew.

Ruth's hands were clammy, but she still gripped the stock of the musket and couldn't force her hands to loosen their hold on the smooth wood, so she couldn't wipe them on her skirts.

With one last quick glance around, Daniel took her arm and walked them away from the area and back toward the trail.

The look the cat gave her kept playing in mind. It recognized her. She would swear an oath to it. Catamounts were loners, and it wasn't as if there would be more than one in this area.

A shiver of ice ran down her back. "Why is it coming after us?"

Catamounts were shy. For all that they could easily kill a person, they usually kept their distance.

Daniel hustled her along. "The Penobscot were right. She must have cubs nearby."

Well, she couldn't very well blame the cat for that. But fear still drummed through her chest, making her heartbeat spike. She would steer well clear of that section of the woods when she collected herbs.

Just before they reached the edge of the fields, Daniel pulled her to a stop. He laid his hands on the musket she still clutched in both hands and tugged it out of her grasp. He slung it over his shoulder and looked at her.

"Did the catamount get him?"

"It was her claws. They match the wound." She closed her eyes and saw the rent flesh of Cook's leg clear as if it was right in front of her now. She opened them.

It could have been her.

Daniel ran his hand over her hair like he could read her mind. "Cook's hound probably made too much fuss for it to stick around and hurt you while you worked on him."

She hadn't even considered it at the time. But then, she hadn't known how Cook had been hurt. She said a silent prayer of thanksgiving that the Penobscot had come along. Their additional numbers had certainly helped keep the cat at a distance.

She looked at Daniel. He still wasn't chastising her for putting herself in danger.

Perhaps he was biding his time.

The light was getting low. Even as they emerged into the field, his face was in shadow.

He said nothing else as they approached the house.

He unlatched the door and gave her his arm as she went through it like he thought she needed help over the doorjamb.

As soon as they were through it, he closed the door, drew in the latch strap, and placed the bar across its brackets.

Then he turned to her and flung his arms around her with such force she could barely draw a breath.

He held her tight to his chest, the warmth of her body pressing against his, proof she was safely home. "You should not have gone."

She stiffened in his arms and shoved him away. "Why? Because they are Indians?" Her eyes were flint as she glared at him.

"Because we are in a delicate diplomatic situation."

She shook her head from side to side, her eyes never leaving his. "How is helping save the Sagamore's father-in-law hurting our relationship with the Penobscot?"

A buzz of energy coursed through his body, and he couldn't stay still. He turned and walked to the door, then turned back. "That is for the selectmen to handle." His breath heaved in and out, and it wouldn't slow, no matter how he focused on it.

"The selectmen were going to set his bones and sew up his wounds?" Her hands rested on the swell of her hips, and she thrust her chest forward.

So help him, his cock responded to that.

It wasn't her place to take that sort of matter into her hands. It was his and the other selectmen's.

But only she could heal the man.

Her eyes flicked down to his cockstand and back up. Her expression didn't change.

His neck grow warm as she watched his body act like it belonged to an undisciplined boy.

She appeared to be entirely unaffected by the day's events.

"You could have been killed." And he wouldn't have known.

Without a word, she turned and left the room.

He charged through the bedroom door after her, and she spun to face him. He spoke before she could. "What if it had been a ruse to lure you away?"

She didn't answer.

"What then?" He stepped in so close that his chest brushed hers when he inhaled. It just made his breath come harder.

Her eyes narrowed. "Would it have mattered to you?"

"Of course it would have."

"You would have cared that your wife had been taken, not that *I* had been taken." She tried to turn away from him, but he wouldn't let her. She was talking nonsense.

"You *are* my wife." He had almost lost his mind when she appeared in the Sagamore's doorway.

She stared at him.

Then, her body seemed to fold in on itself. "And you could have widowed me again today and left me to the mercies of the town." Her eyes were glassy.

His jaw fell slack.

He reached for her and pulled her hard against his chest again. His hands stroked her back to reassure her they were both home and safe.

"That won't happen." They both knew that was a promise he could not make, but she relaxed in his arms.

Her breath was warm against his chest, even through the wool of his clothes.

The air in the room was still as he held her.

Then her arms went around his waist, and his skin tingled. His cock jumped when her belly shifted against it.

She was so tiny in his arms.

His lips found the top of her head, and he kissed her. Then his hands shifted lower to the curves of her arse and pulled her even closer.

She pulled her body away slightly, and he missed her heat. Before he could pull her back, her hand grasped his cock through his trousers, and his entire body went still.

His breathing stopped. His heart might have stopped. His brain definitely stopped.

Then her other hand went to the button of his trousers. That shocked his body into motion.

He backed her to the edge of the bed and reached for the hem of her skirts. Then he hiked them up above her hips and reached for the tapes of her drawers. He managed to untie them without creating a knot and tugged them down around her ankles as he lay her down on her back.

She pulled one leg free of her drawers and, in the process, exposed herself fully to him. He had never seen a woman's privates. He had imagined them—oh, had he imagined them—and the effect the view had on his body was excruciating.

He shoved his trousers and drawers down as one and was on top of her before he could even think how to approach her.

Her hand grasped him, and his sight got blotchy for a moment as she guided him in. His hips took over as he thrust himself home. Sliding into her tight, slick body set off lightning in his bollocks.

He chanced a glance down at her and realized his chest was smothering her. He shoved his elbows into the bed to lift his chest up off her so she could breathe. Her eyes were hooded, and she grabbed the back of his thighs and urged him back into motion.

His hips obliged. He couldn't have stopped them if he tried.

The sound of his cock sliding in and out of her wet center drove his hips harder.

He grunted with each stroke. He couldn't help it. His body was acting on its own.

He forced his eyes to her face. She was straining, reaching.

He should help her feel what he was feeling. His brain was not cooperating.

Her heaving breast was right beneath him, and he rocked onto one elbow and grabbed hold with the other hand. Her woolen dress was rough under his palm, but she pushed up into the pressure as her mouth dropped open. Those lips. He almost finished right then.

Then she grasped his hand and removed it from her breast.

Shite. Maybe he had misread her expression.

His thrusts slowed, but she dragged his hand down between their bodies, holding his fingers just in front of where their bodies joined.

She pushed his thumb against the small, slick nub in her folds and arched her back like she had just been shocked.

He couldn't pull his eyes from the sight of himself disappearing into her body again and again and his own hand on her most private center. He was her husband. This was their right.

The air filled with the sound of skin slapping and moans blending together.

She writhed under his hand, and his mind went blank. A sensation verging on pain shot down his spine, squeezed his rocks, and his body spasmed as he shot his seed into her.

The convulsions lasted and lasted, and it took a few moments to register that she was still rocking hard against him. He was sated, but she was not.

He pushed harder with his thumb.

His seed seeped out of her body, and it made his thumb as slippery as her entry. He let his thumb circle around her swollen nub, and she let out a moan, so he did it again. This time, she almost growled, which set his hips flexing against her again.

She threw back her head and grasped the mattress ticking with both hands. Her face strained as though she were in pain. Maybe he pressed too hard.

She grabbed his hand and pressed it harder against herself. Her breath rasped. Then she went stiff and screamed.

He tried to pull his hand away, but she wouldn't let him. She held it fast against herself as she writhed under him. Her body pulsed around his softening cock, which set it to hardening again. Her body was milking him, and it turned his brain to pottage.

At last, her body relaxed, and she dropped her head back onto the mattress. Her face was soft now, softer than he had ever seen it.

His lips curled up in a smile.

He had put that expression on her face.

He shifted his weight to the side and lay next to her, arm across her chest, and then he pulled her close, tucking her head beneath his chin. His heart drummed against her ribcage, and her breath matched his as they lay there as one.

He worked hard to forgive his father for keeping this from him for so long by not giving him access to his lands until his father was gone.

If she would let him, he could lose himself in her body day and night.

She turned her head and kissed the base of his throat. Her lips were soft against the sensitive skin of his neck.

He stroked her hair, which had come half out of its pins. She looked wild. Unrestrained. Ravished.

She was wild.

He was supposed to be helping her rein herself in and become his helpmeet. Keeping her out of trouble.

He looked down at their still, almost fully clothed bodies, then to the sated look on her face.

The remnants of daylight lingered, and he had work to do.

And witches still afflicted him at night. Witches, it was his job to find.

He rolled onto his back and studied the rough beams in the ceiling. He had no business lying in bed with animals still to be fed. His eyes closed for a moment. He couldn't let himself be distracted from his duties.

He rolled to his side, swung his feet to the floor, and stood. The floor was solid beneath his feet. He yanked his drawers and trousers up and fastened them. He had behaved like a rutting bull.

No more.

He stood and walked to the door. He had livestock to tend.

11

Ruth's back ached as she reached the sickle forward, pulled yet another bundle of cornstalks together, and bound them off. Her fingers were stiff with exhaustion, but so accustomed to the motions they could manage them without her brain engaging.

Daniel had likely been out since dawn. Not that she knew for certain since he slept in the barn again.

She hooked another shock of cornstalks, pulled them in, and tied them off. Daniel's fields were much better off than hers, so at least she would eat this winter.

The wheels of Daniel's wagon rattled in the distance, and his mare's hoof beats got closer.

Ruth reached for yet another shock. She was almost at the end of the row, and now Daniel could help her stand the shocks upright to dry. They were too unwieldy for her to manage by herself. She lifted her elbows away from her body to let the breeze cool her off while she worked. It might be a crisp October day, but it was hot work.

The mare pulled up behind her and cleared her nostrils with a long, hearty series of snorts. The spray hit the back of Ruth's neck, and she turned and glared at Daniel for letting the mare blow horse snot all over her. He gave a half smile and shrugged in apology.

Her heart gave a little extra beat, and she turned away. She didn't need her heart getting itself worked up over a man who slept in the barn instead of with his wife.

Daniel jumped down from the wagon. He bent down and grabbed a shock of corn, and stood it upright. His muscles flexed under his shirt. His shoulders were almost as broad as Matthias'. She hadn't noticed that before.

She went to the back of the wagon and emptied the fresh load of rye straw to tie off the next million shocks. Ha! They should be so lucky.

As she was about to bend down and gather in the next shock, he took her sickle from her.

He unloaded all the rye straw twine from the wagon and then looked her up and down. "You drive the wagon back to the barn. I'll keep going here."

Her mouth opened, then she closed it before something stupid could come out. He was going to let her drive.

Alright then.

She turned to the wagon and realized there was no step to get up. She reached her foot to a spoke in the wheel like she had seen him do before, but her legs were too short.

Then he knelt down before her. She searched his face to see what he was on about.

"Step on my knee, then step to the spoke and up."

Oh. That made sense. She stepped her left foot carefully on his leg, grasped the side of the wagon with both hands, then stepped her right foot up on the wheel spoke and reached her left foot up to the wagon bed. Daniel's hands pushed her backside up and into the wagon.

She turned just in time to see him blushing and busying his hands with the sickle.

Heat crept into her own cheeks, and she had to work to strangle a nervous chuckle before it could escape. He had had his hands in far more intimate places.

But now was not the time to ruminate on that. They had too much work to do. She turned and reached for the reins.

"Alright, move up another five shocks and then stop. Just make sure she is listening to you before you go all the way to the barn." His voice sounded a little tight like he was flustered. He bent to grab another shock of corn, and his arse filled out his trousers quite nicely.

She turned to the mare in front of her, clucked her tongue and gently flapped the reins on the mare's rump. The mare stepped right out. Ruth pulled her up when they had moved just a few strides. She stopped. Apart from spraying Ruth's neck with snot, the mare was very well-mannered.

She glanced back at Daniel. He nodded in approval and gestured her to go on to the barn.

"Daniel," a voice called from the far edge of the field. They both turned to see who it was.

Jacob marched toward them, using his musket as a walking stick. If it was loaded, he might regret that.

Daniel heaved some more corn upright while Jacob made his way down the harvested row toward them.

Jacob drew close, and he and Daniel gave each other a tired nod.

"Cook said he saw Penobscot in the woods behind his barn and that they might be the ones that attacked him."

Ruth swallowed a snort and covered it with a cough when they both looked her way. Cook was an idiot. She couldn't possibly be the only one who understood that. But everyone's nerves were frayed, and Cook had always had an instinct for playing their fears to his advantage. He probably didn't even realize he was doing it. Their neighbors certainly didn't. He probably believed the fear-mongering that spewed from his mouth as much as the rest did.

"No one attacked him." Daniel leaned against the wagon and wiped the sweat from his face with his shirtsleeve. "I went to the Penobscot village, and they satisfied me they didn't attack him. It was a catamount."

Jacob raised his brows and tilted his head like a dog, trying to puzzle out Daniel's meaning, but he said nothing.

"He set up his trap right by her den. She has cubs. And Ruth said the gash looked right for having been made by a swipe from a big cat." Daniel gestured in her direction.

"You believe them?"

Jacob had just ignored her contribution to the explanation, even though it came from Daniel.

Daniel shot her a stern glance.

"I do," he said, turning back to Jacob. "And they are favorably inclined toward us right now because Ruth helped set and stitch the leg of the Sagamore's father-in-law."

Jacob straightened. "I don't know how folks will take you believing their word over Cook's."

It was Daniel's turn to raise his eyebrows. "They had a far more convincing explanation than Cook did."

Jacob was right. People might not appreciate Daniel's judgement on this. But he stood by it. He took the Penobscot's word—and hers—over Cook's.

Her throat got a little tight, and she cleared it. He should take her word. She was right.

Jacob looked from Daniel to Ruth and then back to Daniel. "Are you going to tell him that?"

"Not right now. I still have corn to get down. As do you. As does he, I assume, unless his hogs ate that, too." For an instant, Daniel's body sagged. He had to be exhausted. Then he took a deep breath and straightened his back. "I will visit him tonight if he is in that much of a lather about it."

Jacob shrugged and turned away.

"Goodman Kendrick!"

Their heads all turned to see one of Mr. Aldrich's men run toward them.

People were ridiculously intrusive on a selectman's time. It was a divine miracle Daniel got anything done.

She glared at Mr. Aldrich's man, in his loose coat and trousers. They had had too many lean winters with the war, and she was in no mood for another one. They had to finish getting the corn cut and stood up to dry so they could get it in before the snow flew.

The man ran up to them, then stopped, bent over with his hands on his knees, sucking in air. "Goodman Kendrick," he gasped. "Mr. Aldrich's stud," he gasped again, "is cast in the barn, and they can't get him free."

Daniel put his hand on the man's back. "Catch your breath."

"No time," the man wheezed, "the horse is kicking the barn to timber. The beast is possessed. I think it broke Ned's leg."

"I can set that so he doesn't have to wait for days for the doctor," she said to Daniel.

His eyes met hers for a moment. Then he nodded and swung himself up on the wagon next to her, and reached out his hand. It was warm when it brushed against hers as she relinquished the reins to him.

"Get in," he said to Mr. Aldrich's man.

"I'll try to smooth Cook's feathers," said Jacob as he turned back the way he had come.

"Everyone sit down." Daniel clucked to the mare and slapped the reins against her haunches. "Git up."

He steered her toward the end of the field.

Ruth put her hand on Daniel's arm. "The house. I need my splinting materials."

He looked at her, then nodded again. "Right." He pulled hard on the left rein and redirected the mare's path, then slapped the reins again. The mare broke into a strong trot, which was about all the wagon could handle over the ruts of the field without coming apart.

Ruth glanced back over her shoulder. The man in the back of the wagon was holding the side so hard his knuckles showed white through their grime, and he still bounced right up off the bed of the wagon with each good lurch it took over a rut. His face had gone slightly green. He would no doubt prefer walking back.

Daniel pulled the mare to a stop right in front of the doorstep. "Hurry." As she swung her leg over the edge of the wagon, he reached for her arm and helped her down so she didn't land in a heap.

As soon as her feet were on the ground, she did as he asked. She raced into the house, grabbed her medical basket and was back outside before the horse had even caught its breath.

Daniel reached over and took her basket, then reached down again with both arms this time and hauled her up bodily. Her chest slammed against his as she cleared the edge of the wagon. They both froze. His face was just inches from hers, and his breath lifted a stray lock of hair off her forehead. Her heart pounded harder as his eyes dropped to her lips.

The man in the back sneezed, and they both jumped. Daniel blinked hard and then swung her around to the seat next to him, clucked to the mare, and they took off down the path toward the Aldrich farm on the other side of the village. They had to get there before the horse injured anyone else.

The stallion screamed its frustration and flailed its legs against the side of its stall. It had lain down and rolled and now was too close to the wall to get its legs under itself to get up or to get enough leverage to roll itself back over. The horse was stuck, well and good. And it wasn't happy about it. Neither was Aldrich.

"That horse cost more than your passage across the Atlantic."

Daniel wasn't sure which of his servants Aldrich was addressing. Ruth was already by Ned's side.

Ned moaned.

"His leg doesn't appear to be broken," Ruth said.

"Obviously. He wouldn't be kicking it so hard if it were, but that doesn't mean he won't break it before we can free him soon."

Daniel looked at Ruth, and she stood, her hand poised to slap Aldrich right across his face. Daniel reached for her arm before Aldrich could see her intent. "Come, take Ned to the house so he is out of the way and doesn't get stepped on or kicked again."

She turned her glare on him, and then she blinked. She didn't need to end up in court again. Her arm relaxed, so he let it go, and she turned and bent to help Ned to his feet.

"If it is not broken, he can stay and help." Aldrich wrung his hands. He was sweating almost as much as the horse.

Ruth opened her mouth to speak, so Daniel interrupted her before she could say anything legally actionable. "Aldrich, just because his leg isn't broken doesn't mean it isn't injured to the point of being useless right now."

Ruth shut her mouth tight but gave him a brief nod. The woman had a temper, but she wasn't a fool.

The horse's hoof banged against the wood again, rattling the wall all the way to the roof. If they didn't get him flipped soon, it would indeed be the end of Aldrich's investment.

Aldrich was foolish to spend so much money on the beast. It was a lovely stud, but there was no need for horses of that quality here. They needed sturdy workhorses, or simply oxen, not fancy saddle horses. It was an ostentatious purchase, but that was between Aldrich and God.

"That 'orse is possessed," said Ned as Ruth helped him to his feet. "He hasn't ever lost his mind like this before."

Ruth's face blanched for a moment at the suggestion of supernatural involvement, but then Ned put too much weight on his injured leg and almost passed out, and it was all she could do to stay upright, with Ned's weight dragging her down.

"John," Daniel snapped, "help carry Ned to the house, then get back as fast you can." Aldrich turned and stared at Daniel for a moment, and yes, he had overstepped giving Aldrich's man orders, but he needed everyone out of the way and didn't want Ruth to have to drag Ned single-handed to the house.

Daniel glanced around the barn and spotted ropes hanging from a peg on the wall. He grabbed two and returned to the cast horse's stall.

Aldrich paced and watched but didn't move to help. Just as well. Daniel had done this before, and Aldrich was a bit too paunchy and soft to be helpful.

Daniel made a loop at the end of one rope since he wouldn't have any help. Then he stepped into the horse's stall. The horse shouldn't have been in the barn at all in this weather, but Aldrich thought stallions had to be penned up like bulls.

At his approach, the stallion snorted a warning and started flailing again. Its eyes were wild, and blood vessels stood out under its coat. The banging began again, and Daniel moved slowly and tried to soothe it with his voice. Any one of those four flailing hooves could put an end to him.

He swung the rope against the horse's neck, and it flung its head and snorted, rattling the boards of the wall even harder with its deadly hooves.

"Stop! You're making it worse." Aldrich was looming in the doorway but too smart to enter. His man had returned from the house and stood well behind him.

"I know what I am doing. That's why you called for me," Daniel said.

He swung the rope along the horse's neck again and again, almost stroking it with the twisted fibers, getting it used to the sight and the feel. Its legs stilled for a moment, and Daniel seized the opportunity to lean in and slip the rope around the front hoof closest to the ground. The horse yanked its foot, and Daniel offered no resistance, so the horse quieted again, the loop of the rope hanging loosely around its shin.

He took the second rope and edged closer to the horse's hindquarters, but the horse started flailing again and kicked higher up the wall, so Daniel grabbed the first rope, still looped around its front leg, and pulled. The rope fibers sawed into the skin of his hand when the horse yanked its leg, but every time the horse's body was as far from the wall as the horse could get it, Daniel pulled for all he was worth and finally, between his efforts and the horse's, the horse rolled over, past the peak of its withers, and its legs kicked toward the center of the stall.

Daniel jumped back out of the way of the deadly hooves and crashed into Aldrich, who rushed into the stall. The horse's fore-hoof caught

Daniel in the shin as the horse scrambled to its feet and spun around the confined space, eyes still bulging and breath roaring in and out. Its hindquarters struck Aldrich and knocked him off balance, but Daniel grabbed his arm and righted him before the man fell and got pulverized under the churning hooves. He shoved the older man out the stall door, then followed him out and slammed the door shut when the stallion tried to follow them. Daniel spun and shoved the latch home just as the horse's chest slammed against the door.

"Yours isn't the only horse that's been witched today."

Daniel turned, breathing hard in the cool air of the barn.

Cook. Of course. The man found trouble like flies found manure.

The man stood there in the barn door, leaning on a walking stick since his leg was still not fully healed from his run-in with the catamount. His mouth formed a crooked smile around the pipe he held in his teeth.

Aldrich's stud was breathing hard and in a sweaty lather, but it was settling now that it was freed. It was a typical high-strung horse, panicked from feeling trapped but settling now that the excitement was over. No reason to believe it was anything but a horse that had gotten cast its stall.

"No one witched this horse." He had no patience right now for Cook getting everyone riled over nothing. "And I trust you have not brought a lit pipe in among the hay?" A barn fire would truly be the work of the Devil, and it was any sane man's worst nightmare, especially as the harvest was coming in. Losing the year's harvest was losing the ability to survive the winter.

Cook narrowed his eyes at Daniel but stuck his pipe in his pocket to show it was not lit. Even Cook wasn't that foolish.

Aldrich's color was a more normal shade of pink now, and he seemed to compose himself. "Thank you," he said. Then he heaved in a breath and turned to Cook. "What can we do for you, Goodman Cook?"

Cook leaned on his walking stick and seemed to want to burn a hole in Daniel's eyeballs with his own. Daniel just stared back and waited.

"Are you so certain your horse wasn't witched, Mr. Aldrich?"

Aldrich straightened and glared down his nose. "You forget yourself, Cook."

Cook tucked his chin down in deference. "I didn't mean any disrespect, Mr. Aldrich." Then he peeked a sideways glance in Daniel's direction. "I am a bit jumbled with the all witching and the Penobscot after me. It doesn't sit right when the Devil is at work. I think his minions take over my mouth sometimes. I beg you will pray with me on it."

As soon as Cook deferred to him, Aldrich went to the man and put a hand on his shoulder. He was too solicitous of Cook when they needed to stop his foolery once and for all, not encourage it. But Cook always knew which thread to pull to unravel logic and create a tangle of confusion and fear in its place.

As warden, Daniel knew the strict parameters of witchcraft law, but after five years of violence, everyone else just knew a deep fear of witches. And Cook convinced himself as easily as he convinced others.

If he knocked Cook's teeth out, it might shut him up for at least a little while. But it was not a good choice for a selectman of the town, tempting though it might be.

Aldrich turned Daniel's way. "What say you, Warden?"

There was a sudden high-pitched squeal from the end of the barn. A fury of motion and then Aldrich's mouser let out a yowl as she turned and trotted right past them, a large mouse in her jaws.

Cook shrieked as it came his way. The man must be feverish and having fever-visions.

"Get that thing away from me!" Cook scrambled out of the path of the little hunter as fast as his mending leg would take him, almost climbing over the nearest stall door. "Satan's minions!"

The man was losing his wits. The mouser was doing precisely what she was kept to do.

Then Cook went white and pointed to the far end of the barn. Everyone's heads swiveled in that direction.

A specter of a woman appeared in the doorway at the far end of the barn, and Daniel's whole body gave a slight shiver. In half an instant, he breathed out and his muscles relaxed again. It was just Ruth, lit from behind and looking other-worldly, but certainly not a specter from beyond.

"I will thank you to stop getting everyone riled up, Cook. That is my wife."

Cook turned his eyes on Daniel, and they were red and unfocused. He opened his mouth, a small drip of spittle leaked out, and then he closed it.

The man was full of histrionics, and if they were in London, he would think Cook had escaped from a troupe of players. Or Bedlam.

Aldrich and his servant, who had remained mute through the entire stage show, were now looking at him, both as pale as sun-bleached linen.

"I suggest you have your man take the horse to stand in the creek several times over the next few days to be sure its legs remain cool." It was time to get back to the actual issues at hand so they could get in their crops and prepare for winter.

"That would do Ned good, too." Ruth approached them. "I don't think the kick broke anything, but he has swelling and heat in the leg, and the creek will help."

Aldrich's wrung his hands, glancing at Ruth but not leaving his gaze on her, like she might somehow hex him if he did. "But the creek is in the woods."

Then Aldrich looked back at Daniel, and his eyes widened. He pointed at Daniel's leg.

His trousers were torn, and his shin had taken on an unnatural shade of purple, and there was no mistaking that it was swollen. Once his eyes saw it, his brain registered the sting of his skin and the stabbing pain beneath it.

Ruth was at his feet before he even saw her moving.

"No," he pulled her back to her feet. "We need to get home. You can tend it there." It was time for him to put an end to chaos for this day and be productive for its remainder.

She stood and held her tongue.

He said goodbye to Aldrich, who still wouldn't look squarely at Ruth, and Daniel forced his gait to remain even as he walked out of the wagon. His leg screamed in protest with each step, and he could hear Aldrich and Cook praying together about the Penobscot and minions of the Devil.

12

"You are not fine," Ruth said. "You almost passed out when you tried to pretend you could walk without a limp." He might be able to fool the men at Mr. Aldrich's farm, but he had turned white as snow when he first stepped on that leg, and then green. "At least you managed not to puke on them."

He stared at her from the wagon, and he blinked at her several times like he was astonished she had read him so easily.

She sighed and waited for him to realize she wasn't as gullible as Mr. Aldrich.

"I can get out of a wagon," he said at last.

"Let me steady you as you climb down so you don't make it worse." She reached her arms up to him.

"You don't need to do that."

"Yes, I do."

He opened his mouth to reply, then shut it and turned to swing his injured leg over the side of the wagon. He balanced his weight for a moment and then swung his good leg over, too. She had to stretch to get her hands on his arse to steady him, then she grabbed hold of his hips as he slid down carefully, landing on his good leg.

Once he was steady on his foot, she took his arm and wrapped it around her shoulders. Its warmth grounded her.

"I can walk."

"You will do less damage if you let me help." She wrapped her free arm firmly around his waist.

He looked down at her, his jaw set like a mule. She gripped his arm and his waist tighter and waited. They stared at each other like that for a long moment.

Then he rolled his eyes and leaned on her to take a step toward the house. He winced each time his leg had to bear weight, and his arm around her shoulders tightened, despite his claim that he didn't need her help.

She got him into the house and sat him down by the hearth.

"Stay there while I put the mare in the barn."

He straightened like he had forgotten all about the horse in front of the house, still hitched the very wagon he had just gotten out of. He tried to rise, but she shoved her hand into his chest and pushed him back down. Stubborn fool.

She grabbed a stool and propped his leg up on it. "Stay."

He snorted.

She left him there to go tend to the mare. She got her unhitched and stowed in the barn with some hay. The wagon would have to stay where it was for the moment. She could get it rolling toward the barn, but stopping it when she needed to might be a different and more serious issue.

She returned to the house and almost burst out laughing when she walked through the door. Daniel was right where she left him, but he had removed his shoe and stocking, rolled up his trouser leg, and poked at his shin like her little nephew would poke at a snake.

"It won't bite you. It's your own leg."

"I don't know. It looks pretty angry." He gave her a lopsided grin. Her insides melted a little.

She went to him and knelt down to get her first good look at his leg. Her smile faded. It did look angry.

First things first. She reached for her medical supplies and grabbed a jar of meadowsweet that had been soaking in brandy. She set a clean jar on the table and placed a cheesecloth over it, then poured the meadowsweet and brandy into the fresh jar and left it to drip.

He watched her movements. "What is that?"

"Poison, it will have you writhing in agony for hours before you succumb. But it will take your mind off how much your leg hurts."

She waited. Then he laughed, and she relaxed.

"Fine. Do what you need to do." He leaned back in the chair, folded his arms across his chest, and watched.

He wasn't pushing back. All the other men in her life kicked up a stink when she healed them. She searched his face and saw only open curiosity about what she was doing. He trusted her.

"It's meadowsweet, and it will help with the pain."

He nodded at that.

"Now I am going to poke around a little to see if the beast's hoof broke your leg." She met his gaze. "That will not help with the pain."

His smile faded, but he nodded to her to go ahead.

She placed her hands along his shin. She pressed a few spots firmly, but nothing felt out of place, and no one spot elicited any more response from him than any other. His whole shin hurt, which was, ironically, a good sign.

She looked up. His face was paler than it had been, and his nostrils flared as he forced air in and out of his lungs.

"I think nothing is broken."

He nodded. "Is the meadowsweet ready?" he asked through clenched teeth.

"It will be soon." She grabbed a salve and smoothed it over the purple skin.

A knock sounded at the door, and Daniel started to rise.

"Sit."

He raised an eyebrow at her and lowered himself back onto the chair. "Find out who it is before you throw open the door and let in a French raiding party."

It would be so nice to call him paranoid, but she couldn't because he wasn't.

"Ruth?" Goody Carter's voice came from the other side of the door.

Ruth's shoulders relaxed, and she swung the door open. Goody Carter bustled in carrying a basket brimming with odds and ends.

Ruth turned to Daniel, who was looking at Goody Carter and her basket like she was more dangerous than a French raiding party.

Goody Carter went straight to Daniel and studied his leg. "I heard you got kicked, but I knew Ruth would take good care of you."

Daniel sighed. No doubt annoyed that she already knew he had been kicked. "I am in good hands, as you can see." He gestured to Ruth, and her cheeks warmed.

Most men only considered themselves in good hands when Doctor Kingsman was called in.

"To what do we owe the honor of your visit?" he asked Goody Carter.

She ignored Daniel and grinned at Ruth. "I told you he was excellent husband material. And is he doing his duty and getting you with child?"

Now Ruth's cheeks were burning. She glanced at Daniel, who was red as a ripe apple and looking like he wanted to disappear into the floor.

"I brought some eggs and some cone flower, just in case," the older woman said.

Daniel's brows bunched together in confusion, thank goodness.

"We have no need of that, thank you." She shoved the plant back into Goody Carter's basket.

Goody Carter's face brightened. "Are you refusing help again, or admitting I was right?"

Ruth grabbed her friend by the arm and pulled her out the door before Daniel could figure out the woman was inquiring about the quality of his cockstands.

Goody Carter searched Ruth's face and then grinned. "He is learning his way around, then?"

"Stop it." Ruth wasn't used to being the subject of such talk.

Goody Carter set her basket down and threw her arms around Ruth. "I am so glad. You deserve to be well taken care of."

Ruth closed her eyes and counted to three before opening her mouth.

"I don't suppose you brought any valerian root? I had to leave my supply in the Penobscot village."

Goody Carter pulled some from her basket, but now she was frowning. "Be careful, Ruth."

She had to be careful of so many things.

"Ruth?"

Ruth spun and saw Matthias approaching. Her heart took a moment to return to its normal pace. How did Daniel ever accomplish anything with people showing up on his doorstep all day long?

"Aldrich has called out the militia."

She blinked, and her heart took off racing again.

Her head got light, and she grabbed Goody Carter's arm to steady herself. "What?" She heard her brother's words, but she didn't want to believe them. How could he look so calm?

She must have looked as terrified as she felt because he rushed to clarify. "To drill tomorrow, not to fight."

Her knees almost gave way as she started breathing again.

Except Daniel couldn't drill. He needed to keep his leg up and rest it, or he would never heal.

Before she could say anything, Daniel appeared at the door. He was in his shirtsleeves now, and Ruth caught Goody Carter gawking. She gave the older woman a jab with her elbow, then turned back to Daniel.

"You are not going." The words were out of her mouth before she could think.

A breeze rattled the leaves in the tree next to the house.

Matthias looked from her to Daniel. "I see you have met my sister." The corner of his mouth tipped up.

Ruth smacked her brother's arm. Jabbing a hot poker into his gut would have been more satisfying.

"We are acquainted," Daniel said.

Matthias chuckled.

Daniel turned back to her. "Every able-bodied man has a duty to serve and keep ready. I am going."

"You are not able-bodied right now." His stupid sense of duty seemed to lack common sense. As did he.

"The militia hasn't drilled since the disaster in Jacob's woods. We are overdue."

Matthias grunted in agreement and shifted his weight from one foot to the other. He had born many insults about how he handled himself that day, but for all his faults, she had no doubt that he had followed orders. He just wanted to live his life unnoticed and unmolested, and breaking rules didn't accomplish that.

Daniel spoke again, the lines of his face etched deeper than a moment ago. "He would only call the militia to train in the middle of the harvest if he believed Cook about the Penobscot attacking him."

She looked from Daniel to Matthias to Goody Carter and back to Daniel. "But they didn't." Her gut spiraled downward toward her feet.

Ruth had dosed Daniel with meadowsweet, smothered his leg in slippery elm she had gotten from the Penobscot, and then wrapped his shin in linen strips from her splinting supplies. It still ached with every step, but at least now he could take a step without puking from the pain. She was right. He should be at home resting it, but at least she had him functional. His wife had skills.

Matthias eyed his leg.

Matthias grunted and said, "Cook probably has Aldrich thinking the Penobscot wedged the horse up against the wall. Nothing else explains dragging the militia out right now." He glanced up at the afternoon sun. "If we starve this winter, it will be our own bloody fault."

So true. Everyone in the militia should be bringing in crops right now. Aldrich's fear of the Devil and his minions led him to give Cook too much credence.

Most of the men of the town were already assembled when Matthias and Daniel arrived. The majority payed them no mind, but many stared at them. "What on earth did we do?" Daniel kept his voice low.

Matthias grunted again but said nothing.

"...and with more activity in the woods, we have to be prepared for them to openly break the treaty, which means we need to get back to our drills so we can defend our harvests." Aldrich stood on a stump as he addressed the militia, and Cook stood right below him, nodding and muttering prayers.

Daniel studied the faces of the gathered men, and his gut tightened. Their faces were eager. Like going on the offensive might somehow end the tension.

"What a load of shite," Matthias mumbled. Daniel took a step toward Aldrich, and Matthias grabbed his arm, dragging him back. "Don't."

"What?"

Matthias pursed his lips for a moment like something in his mouth tasted sour. "Just go along for now."

A younger man who lived near Matthias looked their way. "Ain't serving in your company anymore." And he turned and wedged his way through the crowd and disappeared as it closed in behind him.

Matthias shrugged at Daniel.

They hadn't drilled since the disaster, which was unwise. The law said they needed to drill once a month, and disaster was usually a reliable indicator that they needed more practice, not less. But the timing was poor. No one followed the every-month law during the harvest, especially on the frontier, where their survival hinged on getting crops in.

Daniel's hands ran along the cool wood of his musket stock. It had a little dip just in front of the pan that was particularly smooth, and he ran his finger slowly over it, back and forth. He had probably worried the dimple into the wood during the war, rubbing the stock with his finger like that, but it helped him focus.

The younger man was a reminder of the disorder that had grown over the past five years. Disorder that allowed the Devil a foothold. Eyes shifted toward Daniel and Matthias.

"Assemble by company." Aldrich's voice carried easily across the green.

Daniel's leg throbbed as his company assembled around him. Matthias counted heads and gave a nod. They had the right number despite the defector. Aldrich must have juggled the company rosters before they arrived.

Jacob had his own company now, and Daniel gave him a nod across the grassy expanse, then turned to Aldrich to await his commands. Please, dear heaven above, let it not be marching. Even Ruth wouldn't be able to put him to rights for field work tomorrow if it was.

"Prepare for loading drills."

Relief shot through Daniel's body, and he turned to Matthias, who gave him a half smile as he swung his own musket to the ready. Matthias had gotten a good look at his raw leg when Ruth went to wrap it and laughed at Daniel's bulging eyes as she pulled the cloth tight. If Aldrich had called for marching formations, Matthias would have had to carry Daniel home on his back. But musket drills he could handle.

Reverend Maitland's sixteen-year-old son was struggling with his flint. Daniel caught Matthias' eye and nodded his chin toward the boy. Matthias looked, shook his head slightly, walked over, took his flint from him, and got it inserted correctly.

"Your mother teach you how to witch it in right?" said another one of Matthias' neighbors. Matthias ignored the man's words, took the man's musket and checked his flint, adjusted it, and shoved the musket back into the man's chest, then stepped to the next man and inspected his flint.

"Silence in the ranks." Daniel stepped harder on his bad leg than he meant to, which did nothing to improve his mood. He kept walking until his face was just inches from the other man's. "Order and discipline are how a militia wins. Disorder and disrespect are how you give the Devil a foothold." He stared into the man's eyes until the man finally blinked.

The men were all silent. Daniel looked up and caught Matthias watching. "Are they all correctly primed?"

Matthias nodded. Anyone who couldn't prime his weapon was long since dead unless they were green boys like the minister's son.

Daniel ordered them to load and ready to fire. The man who had mouthed off to Matthias knocked too much powder from his horn onto his flash pan. Daniel stopped him.

"What?" the man said. "I want to be damned sure this musket goes off if one of them is coming at me."

"Blow your eyebrows off, and you won't be able to see if you hit anything."

The man eyed him, then scanned the woods like the Penobscot might be forming up for battle somewhere just beyond his view.

"They aren't coming for you. They will only come for you if we break the treaty, which, of course, we will not do."

"Starved enough on their account. Ain't sending them any corn just to live on my own land," the man grumbled. A few others grunted in assent, but the ones who glanced Daniel's way wisely kept silent.

"A legal treaty is a legal treaty. Keep your focus on your drills." Their discipline had waned near the end of the war and disintegrated during raids after the war.

He gestured to Matthias. "Set a log a hundred paces toward the woods." Matthias looked at him and then did as Daniel asked. As soon as he returned to the company, Daniel addressed them. "Check your muskets. We are going to fire one at a time at the log. For every misfire, the entire company will do an extra ten loading drills."

They all stared at him, then seemed to realize that he was not bluffing. Everyone started double-checking and adjusting their flints and loads.

"By file, first up, stand to the line. Make ready."

The first man stood ready.

"Take aim. Fire."

He fired, and a small chip of bark flew off the log. Not at all bad for that distance.

"Next," Daniel ordered.

The reverend's son stood to the front and readied his musket.

"Take aim. Fire."

He pulled the trigger, and a hollow click sounded. Misfire.

"That's ten extra loading drills. Matthias, help Goodman Maitland prepare his musket properly."

Matthias stepped toward him. Someone muttered something that sounded like 'sister witched him,' but Matthias continued what he was doing, so maybe Daniel had misheard.

"Mind you, prepare your musket right and don't blame anyone or anything if you do it wrong. Blame won't save you in a fight."

The next man fired but missed the log. Not surprising. It was a small log, and it was well beyond some men's accurate range.

They got through the rest of the company with no more misfires, and when young Maitland returned to the line and fired, a chunk of bark flew off the side of the log. The entire company cheered the shot, as well they should. Several men clapped the boy on the back.

"Matthias," Daniel said, "your turn."

The men quieted and watched Matthias prepare. He set his flint, poured powder into his pan and took careful aim.

The wind rustling the leaves was the only sound.

He pulled the trigger, and the top of the log exploded into a fountain of splinters. The men were quiet.

"Glad you're on our side," Daniel said to Matthias so the others couldn't hear.

Matthias shrugged.

They couldn't afford to spend more than one ball of shot a piece on target practice, so it was time for the loading drills the reverend's boy had earned them.

"Alright, loading drills."

They gawked at him like he was speaking in tongues.

"Only one misfire in the company, so only ten loading drills. Prepare."

They kept staring. He stared back.

They came to the collective realization that he wasn't moving until they started.

"How much powder do you expect us to waste today, Kendrick?" Goodman Smith asked.

"You're not wasting it. You are using it productively, so we are ready to defend ourselves. No amount of powder will help with that if you can't load correctly and quickly."

They all looked back at him, some unconvinced and others with resignation. Matthias stood with his musket ready for the drill, and slowly, everyone mirrored his stance.

"Begin." Daniel watched them load. They were slow and not focused. "Clear your muskets." They tipped the powder to the ground and tapped the shot out.

"Again." They were quicker this time.

"Again."

By the tenth time, they were quick and efficient and no longer wasting time looking at each other for reactions. They didn't even have to measure the powder with their eyes. They could tell by feel. They could do it without thinking, which is exactly what they needed to do.

When they finished, one man peered pointedly into his powder horn and then at Daniel. Another caught the look and made like he was weighing his own horn. "We done what you asked. Now how we gonna keep our families safe, from the Penobscot or anything else?"

They broke ranks and milled about. Discipline evaporated.

"We need powder, Kendrick!"

Daniel raised his hand to get everyone's attention before they spun out of control. "I have powder from Boston for the Garrison house, so we can replenish your stores at our next training." It might not be precisely how Boston had intended the powder be used, but it was all to the right purpose in the end.

"They could come for us before then, and our powder will be too low to defend ourselves." It was Smith. Others shouted in agreement. "Let us get our powder now." They crowded toward him. In the span of a few breaths, they had gone from disciplined militia to agitated mob.

"The Penobscot aren't coming for us if we don't provoke them," Daniel said.

Smith took a step forward and raised his chin. He seemed to think himself deputized to speak for the rest. "That is easy for you to say, living in a garrison house with all that powder from Boston."

The men all watched Daniel.

"I have no intention of hoarding the powder. The point is to defend *everyone* in the settlement," Daniel said.

"Excellent," said Smith, "then we will accompany you home and get our powder now." And the entire company turned and swarmed down the road in the direction of the garrison house.

Daniel stared after them, blinking.

"They'll burn the house if you don't let them have their powder," Matthias said.

They might burn it anyway, the mood they were in. And anyone in it.

He had to get there first.

"Help me keep up with them." He swung his arm around Matthias' giant shoulders because he would never catch up with them on his beat-up leg without Matthias' help.

"Hurry. Ruth is home alone."

13

With Matthias' help, Daniel was able to keep the men in sight on the way to the garrison house, but they still arrived first and pounded on the door like they wanted to break it down. Ruth no doubt thought the house was being attacked.

Heaven help them if she responded accordingly and blew the head off the first man at the door. She could load a musket, and even if she had never fired one before, it would be pretty hard to miss someone at that range.

"Hold up," he called, "you'll get your powder, but don't frighten my wife."

At that, they stopped pounding and began jostling each other and trying to avoid being the man at the front. Apparently, it had dawned on them what a person in a garrison house might do in response to a mob at the door.

Before Daniel and Matthias reached the house, the door swung open, and the men all flinched back. If he could just have warned Ruth before they arrived, his stomach might not be about to empty its contents. They deserved to be met with a musket muzzle, but Lord only knew what would follow if that happened.

As they reached the back of the crowd, he could see Ruth on the step, musket in hand, over the heads of the men. She met his eyes, and he gestured with his hand to calm down. With luck, she would understand he meant the men were keyed up, and they needed to de-escalate the situation. Without luck, she might think he considered her answering the door with a musket to be an overreaction. Luck was the best thing for everyone.

"Welcome to the garrison house, everyone," he said. It didn't take a genius to know they weren't really welcome, but it was time to make the best of it. "Please, just let me explain to my wife why everyone is here since she could only have assumed the house was under attack by the sounds and with no warning." He gave a laugh to lighten the mood, but it sounded forced to his ears.

Matthias helped him make his way through the men, who seemed a little less sure what to do now they had reached their destination. They were hungry, tired, and amped up over yet another potential escalation of tensions with the Penobscot, but they had lost some of their mob energy, at least for the moment.

"Meet Company A of the militia." Daniel gestured to the men as he reached Ruth. Then he leaned in. "I'm sorry, but I couldn't stop them, and I need to placate them."

She looked at him and then out at the crowd. The grumbling from the men rose in volume. She met Daniel's eyes once again and gave a brief nod, then she stepped around him and opened her arms. "Welcome. I didn't know to expect company, but I have fresh bread. Please come in."

Daniel hopped in the door. There was no point pretending his leg didn't scream in agony with every movement. Matthias followed him.

"Where is the powder?" Matthias asked quietly.

"Attic."

"I'll get it. You sit."

For all that he was cranky, Matthias did what needed doing. Thank heavens.

The men entered the house, looking at Ruth as if she had sharp fangs dripping with blood. His chest constricted for a moment. He was a fool. They weren't put off by her aiming a musket at them. They were afraid they had just angered a witch.

She smiled and portioned out the bread that would have fed the two of them for weeks. If she realized why they were giving her a wide berth, she didn't show it.

She circulated through the main room, offering everyone bread, while Daniel sat at the table, unable to stand any longer.

He studied her. She smiled, but her shoulders were tense. The others didn't seem to notice it, but he had grown used to her body, and she was not as relaxed as she pretended.

At last, she returned to the table and gave Daniel some bread.

He looked around at his company. Everyone held bread in his hand, and no one was eating.

They all stared at the bread they held as if it were witch cake. And that made his heart hurt. Not only had she given away all her afternoon's work, they weren't eating it because they didn't trust her.

He took a giant bite of his chunk of bread, chewed it, and swallowed. "This is wonderful. Thank you."

She smiled at him, but the corners of her mouth were still pinched tight, and her skin was a shade more pale than usual. But she followed his lead and took a big bite instead of waiting for her guests to eat first.

She startled when Matthias stepped down onto the ladder carrying the cask of powder on his shoulder. She was anxious about the house full of men watching her with sideways glances.

When Matthias reached the bottom of the ladder, he set the cask down well away from the hearth. The men all eyed the powder. They clearly just wanted to get their powder and go. They had gotten their hackles up at the militia training, but their bile had settled, and they wanted to be on their way.

Ruth handed Matthias some bread. He surveyed the scene, sat himself down on the cask as if it were a stool, and ripped a chunk of bread off with his teeth. "I needed this. Worked up a hunger today."

The men watched him chew.

Ruth squared her shoulders and forced a very convincing smile to her face. "You all must be hungry after your drills, and your harvesting before that. Please eat." Ruth came and stood by Daniel's side.

They all looked around at each other, then after confirming that neither he, Matthias, nor Ruth had keeled over from the bread or begun speaking in tongues, they began to nibble at their own.

Ruth and Daniel let out their breath at the same time. He reached for her hand. It was warm in his, and he gave it a little squeeze, trying to convey his gratitude. She squeezed his hand back and then let go and walked toward the hearth. Her touch had been comforting, and he wanted it back.

But Goodman Smith approached him. "How certain are you it wasn't Penobscot that attacked Cook?"

At last, a chance to address the unspoken issue without forcing it. "Very. His wound was consistent with a swipe from a catamount, and the Penobscot have nothing to benefit from attacking him."

Smith chewed on his bread, a few crumbs clinging to his beard. "I don't trust 'em. They don't like us."

The first thought that popped into Daniel's head was they had given the Penobscot no reason to like them. And plenty of reasons not to. Except for Ruth. "They feel kindly toward us right now because Ruth saved the Sagamore's father-in-law."

Smith's eyes grew large. He kept chewing, not saying anything.

"They aren't fool enough to mess with a situation in their favor," Daniel added.

Ruth was offering beer to everyone. They would be drinking water this winter if they kept going through their beer stores like this.

Smith kept eating, but he seemed to be thinking, and his beard didn't jut out as aggressively now.

"How is your leg healing?" Daniel asked.

The color rose in Smith's face. "She healed me good." The man shuffled off to talk with someone else, and Daniel didn't see any limp.

The men were eating more freely, and some even smiled at Ruth as she refilled their beer. But they all eyed the powder cask that Matthias' arse still guarded.

Matthias caught Daniel's eye and raised his eyebrows in question. It was time to dole out the powder and send the men home. Daniel nodded to Matthias and then gestured to the door with his chin. Matthias acknowledged the plan with a nod and rose to his feet.

Daniel followed suit and almost collapsed back onto the bench. The room got a little blotchy, and he leaned his hands on the table to keep himself more or less upright. Foolish not to account for his leg stiffening up as he sat, and searing pain tore through it to make certain he wouldn't forget again.

When the room came back into focus, Ruth was next to him, eyes studying him. She was studying her patient, and she was not pleased by his actions.

"I have to," he said in her ear.

Without a word, she placed his arm around her shoulders and her own around his waist. The firm pressure of her arm steadied his balance and his mind. He leaned on her shoulders and hopped a step toward the door. "Bring the keg to the door so we don't risk the house," he said to Matthias, then he turned to men. "Let's fill your horns so you can get home to your families."

Ruth got him propped up in the doorway as Matthias brought the cask. The men went outside and lined up as Ruth helped Matthias fill each man's horn. Even the ones that were so empty they had to have showed up to drill with only quarter-full horns to begin with.

The men chatted as they waited, and snatches of their conversation reached his ears. "Maybe he'll actually cover this brother-in-law's back," one said to another. Daniel wasn't sure what that meant.

When the final man slung his full horn over his shoulder and walked off in the last of the light toward his home, Matthias sealed the cask.

Daniel slumped against the door frame. Aldrich was a fool to call the militia to drill on the spur of the moment.

Matthias came to stand next to him. "Devil was at work today."

He had the right of it.

Daniel gave Matthias's shoulder a brotherly slap. "Get on home to Anne."

Matthias snorted. "Someone finally understands the point of married life." He turned to go. "At least your wife can heal you again after she breaks you tonight."

Horse's arse.

Ruth came to Daniel's side as Matthias headed away from the garrison house, musket at the ready, eyes scanning the woods. She put her arm around his waist again, but instead of walking him back into the house, she leaned her head against him. Warmth flooded his chest. After a moment, he put his arm around her and pulled her in closer as they both gazed out at the last purple glow before full dark.

"I thought they were here to drag me to the town oak." She almost choked on that last word.

He pulled her closer, and her chest constricted a little.

He looked her in the eye. "I'm sorry." He worked his mouth like he had more to say, but the words had left his tongue dry.

"For what? You weren't part of the mob trying to break down the door." Her vision swam a little, blurring his face. She blinked hard to clear the threatening tears.

He wrapped both arms around her and drew her tight to him. The heat of his body against hers was an anchor, but it also set off flutters of energy through her chest and down past her belly. She buried her face in his chest and drew in the smell of him. Black powder, exertion, fresh air, and pine.

"I've hunted witches for the safety of the community." The hair on the top of her head vibrated as he spoke into it. "And until today, I never considered how terrifying it must feel to be the one hunted." He cleared his throat, which made her throat get tight.

His breath hitched against the top of her head. If he held her any tighter, he would crush her, but it felt safe and right.

She had lived with the looming suspicion of witchcraft since her mother was tried when she was just a little girl. No one—not even her brother—had ever considered how those suspicions affected anyone but themselves.

She tightened her arms around his waist, then tipped her head back to look up into his deep, dark eyes. She swallowed. Then she swallowed again. At last, she got her tongue to move. "Thank you."

He stiffened, and his brows bunched down over his nose. "For accidentally setting a mob on you?"

A little puff of a chuckle escaped her nose, but her eyes stung. Her heart was cracking open, and it was agony. "For acknowledging it." A single tear hung at the tip of her lashes, just in her peripheral vision. "No one ever has."

His face had never been so raw and open. He seemed caught in a whirlwind of churning emotions. Then his hands rose to her face and cupped her cheek. He wiped the tear that had loosed its grip on her lashes.

His eyes burned into hers, and his thumb kept caressing her damp cheek. God, he was beautiful.

Her hands loosed from around his waist and traced a path up his sides to his chest. Her belly flipped, and her fingers burned as they traced his chest. Then she reached up to his face and cupped his cheeks in a mirror of how his hands held her. He blinked, and his chest pressed against hers as he breathed deeply, lips parted.

When she stroked his cheek, he bent down to press a kiss to her lips. A flock of hummingbirds took off in her belly, their wings fluttering against her insides, and she felt his cock grow hard against her belly. How had she been so far up in her head that she had never kissed him before?

He kissed her again, and she ground her belly against his cockstand as she kissed him back, nibbling at his lips. His entire body shuddered against hers.

Suddenly, the world tipped, and she was in the air. He had one arm under her shoulders and the other behind her knees, and he was carrying her across the room.

"Your leg!"

"To the Devil with my leg."

His arms were warm against her body, and he had her in the bedroom before she could protest further. Not that she wanted to. If his leg felt good enough to carry them both, she was willing to trust his judgement just this once.

When they reached the bed, he set her on her feet, but his hands remained on her body, his thumbs rubbing back and forth against her sides, just under her breasts. Her breath hitched.

His face was focused intently on her, but he seemed uncertain of his next step. The doctoress voice in her head reminded her that his leg must be throbbing, so she put her hands on his hips and guided them back to the bed. He didn't resist.

Even with him sitting, she was barely taller than him. His gaze sent heart racing and her belly fluttering.

She reached forward and unbuttoned his waistcoat and pulled it from his shoulders. He watched her hands as she untied the neck of his shirt. He likely did not know when his tongue darted out and wet his lips, but her body noticed, and her breath quickened.

She reached to his waistband and untucked his shirt, then dragged it up, raising his arms over his head until she had slid the rough fabric up and off, freeing his wrists last. His chest muscles twitched, and he had gooseflesh despite the comfortable temperature in the room.

His eyes never left hers as her hands slid down his chest to his trouser buttons. When she reached for the button on his trousers, his cock twitched against her hand. She untied his drawers, and his cock lept free.

The sight of his rock-hard manhood rising from the dark curls between his legs had her own nether regions tingling. She knelt down and removed his shoes and stockings, then urged him to lift his hips so she could slide his trousers off. He hesitated for just an instant, then complied.

Daniel was pale where his clothes usually covered him, and dark where the sun kissed his skin as he worked in the fields. His every muscle tensed under that piebald skin. And he was hers to gaze on.

He clenched his hands into fists on the bed on either side of him, like he was trying to keep his hands in check. A red flush crept up his neck to his face as she ran her eyes over him.

She took a half step back and undid the neck of her bodice. His cock jumped. She removed the bodice and then her skirt and her shoes.

She reached up under her shift, loosed the tapes of her drawers, slid them down to her ankles, and tossed them aside. This was so wanton. She had never undressed like this for Esau. He didn't have the patience for it. But Daniel's gaze was intent, and his cock jumped with her every move, fueling her desire for him and her desire to make him want her. She might burn in hell for it, but the rapturous look on his face was worth an eternity wherever it took her.

Then she reached down for the hem of her shift, and he almost rose from the bed. She pushed him back with one hand, stepped back again, and drew the fabric up her legs, hesitated as the draft in the room reached her intimate center, then raised the hem more slowly up past her own thatch of curls, then up over her belly, and, her breath coming harder, she exposed her breasts to him.

He leaned forward toward her but stayed seated. She raised the shift up and over her head, then tossed it aside.

She stood like that, naked before Daniel for a moment, while his eyes burned a charred path from her breasts to the juncture between her thighs and then up to her face.

"You are magnificent." His voice was rough with emotion.

Then, perhaps the Devil made her do it, she raised her arms to the side and did a slow twirl, feeling his gaze on her even when her back was turned.

The only sound in the room was their combined breath. He stood in front of her. Her head tilted back as he rose so she could watch his face, but her eyes were pulled by the beauty of his rough-hewn body. She had always thought of him as being smart, and everyone knew he was skilled with horses, but she had never imagined his clothes hid a body like this.

Her inner thighs were damp, and her belly pulsed with need just looking at him.

But he was injured. He should not be standing. Or using his leg at all.

"What?" There was the faintest hint of desperation in his voice.

In for a penny, in for a pound. "Lay down on your back."

He stared at her. She stared back at him. Then he sat, scooted himself back on the bed, and did as she told him. Her heart gave a quick double beat. This big, powerful man was laying himself bare for her. He would not regret that trust.

She climbed onto the bed and slinked up his body like a big cat. She placed one knee on either side of his waist and leaned down to kiss his full lips. He groaned when her breasts brushed over his bare chest. Or maybe that was her.

Then she took him in hand and guided him where they both wanted him to be. She slid down until his cock speared her right through. His eyes pulled hers to them. They were filled with such trust and awe she couldn't look away. She rocked forward against his body, the delicious friction sending sizzles of sensation from her core out to her toes and fingertips.

His mouth dropped open, and they both breathed with the rhythm of their bodies. The harder she rocked, the tighter they both wound, eyes still locked together. His hips pushed up to meet her with every thrust, and their bodies glowed with a sheen of sweat.

He grasped her hips hard, forcing their bodies even closer, and their actions became frantic as they both reached for release. She hung as if at the top of a towering waterfall for a heartbeat, two, then her entire body convulsed in waves of pleasure that made her brain go blank. All she could do was feel, and he went rigid under her, and shot his seed, pulsing into her body.

They hung in a passionate cloud, each shuddering occasionally as ripples of tension continued to release in their bodies.

She lay flat on top of his body with his arms around her as their breathing returned to normal. Her limbs were limp. He smoothed her hair and kissed her.

Time stopped registering as they lay in each other's arms.

Then he rolled her to the side. Her body tensed. He couldn't be leaving the bed after that. She raised her head, and his face was still soft.

He was trying to get the blanket free from beneath them. Her body relaxed, and she helped him free it and snuggled further into his arms as he wrapped it around them, their legs still entwined like the ivy on the chimney.

    He pulled her in tight, kissed her, and then buried his face in her hair.

    She nestled her cheek against his naked chest and let her eyes drift closed.

    Once, she woke in the night, and his warm body still held hers. She kissed his chest, right over his heart.

    He stirred in his sleep and pulled her tighter to him.

    She drifted back to sleep in the warmth of his embrace.

14

Something was tickling his nose. He opened his eyes, and he had Ruth's head nestled under his chin, and her loose hair was everywhere. Her body warmed his, and their legs tangled together.

Sunlight glowed through the cracks between the shutters.

Her scent filled his nostrils. Roses? She made tinctures from plants all the time, but he had never noticed her smelling of roses before.

Because he didn't have his nose buried in her hair very often. An error on his part.

She stirred against him, and his body responded. Her chest felt like it was vibrating against his, like she was almost purring. She gazed up at him with hooded eyes and smiled, and his heart took off like a jackrabbit.

She gave a little stretch and then snuggled against his body. Her knee brushed against his cock, which jumped with glee.

He heard their mouser yowl outside as she hunted her breakfast. It was time to feed the animals. He did not have time to lie about in bed.

Ruth's lips pressed against his chest, and he pulled her in tighter. Maybe the pressure of her body would help keep his heart from beating right out of his chest.

She made no move to get up or cover her body, although the blanket had slipped to the side when she stretched. The skin of her breast was warm and soft against his chest, and the sensation did more than arouse his body. It was the most vulnerable she had ever let herself be in his presence, and it made him want to wrap her up, and keep her safe and protected in the garrison house, and not let anyone ever threaten her again.

She would kick him in the stones if he suggested that, which made his lips tilt up in a smile. His wife was fierce.

"I feel you smiling on the top of my head." Her voice was rough with sleep and a little muffled since her face still pressed against him. Her breath tickled the hairs on his chest. "How is your leg?"

He flexed his foot, then pointed it, then rotated it in a circle. The movements shot pain up his shin, but it subsided when he stopped moving it. "Better."

"Than?"

"Yesterday."

"The standard wasn't high for that." She pushed herself up on her elbows and looked him in the face.

He craned his neck forward and kissed her on her elegant little nose. "I felt pretty good at the end of the day yesterday."

His neck burned at that admission, and the heat spread to his cheeks. Then her cheeks went rosy, and he pulled her in close.

She was so tiny in his arms, and he had to keep her safe.

But then she pushed herself up on her elbows again and chewed her bottom lip.

"What?" he asked.

She shifted on top of him, then looked him in the eye. "Why have you always left our bed before morning?"

His muscles lost their languid feel, and his chest tightened. The pain of drawing in a breath was far worse than the pain in his leg. He had nothing to be ashamed of, but shame burned his face, anyway.

She watched his face as he searched for words, then after a few moments, her eyes shuttered, and her smile faded. She had made herself vulnerable to him, and he had not returned the trust. The disappointment on her face crushed his heart.

"Witches." He blurted the word out before he could think of a better way to say it.

Her face popped back up, brows knit, mouth in a tight line.

He took a deep breath. She was his wife. Why hadn't he told her?

"I...." He hesitated. He tried again. "I haven't slept well since the day of the raid."

She cocked her head but didn't speak. She was letting him find his words. "Whatever evil was allowed among us that day hasn't left." Her eyes went wide, but her mouth remained closed. If she would just ask a question, this might be easier. "Whatever witch or witches caused that disaster puts visions of it in my head almost every night."

His eyes went to the ceiling above them and blinked hard several times. He should have found the culprit by now, and his failure put them all in danger. When he looked back down at her, her face had transformed. Her expression was soft, and she reached her hand toward his face.

His cheeks burned hotter, and he flinched away. He didn't need pity. He needed to do his work as warden and root out Satan's minions among them.

She pushed herself higher up his chest until her face was level with his. "You slept last night."

He blinked again. He had slept last night.

But he had slept plenty of nights before. He just didn't know when he would get a peaceful night and when the witch or witches would see fit to torment him.

"Did you sleep the nights you left me and went to the barn?" Her level tone and the look of open curiosity on her face allowed him to think.

He had spent many sleepless nights in the barn since their marriage, but except for their wedding night, on the nights he had lain with her before heading to the barn, he had slept. Well.

"Are you suggesting that you are a magical talisman against malefice?"

She pursed her lips. "Perhaps marital relations are a method of exorcism Reverend Maitland hasn't considered." Her eyes glinted, and she failed to suppress a smile. "Perhaps we should continue the experiment?"

His cock twitched merrily, making its views on the subject clear.

She hesitated. No way could he let her think he disapproved of her suggestion. He reached up and stroked her cheek.

Her skin was silk beneath his rough fingertips. He reached up with his other hand, nudged her face toward him, and brushed his lips over hers.

She ground her body against his, and his hips bucked.

Then, an explosive pounding echoed through the house, and they both jumped. It took a moment to register that it was someone pounding on the door.

"For the love of all that is holy...." He swung his legs down to the floor and stood. His injured leg shouted a reminder that it didn't like that. He took two limping steps toward the bedroom door when something hit him in the back.

He turned. Ruth had tossed the blanket to him.

Right. He was naked. Answering the door naked was not good form for a selectman. Or any godly person.

He picked it up and wrapped the itchy fabric around his waist. She blew him a kiss as she scrambled off the bed to her heap of clothes on the floor.

She bent over to pick them up, and the sight of her bare backside rooted his feet to the floor as his cock sprang to attention.

The pounding began again, and he turned before she caught him staring. No one had ever mentioned how distracting married life would be.

He hobbled to the front door. He took a slow breath and tried to compose his scrambled brain. "Who is there?"

"Open up, you lazy good-for-nothing." The tension in his muscles receded. It was just Jacob.

He swung open the door. "What?" He did not step aside to invite Jacob in. He hadn't thought to close the bedroom door. Who knew how fast Ruth could dress?

He wanted to bang his head against the doorjamb. What sort of useless husband had never been in the room when his wife rose and dressed in the morning?

A cowardly one who slept in the barn.

Jacob erupted in barks of laughter.

He laughed so hard and so long that Daniel hoped he would piss himself.

"Are you done?" Daniel's knuckles dug into the blanket as he gripped it tighter around himself and glared at Jacob.

Jacob wheezed and sat down on the doorstep. After a few more moments, he managed to speak. "I came to ask if you plan to harvest the—" He looked up and threw his arm dramatically over his eyes. "Stop pointing that useless thing at me."

Daniel looked down. His cock still jutted out like a pole. His face burned, and he shifted the blanket. "Ask your question, you arse."

Jacob wheezed and snorted. Maybe he would choke.

"When you are through diddling your wife, do you plan to harvest the scraggly strip of corn next to my field, or should I just burn it?"

He groaned. They hadn't finished harvesting his fields, and he hadn't even thought about hers. But they needed that corn. "I will get there. Burn it, and I will sue your sorry self."

Jacob chuckled again.

"Burn my corn, and I will do worse than sue." Ruth's voice boomed over his shoulder. He turned. She was dressed if not carefully groomed. Her eyes were narrow slits.

Jacob gave her a hard look, then turned back to him. "Your choice." And he got up and walked off without looking back.

Ruth watched Daniel close the door and turn toward her. As her nerves began to settle, her gut grew tight. She shouldn't have threatened Jacob. That was stupid.

She forced her eyes to remain on Daniel's. Her threat may have been stupid, but it was also justified, even if he didn't agree.

"What don't I know?" Daniel stood facing her, shifting his grip on the blanket so that it covered more of his body. The v-shaped patch of skin at his neck where the sun hit when he worked with his collar open highlighted the trench between his pale chest muscles. As did the sprinkling of dark hair on them.

He needed to shift the blanket higher.

"Ruth?"

Her lungs heaved in a breath, and let it go. "I shouldn't have said that."

He took a step toward her. She took half a step back. He stopped.

"Please tell me what I am missing."

She shrugged and turned toward the hearth. She grabbed the poker and stirred the banked embers, then placed a couple of new logs on the fire. "There's nothing you don't know. I am just tired and snapped at him. I shouldn't have." She jabbed at the fire.

What did it matter if Jacob was still trying to control her land? It wasn't hers anymore. It was Daniel's. And Daniel had taken charge and told him not to burn it. She should have let it lie. She was in no danger of being Jacob's ward anymore, and he couldn't take her land, make her his servant, and control her every move. Even though he had felt entitled to do exactly that.

She would not suffer the fate of her mother.

Daniel was a man. He couldn't possibly understand what it was like to have no control whatsoever of your life.

She looked over her shoulder at him. "You should put some clothes on before the next person comes banging on the door."

His neck and cheeks turned pink, and so did his chest. He wasn't used to being seen naked, and somehow, that thought loosened the tightness in her own chest a little. She almost smiled. That view alone made marriage better than wardship.

He turned and disappeared into the bedroom.

She turned back to the fire and made sure the new logs had caught and were burning well. Then she swung the iron arm holding the kettle of pottage toward the center of the fire since Daniel had distracted her from swinging it out over the embers last night. It would have to warm before they could break their fast. Her stomach let out a low growl, and she couldn't help the corners of her mouth turning up a little as she thought about how she had worked up her appetite.

If she didn't eat something soon, she would start to feel queasy from hunger. That thought put an end to her smile. They had had too many years of hunger.

But that was the past. It was time to move forward.

She grabbed some bread from the basket next to the hearth and tore off a chunk for herself and a larger one for Daniel. The man could pack away bread like it baked itself.

The floor creaked behind her. She turned and handed Daniel his chunk of bread. "The pottage will be warm soon. If you can wait, then you can have some of that, too."

He took the bread in one hand and her arm in the other and went to the table, towing her in his wake. He sat her down at the table and then sat next to her instead of across from her. She turned and studied his face. Her gut tightened again.

He took a bite of bread and chewed, so she did the same. No point in waiting to eat if he was going to think himself to death before announcing his reason for dragging her to the table with him. She swallowed, and the bread stuck in her dry throat. She should have grabbed some beer.

Focusing hard, she swallowed a few more times, and finally, the bread went down. Then it sat in her stomach like a stone.

He was still contemplating her. She bit off another, much smaller chunk of bread and chewed it carefully before trying to swallow this time.

"When you were offered wardship until you could find someone you wanted to marry," his cheeks colored a little, "you looked like the idea of being Jacob's ward was worse than embracing Satan himself."

She stared down at the table. He had read that disturbingly well. She picked a piece of crust off her bread and broke the little piece in half.

"I thought you had bad blood with Jacob, but then you reacted the same way to the option of becoming your brother's ward."

She broke tiny pieces of crust into even smaller pieces. A tightness rose in her throat just thinking about that day. All of her autonomy was gone in an hour. The tightness threatened to choke off her breathing. She focused on the pieces of crust in her hand and on getting air to her lungs.

"Someday," he said, his voice a little tighter, "I would like to know why you chose marriage to me." He swallowed. "But right now, I think I need to know why guardianship caused you such panic." He put his hand over hers and stopped her destruction of the crust.

Removing the outlet for her hands cut off her only mechanism of control. Tears welled up and blurred her vision. She could never make him understand. Matthias hadn't understood. Esau hadn't understood. Jacob hadn't understood. And asking for help had almost proved catastrophic.

She trembled, and a cold sweat broke out all over her body. Her dead mother's face, gaunt and shadowed, appeared in her mind. A sob broke free from her throat.

She clamped her hand over her mouth. Her stomach was knotting in reaction to the feeling of helplessness.

Then, her stomach gave a big lurch. She leapt up from the bench, hand clamped even harder over her mouth, and ran to the door. She swung it open just in time to heave the contents of her stomach onto the grass beside the doorstep. And her stomach kept heaving long after it was empty. It might turn itself inside out and come hurtling out of her mouth itself. Her fingers gripped the wood of the doorframe, clinging to it as her body convulsed.

As the spasms decreased in violence, she became aware of the world around her again, including a hand rubbing her back. He might have been doing that for the whole time she had been vomiting, but she didn't know. Panic did that.

She stared at the ground in front of her as her head regained its equilibrium. She hadn't panicked so badly that she vomited since she was little.

Daniel continued to run his hand over her back in warm circles. The choking sensation in her throat loosened. Her heart rate subsided, too. Leaving her sweaty, exhausted, and shivering in the chill fall air.

Daniel's hand disappeared, and she heard him rummaging in the house. She leaned against the door, unmoving, apart from the shivers. She heard him return a moment later, and a mug of beer appeared in front of her face.

"Just rinse your mouth. Don't drink it yet." His hand returned to her back, rubbing warm circles again.

She took a small sip of beer, swished it around, and spat it in the grass before her stomach could get the wrong idea and start lurching again to keep her from swallowing it.

She could hear Matthias' childhood voice in her head. "Pukey Ruthy."

Tears threatened again. For years, she had been able to keep the panic at bay. The stupid war and the stupid paranoia it brought with it had unraveled everything.

No.

She raked her sleeve across her eyes. She was not a helpless little child.

At least she was not a ward, even though she didn't control her land anymore. She had a future. Daniel hadn't stopped her from her doctoring, not yet anyhow, so she still had some control over her life. As long as she stayed strong, she would survive. It was always her own doing when she allowed people to take advantage when she acted powerless and begged for help, and she knew better now.

Daniel slipped his arm around her shoulder and pulled her to him.

She tried to lean in, but she couldn't breathe when she did.

She pushed away. "I need to get some chamomile from Goody Carter and help her hog-proof her garden."

Daniel's eyes searched her face.

She turned her head away. She must look like a harpy, with red eyes and a blotchy face. It didn't matter.

She went to grab a basket, and then she tucked a small loaf of bread into the basket. They could spare it.

When she turned, she almost slammed her face into Daniel's chest. She stepped back.

"When will you be home?"

She felt the hair on her neck bristling like an angry cat's. "When we are done."

She stepped around him, but he reached for her shoulder and spun her back to him. Then he handed her a musket and powder horn.

He wasn't trying to stop her. He was trying to keep her from doing yet another stupid thing today.

Her face flushed warm.

He handed her the remaining bread she had left on the table. "Don't eat this until your stomach settles. You need the sustenance."

She wasn't a fool.

She grabbed the bread and headed for the door.

"Ruth..."

She started running.

15

"Don't tell her I am helping you." Matthias hacked at the corn with his scythe.

Daniel couldn't pretend to understand Ruth and Matthias' relationship. Or Matthias' relationships with anyone, including himself. He had been so shocked when Matthias turned up on his doorstep offering to help harvest her corn that he almost turned him down.

He stood straight and studied the spotty tufts of corn in the field. A little shiver crept up his spine as he thought about Ruth trying to help Esau plant it. His wife was the wife of another man when this year's crops went in. The world had turned upside down. And he *would* right it.

He looked at Matthias again. "Why does she panic at the thought of being a ward?"

Matthias turned and looked back at him. "She isn't a ward. She's your wife." His brother-in-law stared at him for another moment, then went back to hacking at the corn, but with greater violence.

"Why were you so opposed to her becoming Jacob's ward?"

Matthias swung the scythe so hard that the corn he cut flew a good six feet.

"You wanted her under someone's legal control. But you almost ripped Jacob's head off when he suggested her becoming his ward." In fact, Matthias had reacted almost as badly to it as Ruth had. Daniel rubbed his hands through his hair to get his brain working better. He had been so knocked off kilter by finding himself betrothed a moment after that Matthias' reaction was only now registering.

He reached for Matthias' arm, and then danced away from the scythe's backswing.

Matthias spun toward him. "What did you do?"

"What?"

"Why are you bringing this up?"

His wife went into a full-blown panic attack when he asked her about it, and now her brother was about to take a swing at him with the three-foot blade of his scythe. "I asked her about it, and she went into a fit, and now you are trying to kill me. What don't I know?" He planted his feet right in front of Matthias'. He was inches from the man's face and couldn't miss Matthias' eyes going wide.

"Tell me you didn't make her puke." Matthias must have seen the answer on Daniel's face. "I said to keep her out of trouble." He shook his head and turned away.

Daniel was ready to spike Matthias in the back with his sickle. When Matthias told him to keep her out of trouble, they had been talking about witchcraft. "What does being a ward have to do with witchcraft?"

Matthias flinched at the last word but swung the scythe into the next stand of corn and the next. After seven more swings, he stopped. He lowered the blade to the ground and leaned on the handle as if their discussion had worn him out. "I don't know what my mother taught her," he said to the corn in front of him. "I don't know for certain if she even had anything to teach."

Daniel watched the back of Matthias' head. The muscles in his neck and shoulders flexed tight and gave away his tension.

"What does Jacob have to do with any of this?" Daniel asked.

Matthias flapped his hand, gesturing to the fields. "He wants this land. When Ruth asked him for help when Esau was on his deathbed, he tried to buy it from Esau and offered to take Ruth in as a servant after he died." Matthias turned and looked at him. "And he thinks his brother died because I didn't cover him in the woods." His eyes fell. "He already thought he had a right to the land and to Ruth's labor when Esau died, and I'm afraid he will take Esau's death out on her in my place."

Matthias had been a rock that day. "But he was supposed to cover Esau. You were one of the few who followed orders."

Matthias sighed. "He told me to cover Esau so he could circle around to catch the Penobscot from behind. I stayed to cover him, but there wasn't much I could do when our own men opened fire on us in the confusion. The Penobscot weren't even there. Which one of our men was I supposed to shoot at?"

Daniel stared at Matthias for a moment. That meant Jacob had disobeyed orders. Not only had he disobeyed orders, but he unknowingly created the confusion that led to the death of his own brother and Daniel's father. If Jacob realized that, it would kill him.

Matthias squirmed under his gaze. The man had never said a thing, but it finally made sense why Jacob had always implied Matthias had been unreliable in the militia. Matthias had born more of a burden from that day than anyone realized.

"You did right, Matthias."

Matthias shrugged. "You are the only one who thinks so."

A lone crow flew overhead.

Matthias' eyes were pinched at the corners, and he rubbed at his chest. "I was our mother's guardian. She didn't take it well, and Ruth took it even worse." He paused. "Just keep her out of trouble." Then he turned back to grimly reaping the corn.

Daniel stared at him as he hacked his way through the tough stalks. Daniel rubbed his head again and almost stabbed his eye out with the sickle he forgot was in his hand. He threw the sickle to the ground, and it took every bit of restraint he could muster to keep from kicking it across the field.

How did she not take her mother's wardship well? What did that even mean? Ruth had apologized when she returned home that day, but after that, they hadn't talked about it.

He bent down, grabbed the sickle, yanked a bundle of corn together and tied it off. Not that they had had much time to talk as they worked from sunup to sundown every day harvesting his fields. They were too tired to talk beyond basic necessary communication.

He hooked another bundle and pulled it toward himself with such force he almost stabbed himself in the ankle with the sickle. He was going to maim himself if he wasn't careful. Paying closer attention, he reached his arm out again, gathered in the next bundle, and tied it off. After a few more bundles, he got back into a rhythm and started to catch up to Matthias.

At least with this corn, he could pay the Penobscot their bushel and still have plenty for the winter and for next year's seed. He was lucky. He was more than that. He was grateful. Perhaps they were, at long last, returning to divine favor.

At the edge of the field, Matthias had stopped and was stretching out his arms and shoulders. Daniel stood next to him and bent his torso backward to counter the stooping he had been doing. His back cracked twice like a dry twig. Adding Ruth's fields meant more corn, but it also meant more work. He wouldn't have been able to get it done without Matthias' offer to help.

"How was your harvest this year?" If he needed to give Matthias some of the corn from Ruth's field to help with what he owed the Penobscot, he would.

Mathias swung both arms across his chest, then back behind his back a few times to un-kink his shoulders. "Compared to the last few years, good."

Just enough to get his family through the winter was 'good' compared to the last few years. But he didn't want to insult him. Then again, better to risk that than let him suffer when Daniel and Ruth had enough. "Do you need some of this," he gestured to the corn at their feet, "for the Penobscot?"

"For the Penobscot?" Matthias blinked at him for a minute, like he had just spoken Portuguese or French. Then he sucked in a deep breath. "You're serious." He threw his hands out to the side in a gesture that could mean frustration or confusion. Or both. "I thought the consensus was that we did not have to pay them?"

"Since when does the consensus get to decide what laws to obey and what laws not to obey?" That, in a nutshell, was why they had fallen from divine favor, to begin with. "The treaty says we give the Penobscot a bushel of corn per household, so we give the Penobscot a bushel of corn per household."

Matthias groaned and rolled his eyes. "You realize everyone thinks the Penobscot are in league with the Devil?"

"Do you?"

Matthias stared down at the scythe blade by his feet. "I don't even know if my own sister is a witch."

Daniel heaved in a deep breath. He didn't know either. Really. But if she had been, she seemed to have mended her ways. Nor did he find the Penobscot to be anything more than another group of people with different political interests. "It is not for us to judge. We don't have legal jurisdiction, so we obey the treaty."

"And how will that go over with the rest of the town?"

"Is that what determines whether you follow the law?"

Matthias shook his head and started hacking at the next section of corn. "I just keep my head down."

He slashed the scythe through the corn with deadly force and speed, so Daniel bent to gather it with his sickle. He was already falling behind. "You could set an example and do what you think is right. Then others will follow."

Mathias turned his head over his shoulder as he kept slicing his blade through the stalks. "Follow the son and brother of witches? Into giving up corn to the Devil?"

Daniel froze. His breath went still. Even his heart seemed to go still. Others had mocked Matthias about his mother. Even about Ruth. But they didn't suspect steady, if somewhat grumpy, Matthias. Did they?

Geese honked overhead. He looked up to see them flying in a V toward more hospitable climates for the winter. Despite the exercise, he shivered in the chilly breeze.

No one in town had ever mentioned Matthias in connection with selectmen or any other office. He would make a perfect constable, but again, no one had ever so much as suggested it.

Not even Daniel.

Mathias was a good twenty feet ahead of him now and striding across a bare patch in the field to get the next stand of corn.

But Daniel just stood there, feet rooted to the ground.

Ruth stirred the pottage in the kettle over the fire. The heat in the hearth was a dry wall of pressure against her face and the front of her body.

A cold burst of air hit her back as she heard the door open and then quickly close. They already had days that felt as cold as winter, even though it was not quite November. The skin on her back pebbled from the cold, as her face burned from the heat in front of her.

She turned to Daniel. "Jacob was here." He had been complaining about her field, which she would have to help Daniel harvest.

Daniel hung up his outer coat and flapped his hands to warm them. "I didn't see him. We were right by his fields. What did he want?"

"You were by his fields?" He had said he was going to mend some equipment with Matthias.

Daniel came up next to her and warmed his hands at the hearth. "We harvested your corn."

She almost dropped the spoon. He harvested her corn. It still felt like hers, even though it wasn't, legally. "I want to help."

He shifted next to her, and out of the corner of her eye, she saw him studying her face. "We got it all down, but you can help us bring it in."

"You got it all down in one day?" She was gawking at him like an alewife caught in a net. "Who is 'we'?"

She turned back to the kettle in front of her and gave it a hard stir, almost sloshing the contents on the hem of her skirts.

She focused her eyes on the kettle so she wouldn't see Daniel's expression, while he no doubt considered what sort of possessed she had become. But she felt his eyes on her and finally turned to confront him.

Before she could get a word out, he said, "Matthias and I harvested the field. There wasn't too much salvageable corn there, but enough to make a difference."

He reached out his hand to her cheek, and her body couldn't decide fast enough if it should flinch away or lean into the comfort, so she froze in place like a block of granite.

His thumb smoothed over her lips, and she stared into those searching eyes. He wasn't trying to take anything from her, so why did it feel like he was ripping something from the center of her chest?

She was getting irrational. Maybe she *was* possessed.

She took a deep breath and smiled at him.

"Why does the idea of anyone trying to help send you into a panic? Matthias wouldn't say and said to ask you. And you aren't supposed to know he helped."

Her cheeks fell, and she felt a little lightheaded. She needed air.

She stepped back from the hearth and fanned herself.

A bucket appeared in front of her. How dare he assume she was having a panic attack?

Because she was, she had, and he had been prepared after just one attack. Flinging the bucket at his head had an indescribable appeal at the moment, but she didn't. None of this was his fault. It was hers.

His hand was rubbing her back in circles. The warm, gentle pressure was so sturdy, so secure. It was so comforting she wanted to fling it away. He was so sure he could fix everything by applying logic, rules, and brainpower.

She let her head fall back, and a primal scream of frustration escaped from her lungs.

He flinched but kept up the comforting motion of his hand on her back.

She let her head fall forward. Fine. Let him fix what was wrong with the world if he could.

"The town 'helped' my mother after she was acquitted. To save her from being independent and having any autonomy whatsoever, they forced her to become Matthias' ward. Told him he had to keep her out of trouble. Keep her locked up. Everyone had been so nasty during the trial that he did whatever the selectmen told him to do. He wouldn't let her make any decisions, leave the house on her own, plant her garden without explaining what each plant was and what it was for, or do anything. She had to rely on him for every single thing in her life. Those were the rules. He followed them. It killed her."

Her face was wet, and her breath was ragged.

"She was made a ward to protect her—"

She flung his hand off her back. "From what?"

He gaped at her, jaw hanging loose.

"What were they trying to protect her from? Having her own opinions? Her own judgement? Trying to support herself?" She was yelling, but she couldn't make herself stop. "She was acquitted!"

Her throat felt like it was closing, and she gasped for air.

He pushed the bucket closer.

She kicked it across the room. Pain shot through her toe and into her foot, and she welcomed it.

He went back to rubbing her back in soothing circles. "She had no one else to be legally responsible for her."

She turned and glared at him. "Would a widower who was acquitted in court need to be made someone's ward so someone was legally responsible for him?" Yes, she was being too bold. So she had been told all her life, and right now, she didn't care one corn cake. The Devil could take her if he felt like it, but he would probably find her wanting, too.

Daniel's brain was clearly working hard to find a way to explain what he felt was obvious without triggering her to rip his head off. His face was moving like he was having a conversation, but it was all inside his own head, between him and himself. He was so used to having the privilege of making decisions he couldn't possibly understand what it was like to have so little of that and then to have even that little leeway taken from you.

The Quakers understood. And now, for even thinking that, she would most certainly roast in hell.

She covered her face in her hands and leaned into the pressure of her own palms. She should just surrender herself to the judgment of the man legally responsible for her actions.

But she couldn't. She wouldn't. So, she probably *would* rot in hell.

All of her life, she had been the only person she could rely on, and that would never change.

If only she believed in witchcraft, she would take it up and have some fun since she was already paying the price anyhow.

Enough.

She turned and went back to the kettle and stirred before it bubbled over. It was probably burnt on the bottom.

She grabbed two bowls and ladled stew into each without sloshing it all over the hearth.

She reached out with one bowl toward Daniel, and he was looking at her like she was a stranger handing him suspect food or perhaps a witch handing him poison. For heaven's sake.

She reached the other hand out and offered him the second bowl instead.

He shook himself, like he was rousing himself from a daydream, and reached for the first bowl. "You wouldn't poison me. You heal."

She did not know what to make of that, so she turned and reached for a spoon. She turned back and handed it to him. He brushed his hand against hers as he took it from her, and his skin scorched hers. Maybe he was Satan, sent to tempt her.

He took his bowl and spoon and went to sit down at the table. He took a spoonful of stew and slurped it.

Then he looked up at her, standing there watching him like an alien from a faraway land and patted the bench next to him, inviting her to sit.

Part of her wanted to go to him, but another part insisted she resist. But she was hungry, and there was still harvesting to be done, and she needed her strength, so the practical won out.

She went to the table and sat. She spooned the stew into her mouth.

More rosemary next time. It was a little bland.

They ate in silence.

"How did she die?" His voice was soft, but insistent.

She took a deep, shuddering breath. "She ate a bad mushroom."

His eyebrows rose in confusion. "But she knew mushrooms...." His voice trailed off as that information registered. Another sin against her mother's long tally.

"Don't tell Matthias. He doesn't know. At least, not for certain." She spun her spoon in her bowl, watching the pattern it made in the last bit of stew at the bottom. "Everyone assumed she died of the bloody flux, and I think he was relieved." She couldn't really blame him. He hadn't wanted any of it.

"You were there?"

"She apologized."

"I'm so sorry, Ruth." Daniel placed his hand on hers. "I promise I *will* restore order so the Devil will no longer walk among us."

Her head snapped up. "And what unprotected woman will take the blame?"

16

Daniel could see the smoke rising above the trees as he slapped the reins at his mare's flanks, urging her faster. He'd seen it first from the garrison house and raised the alarm, and it was already much thicker.

Ruth sat next to him in the wagon, clutching her medical basket full of remedies for burns and other related injuries. Her mouth was set in a firm line, no doubt a mirror of his own. A barn fire at harvest time was a farmer's worst nightmare.

He reined the mare in as the turnoff to Cook's farm neared. Flipping his wagon taking a corner too quickly would help no one, and it would block the way for others to get to the fire to help.

The mare had her blood up but, after a little persuasion, slowed and swung around the corner onto the new, more rutted path.

The wagon bounced over an ungainly rut, and Daniel slowed the mare further. A broken axle on this narrow path would be even more of a traffic disaster.

Now Ruth had her basket braced between her feet so that she could hold it steady, hold the side of the wagon with one hand, and still have one hand free to rummage through the basket's contents.

He returned his eyes to the path. Matthias's wagon was ahead of his, so at least one competent person would be on the scene when they arrived. It was uncharitable not to count Cook in that number. Uncharitable, but not unrealistic.

The smoke was in his nostrils now, and the mare tossed her head. She kept moving along, but the smoke made her uneasy. When Cook's homestead and barn appeared in front of them, he pulled the mare over to a tree near Matthias's wagon and well away from any structures. Horses and fire were a terrible mix.

He set the brake and leapt over the side of the wagon to tie the mare up, not trusting even his well-trained horse to stand quietly in the commotion of a fire. Ruth was right on his heels. As soon as his hand dropped from the mare's tether, Ruth thrust a strip of heavy fabric into it.

"Tie it over your nose and mouth, but dunk it in some water if you can before you go into the barn." Her voice was steady and sure, and she was right. The water would help, even though it would make breathing harder.

He tied the fabric over his face, and she thrust a second piece of it into his hand.

"For Matthias." She had to raise her voice to be heard over the racket.

He nodded, raised the cloth in his hand in salute, and then bolted toward the barn, where he could see Matthias ahead of him, setting the hogs free from their pen up against the side of the barn. The one time the man had his hogs contained was the one time it wasn't safe for the hogs.

He flapped his hands at the hogs to get them running and swatted the nearest on its rump. It squealed, but it wasn't going to argue, and it took off as fast as its stubby legs would take it, which was shockingly fast. Cook's hound set off in pursuit, which only made the hogs run faster.

He turned to Matthias and handed him the strip of cloth from Ruth. He took one look and tied it around his face like Daniel had done. Then he gestured to the barn. "Horse!"

Shite. Daniel sprinted to the door. Cook had gotten the beast as far as the aisle of the barn, but it had planted its feet and would not take another step. Its eyes rolled in panic, and it screamed as it tried to yank its head free. Goodman Smith was there, shoving at its hindquarters, making the situation even more chaotic.

Smoke filled the barn, but the flames were contained in a small area by the horse's stall. If they could get the horse out and start putting out the fire, they could save much of the barn.

Cook yelled at the horse, making its panic grow worse. Daniel went to the horse's head, ripped the fabric from his own face, tied it over the horse's eyes so it couldn't see which way it was headed, and tugged it in a circle to disorient it.

The noise from the fire almost deafened him.

He gestured to Cook to pull the horse's lead toward the door, and then Daniel went to the horse's hindquarters. Its tail was smoldering, and with every agitated flick of that tail, it threatened to spread the fire. Daniel grabbed the tail and smothered the embers. His hand caught on a pipe.

He ripped the pipe free from the singed tail hairs and tossed it away. He slapped the poor beast's rump as hard as he could, and the horse lunged forward, dragging Cook toward the door. The horse couldn't see, so it bumped into the doorframe, slamming Cook against the wall, but then they both disappeared out the door to relative safety. Smith followed them.

A quick glance around assured Daniel that there were no other animals inside, so he ran for the door himself.

His eyes stung, and he could barely see Matthias, who had caught the horse and was trying to wrestle it to a stop at a safe distance from the barn.

Others had arrived and were set to put the fire out with buckets from the well. Smith veered off to go help them, so Daniel ran to Matthias, grabbed the horse's lead, and brought it to a quivering stop. He left the blindfold in place, handed the lead back to Matthias, and soothed the horse with his hands, rubbing its neck, its back, and making his way to its hindquarters. It had singe marks in its coat where it had flicked its smoldering tail in a panic, but only a few spots were burned.

Now that they were out in the light, he saw just how much of the horse's tail had burned. Cook was lucky it hadn't burned more of the horse's flesh and seriously injured the beast or spread the fire to the rest of the barn and the corn cribs. As it was, he could hope they had headed off the worst-case scenarios.

Cook rushed over to them.

"My horse!"

Daniel tried to calm him. "Your horse should be fine. It just has a few burns on its flanks and a singed tail." Of course, it would not be too willing to go back into that barn anytime soon, but that was a problem for another time. Daniel could help with that.

Ruth joined their little group. "Goodman Cook, you have burns on your hands. You need to let me apply a salve."

Cook stared at her in horror, like she was trying to pour acid on his flesh. "Get that demonic potion away from me."

She glared at him.

"It smells of the fires of hell." Cook's voice rose over the fire.

Daniel tried to calm him. "That is the charred horsehair that you smell. Let her help." He yanked his hand away from her again, then, apparently deciding his horse was in good hands, he ran to the men putting out the flames at the corner of his barn. His harvest was more important than his horse, though if he could use the fire to avoid paying his corn to the Penobscot, he no doubt would.

Daniel looked at Ruth. She looked back at him. "The horse needs your ministrations, too, and I think you will find it a more willing patient." He guided her to the side of the horse, facing its tail, so she could apply her salve out of reach of its hind hooves in case the beast lashed out in pain.

Her touch was sure and must have been soothing because, despite the horse's agitation, it did nothing more than shiver its skin as she smoothed her remedy over its tender flesh. Finished with that side, she went to the other, placing herself exactly as he had placed her so she stayed safe as she tended the horse's other flank.

Cook came running back to them. "Get her away from my horse before she causes more harm."

She ignored him and kept doctoring the horse, so Daniel stepped in to distract the man.

"What happened? Were you smoking your pipe in the barn?" Only a fool would do that, but this was Cook, and he fit that description pretty well.

"Of course not. I was trying to cure the beast of colic."

Daniel stared at him.

Cook snorted. "You call yourself such an expert with horses. Goodman Smith taught me that you stick a lit pipe up its fundament, and that gets the colic to pass," he said like he was explaining it to a child.

The man was a complete and utter idiot. That was the only explanation.

"What happened then?" Daniel asked.

"A blue flame shot out and lit the barn on fire." Cook was flailing his arms and gesturing to the barn like it should be obvious what started the fire if you just looked. "More witchcraft that you didn't stop in time." He spun on his heel and returned to the group putting out the last of the fire, apparently no longer interested in the fate of his horse.

The man was delusional. What other explanation could there be?

He glanced at Ruth, whose face was paler than usual. She was looking in the direction Cook went.

What unprotected woman would be blamed? Ruth's words kept bouncing around in his head.

He was the warden, and Cook, at least, thought he wasn't doing his job. It was a thought that had plagued him for months since he had found no new leads on the potential witches still active among them.

But Ruth's words, and watching the fear in her face, pounded home how important it was to get it right and not ruin an innocent person's life.

For the first time since he became warden, he didn't know what to do.

Ruth scrunched her shoulder up to her cheek to scratch an itch. With her hands, she continued to grind the apples Goody Carter cut and tossed in the tub.

Daniel had agreed that since their trees were close to Goody Carter's house and because Cook's hogs had eaten so much of her garden, she would make her cider at Goody Carter's, with the older woman's help, and pay for that help in cider to help her through the winter.

Goody Carter set the last handful of apples to cut on her board. "Mmm. My house will smell divine for days."

The wind whipped the trees outside, and an occasional gust came down the chimney, blowing smoke from the hearth into the little room.

But the apples did smell sweet.

Apart from those occasional gusts down the chimney, the house was snug. And standing by the hearth, using the strength of her entire body to crush the apples, made her warm and her head a little light.

"Does he know you are with child?"

Ruth's head snapped around toward the older woman, and her breath caught. She wasn't sure herself, and she certainly hadn't planned to say anything to anyone until she was.

She gaped at Goody Carter, who tipped her head back and let out a full-throated guffaw at her reaction. Her cheeks burned even hotter. Thank goodness they were likely already so red from exertion that a little more wouldn't be noticeable.

Who did she think she was fooling? Whether her blush was visible made no difference. Goody Carter was laughing so hard she almost stumbled into the fire.

"Careful." Ruth pulled her upright. Maybe her stumble would distract her.

"You couldn't have thought no one would notice?"

"I..." Did Daniel guess, too? She was a doctoress, and apparently, she was the only one unsure of her own condition. She ducked her head and went back to grinding the apples.

Goody Carter patted her on the shoulder. "The men wouldn't notice the veins around your eyes, though surely he noticed your breasts growing?" She clucked her tongue. "Why do you blush? This is wonderful news."

It *was* wonderful. Her shame came from not knowing. Other women knew. It felt unnatural to be unsure.

"Think you that Daniel will not be happy?" Goody Carter's face was serious for the first time since Ruth had arrived at her doorstep this morning.

Ruth shook her head. "No. He will be pleased. I have said nothing because I wasn't sure." She glanced down. "I didn't want him to be disappointed if I was wrong."

At some point, she *had* started to worry about disappointing him.

Or maybe it was the fact that a baby put an end to any thought of being self-sufficient. She hadn't even realized she might be with child until a few days earlier, and now she felt stupid for being so oblivious. Her head hurt.

She drew in a deep breath to steady her mind, then went back to pulverizing the apples.

"Where is he right now? If you don't tell him, I will." Her wrinkles deepened and multiplied as she grinned. Ruth knew it was an empty threat. Just the sort of flippancy that got her into trouble when the wrong people had no sense of humor.

The sort of people who would not be happy about where Daniel was right now.

Tears welled in her eyes, and her breath caught. Gah! How had she not been certain she was with child? She never cried. And now she said a silent apology to every pregnant patient she had ever lost patience with or thought they were being manipulative when their moods had swung from one extreme to the other. Were her hands not occupied, she would have smacked her own forehead.

"Daniel is going to the Penobscot with his bushel of corn to fulfill the treaty provision."

Goody Carter's eyes widened. All mirth had gone from her face.

Ruth's tears threatened again, which was foolish. He wasn't going alone. He had badgered Matthias into going with him, bringing his own bushel of corn. It was the right thing to do. It belonged to Marie's people by right, and setting the example would help others follow.

But seeing Goody Carter's reaction confirmed her fear that it wasn't just her emotions slipping their moorings that had her worried.

"After Cook's fire?"

It was the right thing to do, and people needed to get their heads out of their arses and realize what jackals they were being.

She threw her shoulders back and straightened her spine. "Yes. The matters are unconnected, and he is following the law." She jammed the dash into the tub for emphasis.

Goody Carter yelped and dove for the tub.

Ruth had unbalanced it and Goody Carter just grabbed it before the tub tipped off the stool it sat on, and the entire sticky mess spilled over onto the floor.

Ruth's heart pounded at the near disaster she had created by getting caught up in her head. "I'm so sorry." She grabbed the dash and began mashing with renewed focus. The ache in her shoulders was a lovely distraction from anything else.

Nothing had slopped over, thank goodness. Goody Carter had salvaged her floor. They should be doing this outside, but it was simply too cold today.

The older woman started folding the cheesecloth they would use to strain the cider. Ruth reached for the press so they could squeeze the juice from the crushed apples. Goody Carter shoved a barrel under the tap hole of the tub, then Ruth laid the press board on top of the crushed apples. Juice flowed from the tap hole and began to fill the storage barrel.

As Ruth leaned all her weight onto the board, Goody Carter made sure no chunks snuck through.

They needed a screw press, but that would have to wait for more prosperous days.

Goody Carter gave an exaggerated and very satisfied nod as the flow of the juice at last dropped to a trickle and then to just a few drops.

Ruth lifted the board and peered into the bottom of the barrel. The pomace was flattened, and even Matthias wouldn't have been able to wring any more juice from it. She went to lift the tub to take it outside to dump.

"Don't even think about it." Goody Carter's voice was deadly serious.

"But—"

"The tub can wait. That," she pointed at some cakes next to the hearth, "is our reward." She reached for the corn cakes, then returned with a glint in her eye and a triumphant smile, holding them out to Ruth. "Unless your stomach can't handle it?" Her eyebrow cocked in challenge.

Ruth snorted and grabbed a cake.

Goody Carter chuckled.

Then Ruth's stomach gave a rumble and then a growl so loud it drowned out the wind outside. She had to force herself to be mindful of the older woman's limited food stores and only take one cake.

Goody Carter laughed so hard she doubled over. "A hearty appetite, I see." She let out a fart, which made her laugh even harder.

The woman was truly impossible. And Ruth loved her for it.

Goody Carter rummaged through the pomace, careful to avoid the stems and seeds, popped a handful of crushed fruit into her kettle, and added a little honey and water. Within a few minutes, she had a hot, sweet apple spread for their cakes. She swung the kettle out to cool, and they both began to mop up the gooey sweet treat with their corn cakes, not caring that they were double and triple dipping.

The hot cake felt like manna from above. Ruth reached in and dragged the last bit of corn cake up against the edge of the kettle, getting a big glop of apple. She stuffed it in her mouth and chewed, savoring the sweetness rolling over her tongue.

Goody Carter caught her eye and smiled as they both chewed with over-full mouths.

Then Goody Carter thrust another corn cake into her hand. She tried to push it away.

"We worked hard. We earned this." Her wrinkled hand grabbed another cake for herself, and she dipped it into the kettle. Her face wore the same expression Ruth's nieces and nephew did when she snuck them a sweet.

Ruth took the second cake and dipped it into the kettle.

They ate without talking. The only sounds were their moans of appreciation.

Her belly felt well and truly full for the first time in weeks. They had been working so hard until well after sunset, bringing in the harvest, that they both ate just enough to stop the hunger pangs, and then they collapsed into bed.

"I trust you will not let Goodman Kendrick slack off on his marital duties when you tell him you are with child?" She leaned in to study Ruth's face. "He got a late start. He needs practice."

Ruth's face burned. He had been practicing. And she was more than pleased with his progress.

But she was not going to discuss it.

Goody Carter nodded and smiled. "A quick learner, I see. Good." She patted Ruth's hand. Then her smile faded. She fiddled with her apron and wouldn't meet Ruth's eyes. "You deserve a good man to grow old with."

Ruth waited. "What?"

Goody Carter studied her feet. "Let's just hope he stays alive longer than the last one."

Ruth sat up straight, good cheer gone. "The Penobscot have no good reason to hurt him."

"No, they don't. No one does." Goody Carter sighed. "But not everyone needs a good reason."

17

Daniel and Matthias walked through the woods. They carried two bushel baskets of corn between them, wooden poles threaded through the basket handles so they could carry the baskets more efficiently between them without breaking their backs before they got to the Penobscot village. Matthias' shoulders were hunched as he walked in front of Daniel, carrying the ends of the two poles.

But the man was decent at heart, and an evening of persuading, plus a few stern looks from Ruth, had convinced him to join Daniel today.

"We starve for years, and now we finally have a decent harvest, and I am taking a bushel of it to the Penobscot." Matthias looked even grumpier than he sounded. Only Matthias could look that miserable from behind. He was barely even picking up his feet with each step.

"We have to set an example and fulfill our end of the treaty." If he said that sentence one more time, either his own brain would melt, or Matthias would cold-cock him.

Matthias shot him a glance over his shoulder. The man left no doubt he wanted to kill him.

Matthias' steps slowed.

Daniel shoved at his end of the poles to get him moving faster. As if Daniel could out muscle Matthias. "Did it occur to you, brother," Matthias groaned out loud at being called brother, "that the treaty is why we could grow our crops at all this year?"

"No."

This was getting old. "We didn't start the war, neither did the Penobscot. But when it spread here, they kicked our arses."

"No, they didn't."

"Really?"

"Fine."

Matthias was probably just agreeing to get Daniel to shut up.

Then Matthias stopped, so suddenly Daniel almost lost his grip on the poles. Matthias' head swiveled, scanning the surrounding area.

Daniel did the same.

Trees, dead leaves, undergrowth.

No birds. The woods were silent.

Danial looked behind them. The trail was empty.

He looked forward. Three Penobscot men had materialized in front of Matthias.

Daniel's pulse pounded, and he tried to slow his breathing.

They were near the village, and the Penobscot kept a watch even though the war and raids ended. They had to keep alert for both English and French, so they couldn't afford to be trusting neighbors.

Matthias' bulk blocked his view, so he craned his neck and leaned to the side to get a good look at them. His shoulders quivered from the exertion of holding up the corn. It was easier when they moved.

The three men watched them without speaking. None of them were any of the men he had met the last time he visited the village.

The weight of his musket felt futile on his back. With his hands occupied in holding up the corn, he couldn't reach it if he had to.

Matthias' shoulders twitched with tension.

"Easy. Don't move quickly, Matthias. It's just the watch." With luck. "Let's set the corn down and keep our hands visible to them."

They lowered the corn to the ground, and both kept their hands in clear view.

Daniel stepped forward next to Matthias and looked at the men. He tried to keep his face neutral.

He was wrong. One of the men was familiar. The jagged scar was a giveaway.

He gave the man a nod. "Do you remember me?"

"Your wife healed the Sagamore's wife's father." The man's face relaxed just a fraction, and he spoke to the others in their own language. Ruth was right. They should have made an effort to learn to speak with their neighbors.

"You bring corn." The man nodded to the baskets of corn and pursed his lips in thought. "Come to the Sagamore."

Matthias caught his eye. Daniel gave him a nod. The muscles in Matthias' temple flexed, and his eyes narrowed at Daniel, but he resumed his place between the poles, and Daniel resumed his own spot.

"One, two, three, lift." The muscles in Daniel's shoulders felt like they were ripping as he lifted the weight. They were tight and tired. He had felt worse.

The man laughed at him. "Your wife can fix that when you get home. She is a good healer."

Matthias didn't relax, but at least now he didn't look like he was going to drop the corn in order to club someone.

The man with the scar led the way, and the other two took up position behind Daniel. As if he could run with two bushels of corn.

They walked the rest of the way to the village in silence.

By the time they reached the gate in the palisade, Matthias was so tense that his arms almost jerked the poles right out of Daniel's hands with every step.

Daniel called to the man with the scar. "May we present the corn to the Sagamore ourselves?"

Matthias glanced over his shoulder, eyes a little wild. No doubt he would prefer to drop the corn at the gate and get out of there.

"Wait here." The man with the scar gestured to his fellows, and they took up positions on either side of Daniel and Matthias, while the man with the scar disappeared down the path and into the building that Daniel remembered belonged to the Sagamore.

They waited.

The men stared at them.

Matthias' neck muscles trembled, either from tension or from holding up the corn.

Daniel looked at their frowning guard. They still had their muskets at the ready. They didn't look ready to entertain a request to set the corn down while they all waited, so Daniel gritted his teeth. It would be rather embarrassing if they dropped the corn.

After many minutes, the man returned and gave them an approving nod. Perhaps it had been a trial of strength. Or respect. Or just a trial.

He waved them forward. Once again, Matthias glanced over his shoulder at Daniel. He nodded back. Matthias started walking as if he were being led to the gallows. Daniel was a fool not to have taken the front position when they left home.

When they reached the Sagamore's door, Matthias came to a halt. The top of the doorway was only as high as the middle of his chest.

"Let's set it down and take in just the baskets."

Matthias' answer was to more or less drop the corn right there. Daniel pulled the poles from the basket handles and laid them alongside the outer wall of the building. He grabbed his basket's handles, picked it up, ignored his aching muscles, and ducked through the doorway. Matthias grunted, so he must have followed suit.

The Sagamore sat in the same spot on the far side of the fire as he had the last time Daniel stood here. The older man's smile created small folds in the skin around his mouth and eyes.

"I am pleased to see you, Daniel Kendrick." He cocked his head to the side, looking at Matthias. "Who is the big man you bring with you?"

Daniel gestured with his chin, since his hands still held the corn. "This is my wife's brother, Matthias Derwin. We bring you your bushel of corn from each of our households, as the treaty spells out."

The man smiled and nodded, but said nothing.

"Where would you like us to set the corn?" He had had enough of standing and holding corn for the amusement of others. He would be unable to lift his arms to even get dressed by tomorrow, let alone get anything productive done.

The Sagamore spoke to the two men who had escorted them in, and they took the baskets and left the building.

"You have proven to be a good neighbor, Daniel Kendrick. We respect that."

Daniel acknowledged him with a nod.

The Sagamore appeared to be done speaking.

He did not know what the protocol was now, and he glanced over at Matthias, who had his teeth clenched and was apparently going to remain mute for the duration.

He turned back to the Sagamore and did his best to smile benignly.

The Sagamore shifted on his seat of piled blankets.

"When do the rest bring their corn?"

Daniel shot Matthias a look, but the man was just staring straight ahead. Matthias was certain no one else would follow their example, but at least he didn't seem to want to share that belief with the Sagamore.

"Others are still finishing their harvests." This was true, even though it implied they would bring their corn when they were done, which might not be true.

The Sagamore grunted. "Most are done with their harvests. Why do they delay?"

Matthias still steadfastly stared over the Sagamore's head and at the far wall. Clearly, he meant it when he told Daniel this morning that Daniel was on his own making any excuses.

Daniel had hoped their bringing the corn today would buy him a little more time to convince everyone else they had to follow their example. That did not appear to be the case.

"We had a fire in town, someone's barn burned, and folks are still dealing with that."

The Sagamore waved his hand in the air as if he was swatting a fly. "The man Cook is a devil." Others in the building grunted at the sound of Cook's name. "He lets his hogs destroy everyone's crops but his own. He lets others starve. Besides, his corn was not in the barn when it burned. He can still pay his bushel."

Daniel glanced at Matthias to gauge his reaction to how closely the Penobscot had been following their daily activities, but he still stared at the wall like he was trying to drill a hole through it with just the power of his mind.

And this conversation had gone on long enough. "We will convey the urgency of the matter to everyone in town. If you will excuse us, we need to return home and tend to our work."

For a moment, the Sagamore just studied him. If he didn't want them to leave, this could get tricky. Daniel's aching shoulders tensed, and he tried to force them to relax, but they refused.

The cool air in the room was still.

Then the Sagamore stood. "You may go now."

Daniel let out a big breath. He had not considered the possibility that the Sagamore would keep them there until that moment. Poor planning.

"We thank you." He gave the headman a deep nod and turned to follow Matthias out the door.

"Tell the others that the treaty holds only as long as they keep their end."

Daniel turned. "Of course."

Now, he would find out how much pull he had with the town.

Ruth sat on a stool by the hearth, mending her stockings in the firelight. The warmth of the fire eased her muscles and mind. She glanced at Daniel, who sat at the table sharpening his scythe with a whetstone. Her cooking knife and his hunting knife lay on the table, waiting their turn.

He glanced up at her and smiled. His face bore weary lines from his day tromping through the woods with Matthias to deliver their corn, but his demeanor was more settled since they had returned. He said he felt the peace of having done right.

He was a good man. She could have done far worse.

With luck, the rest of the town would do the same, however grudgingly, and they could have a peaceful winter for the first time in years.

Her needle followed the rhythm of Daniel's stone across the blade. She had been working on this stocking for three nights now, and she was almost done mending the holes she had made back when she raced through the woods to find Cook and stitch him up.

The man was not worth it on his own, but she could feel a bit of the peace Daniel spoke of from doing right.

She tied off her thread and bit it to break off the excess.

It was time to tell Daniel.

Her palms got a little clammy, and her heart rate picked up. She had never been with child before, but Goody Carter's confirmation made her realize she was right, and she needed to tell Daniel they were going to be parents. And have another life to be responsible for. Excitement and sheer terror warred in her chest.

She took a deep breath, set her stocking aside and stood.

Her hands trembled, so she balled them in her skirts at her sides to steady them. She would have to rely on him to keep her and their baby safe. Her throat got a little tight.

She walked over behind him, set her hands on his shoulders, and squeezed.

His head dropped forward, and he moaned in pleasure. She suddenly needed to hear that sound again.

She rubbed her hands over the muscles in his shoulders, then dug her thumbs into the tightest muscles. The sounds from his throat were identical to the ones he made in bed, which set her own belly to fluttering.

She rubbed her hand up the muscle from his shoulder up the back of his neck, and he dropped the whetstone on the table with a thud as he leaned into the pressure. She could at least control some things in her life, and making him feel good felt good.

His skin grew warm beneath her hands, and the muscles grew more pliable, and his moans grew even more appreciative.

Perhaps they could remove themselves early to bed.

Banging on the door made her jump almost out of her skin, and the muscles in Daniel's shoulders went from pliable to taut as ropes under her fingers.

They glanced at each other for an instant, and then Daniel stood and went to the door, grabbing his musket before calling out. "Who is there?"

Multiple voices rumbled, but one came through clearly. "Aldrich. Open the door."

Was his farm being attacked? His home was fortified, just like this one, so he had no reason to risk leaving cover to come here unless his home was lost. Her heart pounded harder.

Daniel unbarred the door and flung it open. Torches shone in the doorway and gave the men's faces an eerie look of the Devil.

Ruth took an instinctive step back, her hands going to her belly.

They weren't frightened. They were angry.

Daniel set the musket against the wall and stood in the doorway. "What has happened?"

Her throat grew tight, and her eyes stung with threatening tears. Why could they not have one quiet evening without people banging on their door with selectman business for Daniel?

She breathed and forced the muscles in her face to relax. This would pass.

Aldrich stood to the front of the small group of men. "I am sorry, Daniel. We are here to charge your wife with witchcraft."

Her vision narrowed and went a little blotchy, and she could barely draw breath as her throat closed off, and her heart wouldn't keep a steady rhythm. Not again. She could not have heard him right.

Her knees felt unsteady, and the men's voices were distorted as they started talking, and she couldn't make out what they were saying.

She grabbed at the table as tears blurred her vision. Then, the floor seemed to rise toward her, and a sharp pain on her chin came from nowhere.

Then Daniel's arm was around her, lifting her to a sitting position on the floor. His face was blurry at first, but then it came into focus. His look of concern registered before his words did, and she tried to raise a hand to comfort him and then saw a drip of blood on it and stopped and stared at it.

"Your chin is bleeding. You hit it when you fell." He pulled his shirttails out of his trouser waist and leaned in to use the hem of his shirt to press against her chin and contain the bleeding.

She felt the cold air from the open door on her face. It was oddly refreshing. Then she thought of Daniel's bare stomach and could feel the cold as if it were her own bare torso pebbling with cold. "Shut the door." Her voice was muffled by Daniel's shirt and his hand pressing on the underside of her jaw.

At first, they didn't seem to have heard her, then they doused their torches in a pail of water by the door and filed in, closing the door behind them.

She looked back at Daniel, and his eyes were searching hers.

"What happened?" he asked.

She searched for an answer, but her brain was fuzzy. Then it latched on to a word, and tears spilled over her lashes and streamed down her face, stinging her chin when they reached the cut there and seeped through Daniel's wadded shirttail.

Witchcraft.

A chill seeped into her bones.

She looked over Daniel's shoulder at the men assembled in her home. Mr. Aldrich, Cook, of course, Goodman Smith, and Jacob at the back of the group.

Daniel's voice hummed in her ear. "It will be alright. They have no evidence. Everyone is just tense right now after Cook's fire." He stroked her hair with his free hand. Then he carefully removed his shirt from her chin and peered at it.

He seemed to be satisfied because he didn't press the cloth back into place, but let it fall to his waist. It wasn't a large patch of blood. It wouldn't be too hard to get out.

Heaven only knew why her mind went there. Perhaps to distract her from the more pressing reality.

"Don't get up." Daniel smoothed his hand over her hair one more time, then rose and turned to face the men.

He gestured with his hands as if to calm everyone. "I know with everything that has befallen us, everyone is tense. But I can assure you Ruth is not in league with Satan. I can vouch for her behaving as a godly woman since our marriage."

He looked at Smith, then at Cook, then at Aldrich. "She has helped every one of you, not hurt."

Smith shifted on his feet. Aldrich stood, calm and resolute.

Cook bristled. "She witched my horse, gave him colic, then burned my barn."

Daniel's shoulders rose and fell, as he must have taken a deep breath. "Your pipe burned your barn, Goodman Cook."

Cook took a step toward Daniel. "How dare—"

Mr. Aldrich's hand on Cooks' shoulder brought him up short.

"Daniel," Aldrich said, voice level, "we come as a courtesy to you to let you know we will bring formal charges."

Ruth almost snorted. Courtesy, indeed. And to Daniel, not even to her.

Her head still floated a bit and didn't feel well-supported on her neck.

Witchcraft. Again. Marrying Daniel was supposed to be the end of that.

She looked at his strong, broad back. He stood between her and the men who invaded their home. But what could he really do to protect her?

He took a step toward her accusers. "We will sort this out. You will see she is no witch." He spoke in the same tone he used with a nervous horse, level and reassuring.

Smith and Cook glanced at Aldrich. Aldrich leveled a steady gaze at Daniel. "We will take our leave and let you tend to your wife. She is bleeding again."

She glanced at her lap as a drop of blood fell from her chin and landed on her skirts.

Daniel glanced over his shoulder at her, and she gave him a brief nod to know she was alright. He turned back to the men and ushered them to the door.

Jacob was the last to the door, and Daniel appeared to say something in his ear before he went out. Then Daniel closed and barred the door.

He turned to her. "You fainted."

"I did not." Even as the words were out of her mouth, she realized that was the only explanation for her sitting on the floor with a bloody chin. Her head was suddenly rather heavy. "Perhaps I did."

Witchcraft. Again. The very idea drove every other thought from her head.

She was going to hang, and there was nothing she could do.

He came to her and gathered her in his arms. He lifted her up to her feet and kissed the top of her head. "Don't worry. I will sort this out, and it won't amount to anything."

She buried her face in his chest and breathed in his woodsy smell.

She wanted so very badly to believe him.

18

Daniel sat by the hearth, watching the embers glow red. He had convinced Ruth to go to bed, so he was alone.

Seeing her face go whiter than snow as she crumpled to the floor still had his nerves jumping.

The wind whistled around the chimney as he stared at nothing.

A quiet tap sounded at the door.

He rose and hurried to the door before the knocking got louder and woke Ruth, or worse. She had already had enough trauma for the evening. He slid the bar and unlatched the door.

There was Jacob in the dark, huddled in his cloak, alone.

Daniel stepped aside to let him in and gestured with his finger to his lips to be quiet. Quiet was not Jacob's natural state, so Daniel would not take on faith that because Jacob did not immediately see Ruth, he would realize that she was asleep.

Jacob stopped just a few steps into the house. "I couldn't stop them."

Daniel took his cloak, hung it up, and then gestured to the hearth. They could stay warm, and the crackling fire would drown out some of their conversation, so they were less likely to wake Ruth.

He pulled a stool up for Jacob and sat back on the one he had abandoned when he answered the knock. The wood of the seat was hot from sitting so close to the fire. He shifted until his flesh adjusted to the heat.

He looked Jacob in the eye. "What happened?"

Jacob glanced down at his hands and then into the fire. "Cook has been in Aldrich's ear about witches since Aldrich's stud got cast. I had thought Aldrich steadier than that, but apparently Mrs. Aldrich," he looked up, "the second one, was very much concerned with witches, especially since the war started. But then, are they really so far wrong?"

She was wise to have been concerned with devilment during the war, and so was he. "But why did they suddenly show up tonight?" There had to be a logical sequence of actions he could follow to figure this out.

Jacob shrugged. "They just showed up at my house. I guess they wanted me to come with them since you are a selectman."

"They just showed up at your door?" Ruth's voice made them both jump.

She was standing at the bedroom door, a blanket wrapped around her shoulders. Her skin was still pale, except for the dark patches beneath her eyes and the fresh scab on her chin. Every line of her body slumped with exhaustion. Not sleepy, just bone weary.

He got up and went to her. "You should be in bed."

She swatted her hand at him but softened the gesture with a smile. "I'm fine."

"Well, I'm not fine. You collapsed in front of my very eyes tonight, and I am still recovering." He wanted to take her in his arms, but with Jacob there, here merely brushed her cheek with his thumb.

She lifted her chin and surveyed his face. "Do I need to make a sleeping drought for you?"

That was the first spark of humor he had seen from her since she fainted, and he let out a breath. "What I need is for you to go back to bed so Jacob and I can finish our business, and I, too, can go to bed."

The legs of Jacob's stool scraped on the floor as he shifted himself further from the fire. "I do not need to hear about your bed habits." He was probably trying to be funny, but the corners of Ruth's mouth turned down, and Daniel wanted Jacob to stop talking.

They both ignored Jacob. Daniel studied her face. "Please," he said, voice pitched so only she could hear it. "I'll be in as soon as I can."

For an instant, she raised her chin as if to refuse, then she seemed to change her mind. "Don't be long." Then she turned and disappeared into the bedroom and closed the door behind her. The latch gave a faint click as it settled into place.

Unease haunted him. He wanted to go after her.

But he turned to find Jacob watching him. So he returned to the hearth and sat down heavily. "She doesn't deserve this."

"They don't trust her."

His gut tightened. He was part of the reason they didn't trust her. He had taken Cook's accusations seriously instead of believing her and the evidence of his own eyes.

But he had followed the law, as was his duty. He didn't know her then. He raked his hands over his face and through his hair.

Jacob snorted out a little laugh.

Daniel's head popped up. "What?"

"Has anyone ever told you how entertaining it is to watch you wrestle with yourself inside your own head?"

"Fuck you. I'm trying to figure out how we solve this mess."

Jacob's eyes grew wide, and then he gave an outright belly laugh.

Daniel shushed him. "This is not the time, and if you bring Ruth out here again when she should be asleep, I cannot account for what I will do to you."

Jacob's face grew serious. "I can see you have grown fond of her, but remember your duty here."

The unease from earlier crept back up his spine. "What exactly do you mean?"

Jacob flapped his hand in Daniel's face. "Don't get yourself in a lather. I just mean that you are a selectman and the warden. You are the theories and evidence man. Do your theories and evidence thing. Figure out what caused all the issues they are concerned about."

Daniel sat on his own hands to keep them from smacking the smile off Jacob's face. "Is that all? Because I haven't been trying to do that for months, along with finding causes for all the other devilry, while also getting in crops, keeping the peace with the Penobscot, and figuring out how to be a husband to a woman we bullied into becoming my wife." His hands escaped, and he flung them in the air. "I have been trying to do all those things for the past months."

Jacob's eyes widened. They stared at each other. "I've never seen you flustered." Jacob smiled, and a snort of laughter escaped his nose.

"Fuck off."

"That's two."

"Are you itching for three?" Daniel closed his eyes and took three deep breaths. Jacob was right, he was losing his calm. That wouldn't serve. He opened his eyes. "I'm sorry. You didn't deserve that."

"Yes, I did." Now Jacob was grinning again. What a pain in the arse to grin right now.

"Yes, you did." Daniel tried to smile at him, but it felt more like a grimace.

He looked into the fire again. It had always helped him think to watch the flames dance around the logs. Tonight, they seemed to mock him. They slowly consumed the logs and offered no inspiration. He needed to figure this out before the whole town got into a panic. Once they started egging each other on, their evidence grew less reliable because their imaginations got the better of them.

"Why do you think it is Ruth they latched onto?" That was really the key question here, now that his brain was functioning again.

Jacob shrugged as if it didn't matter. "She is very forward." Jacob held up a hand as Daniel leaned in to speak. "She makes people feel stupid when she contradicts them in public. And she denies witchcraft's existence."

All valid legal reasons to suspect her.

And exactly the same reasons a person might rationally put forward if they were trying to prove innocence.

Had he really never grasped this conundrum before? He raked his hands through his hair again until it was probably standing straight up on end. No wonder she fainted dead away when she was accused a second time. The miracle was that he had let her off with the punishment of marriage to himself the first time instead of a trial that could have ended in her hanging.

"They have a good case," said Jacob.

Daniel sat up straight. Truth would out. "On the surface. But she is innocent, and I will prove it to them."

Jacob's brows knit together, and he worked his mouth like he was trying to form the right words.

"Spit it out."

Jacob rolled his eyes. "Be careful how you cast your lot."

Daniel waited, but that was all he said. "Meaning?"

"Be careful how you cast your lot."

Daniel's own eyes rolled before he could stop them. "Stunning clarification." He stood and paused. He just needed to think. Everything he had ever read was about prosecuting witches. Nothing he knew of had been written to explain a good defense against such an accusation.

He managed not to kick anything and wake up Ruth, but it was close.

He stood still and focused on the feeling of his feet on the ground. His neighbors were rational. He would find a rational argument that would persuade them.

He turned to Jacob. "What would persuade you if you didn't know the interested parties?"

Jacob shook his head. "I do know the interested parties." Then he stood and went to the door.

Daniel let him leave and barred the door behind him.

Be careful how he cast his lot. Surely he didn't mean for Daniel to abandon Ruth to the charges?

"Auntie Ruth," Matthias' daughter almost sang her name. "Can I get healed, too?"

Ruth tucked her woolen cloak around her legs, sat on the doorstep, and made a big show of removing the little girls' mittens and inspecting her hands. She clucked her tongue, and then she rummaged around in her medical basket. "Aha!" She pulled a bottle from the basket, poured a bit of lavender oil out of it, and rubbed the lavender on the little girl's wrists. "There, that should heal your injury quickly. Give it a sniff."

The little girl bent her head down to her wrists, which she now held immobile, and gave a brief sniff. Her smile spread across her face. "This smells much better than my brother!" She waved her hands in the air and danced around the dooryard.

Her brother was more dour. The plaster she had put on his all-too-real injury smelled rather rank.

"I am so glad you sent your sister to get me when you scraped this. This could have gotten very painful, but because you did the smart thing, it should heal well now." She gave her best imitation of a manly pat on the shoulder. "You have a good head on your shoulders, young man."

The boy smiled for the first time since she arrived. He had scraped his arm badly in the barn, and if it had gotten puss-filled and inflamed, it could have made him dangerously ill. But it should be just some ugly scabs in a few days since she had dressed it in time.

Her nephew met her gaze like an adult. "You healed Papa's hand, so I knew I had to send for you." With that, he turned and went to the barn to continue his chores.

The little girl rummaged in Ruth's basket and asked about the various plants and jars. Then she squealed almost in Ruth's ear. "Papa!"

Ruth's head popped up to see her own brother approaching. He stopped mid-stride when he spotted her and looked over both shoulders to check that no one might have seen him in her general vicinity. Just like with their mother. She didn't know whether to laugh at his predictability or cry.

Her niece sat herself down in Ruth's lap, so she did neither. Instead, she smoothed the little girl's hair and plucked a piece of a leaf that was snagged in a curl behind her ear.

Matthias hurried to where she sat on the doorstep. "What are you doing here?"

Her niece answered for her. "My brother scraped his arm in the barn, so he sent me to go fetch Auntie Ruth. And then, I brought Auntie Ruth back, and she dressed his injury and put a plaster on it. And then she put some medicine on my injuries, and they are already healed. And I smell much better than my brother." She waved her little hands at her father, who looked confused, annoyed, and concerned all at once.

Matthias plucked the little girl off Ruth's lap with one arm and hustled them both into the house and closed the door as if someone might sneak up on them and see her there.

Matthias had put the girl down without even looking at her, and she sniffed and brushed a tear from her cheek. She wanted her father's attention and hadn't gotten it, but she knew better than to pester him.

Ruth glared at Matthias, tilted her head toward her niece, and raised her eyebrows at him.

Matthias rolled his eyes, then bent down to sniff his daughter's wrists. "You smell nice. Where is your brother?"

The little girl was smart enough to realize that was all the victory she would get here. "He went back to the barn."

"Go help him." He scooted her out the door and closed it behind her. Then he turned to Ruth. "You can't be here."

"I am here."

His nostrils flared. He hated it when she did that. Always had. But it was the truth, so he had to deal with it.

"Then you have to go."

"No."

"Yes. Now."

"I assume from your haste to have me gone that you have heard I am to be accused of witchcraft again?"

He half closed his eyes and shook his head. His tiny supply of patience was already close to gone, so she shouldn't toy with him.

"It is already bleeding over onto me."

As if she had done something intentionally to mess up his life. Her hands went to her hips, and heat rose up her neck. "I didn't do anything."

He snorted at her.

"Why did Jacob tell Daniel to be careful how he cast his lot?" She shouldn't know he said that, but Jacob's idea of talking quietly carried through a closed door with uncomfortable ease. And then Daniel had been gone before she woke, so she couldn't ask him.

Matthias stared down at his own feet and shifted his weight. He wouldn't look back up at her.

Her stomach felt queasy, and her chest got tight. "Was he telling Daniel not to cast his lot with me?" She was his wife. Hadn't he cast his lot with her the day he agreed to marry her? Her hands trembled, and her legs felt weak.

Matthias pursed his lips. "I didn't think of that."

"What? What did you think of?" She flung her hands in the air. "What is going on that you aren't telling me?"

Matthias sat down hard on a stool by the hearth, and its legs splayed under his weight. The stool's days were numbered if he did that regularly.

"What did you think he meant when I told you?"

He hated being pressed, but he was her brother, so she had a right to press him.

He was silent.

She kicked the leg of his stool, and he glared at her.

"What did you think he meant?"

He groaned. "The Penobscot. Daniel talked me into going with him to take them corn."

She knew that. And it didn't answer her question.

He stared at her.

She gestured with her hands for him to continue and almost poked his eye out in the process.

He swatted her hand out of his face. "The Penobscot. Throw his lot in with them instead of the town."

Oh. That was possible.

She ran everything she heard of Daniel and Jacob's conversation through her mind. She had assumed Jacob was talking about her. But maybe Matthias was right.

She looked back at him.

He glared again. "You are not the sole subject of every conversation."

"They just accused me of witchcraft!"

He had the decency to duck his head a little at that. Then his foot shot out, and he kicked the empty stool next to him, sending it flying across the room. "He was supposed to keep you out of trouble, not drag all of us further into it." He looked up at her. "Your husband is not as smart as I thought he was."

Her head snapped back like he had slapped her. "He is a lot smarter than you, Matthias Derwin." Though it didn't help her peace of mind that he withdrew to the barn or fields, as he seemed to do when he needed to think. She needed to talk to think, and he hadn't been there this morning.

Matthias' head came up, and he cocked it toward the door, paying her no attention.

Voices.

He turned back to her. "You can't be here."

Her eyes searched her brother's home, which had not sprouted a back door since she was last there.

"As we have already determined, I am here."

The door swung open, and they both froze.

Then her muscles relaxed, and her breath whooshed out of her.

"Woman, you can't do that," Matthias barked at Anne.

She had been married to him long enough not to take offense. She turned to Ruth and smiled. "Thank you for mending my boy. He showed me your ministrations and said how very wise you thought he was." Then she glanced at Matthias. "No one has seen Ruth here."

Anne then went to the hearth and started stoking the fire and warming her hands.

Matthias stood and stared down at Ruth. He knew she hated to have to tip her head back to see his face. "You need to go while that is still true."

She blinked twice. It shouldn't hurt after all these years. She drew in a shaky breath. "Sometimes I think you want me to hang so you can be rid of me."

Anne gasped. Matthias' face went to stone. "I have suffered for other people's actions all my life, especially yours, and I still fought for you."

She leapt to her feet. "How, exactly?"

He crowded in and breathed down in her face now, his toes jammed up against hers. "You're married to Daniel, aren't you?"

"What does that have to do with anything?"

He leaned down so close she could see the spittle in the corner of his mouth. Then he stilled, breathed twice, and straightened. He pointed to the door. "Go, and don't touch my children."

She gasped. Then she glanced at Anne, who smiled apologetically but wasn't about to step in. Then she looked back at her brother. He pointed at the door again but didn't say a word.

Her head was spinning. She took a step toward the door, then reached out a hand to steady herself against the wall. She turned to look back at him.

"Now. And tell your husband to stop kicking over hornets' nests before he gets us all killed." His face was more animated and impassioned than she had ever seen it. "I should have known the two of you would be like tinder and spark. What a fool I was."

She turned and ran out the door, slamming it shut behind her.

19

Daniel entered the meetinghouse, and the buzzing of multiple heated discussions engulfed him.

Some of those discussions ceased abruptly as he walked by. His various neighbors watched him as he made his way to the front of the room, where Jacob and Mr. Aldrich stood.

Murmurs rose behind him as he walked.

This might be a long day.

"Did you take corn to the Penobscot?" Aldrich asked.

The room went silent, and the whole town leaned in to hear his answer.

He waited until he had reached the front of the room, then turned so that everyone could hear him since there was no point in having to repeat himself later. "Yes, I took my corn to them, as the treaty requires."

The silence remained, but the energy in the room shifted. Some of the gathered men fumed with anger, others went wide-eyed with surprise, though whether they were surprised that he did it or surprised that he admitted to it, only they could know.

Aldrich's face grew stony. "The selectmen had not yet decided that matter."

It was hard to give Aldrich his due deference when he said things like that. "Boston decides our treaty terms, not the selectmen."

Besides, the selectmen had raised no formal discussion about it, only informal chatter, with Aldrich and Jacob grousing about not wanting to pay it.

"Traitor!"

Daniel's head whipped around, and he scanned the room to see who had spoken. That sort of disorder, to say nothing of slander, could not be tolerated in the meeting house, even if it wasn't the Sabbath.

Everyone in the audience stared back at him. He turned to look at Jacob and Aldrich. They at least had the decency to look affronted that someone would behave in such an unruly manner.

Aldrich raised his hand for attention, then turned back to Daniel. "We had not yet discussed our reply to the edict from Boston. We disapprove of your presumption."

Daniel worked his jaw to keep it from gaping like a trout's. A treaty signed in Boston was law. "I was unaware there was any reply to a law other than to follow it like the godly community we are."

Aldrich and Jacob both gaped with indignation, as well they might. It was not politic of him to be so direct. He needed to persuade, not badger.

He turned to his collected neighbors. "I can't spare my corn any more than anyone else can, but Boston did not ask us before they negotiated the treaty, and we are bound by any treaty they sign."

"Why should we be bound by a treaty we had no say in and did not agree to?" Cook asked from the front of the crowd. "Boston can pay the corn if they want to, but not me."

Aldrich and Jacob stayed silent, so Daniel replied. "We do not get to have individual input on treaties that end wars."

Cook was glaring at him now. Daniel turned to his fellow selectmen. They knew full well a treaty was a treaty. But they remained silent and left him to defend the position of law and order on his own.

This was madness. He should not have to explain that they were required to follow the law, least of all to his fellow selectmen.

"We won the war. Why do we have to pay a quitrent to the Penobscot to live on our land as a result?" Without a quelling word or look from Aldrich, Cook would not let it go.

Daniel's breath grew quicker and more shallow. "The English won the war against King Philip down in Massachusetts and Connecticut, but as we well know," he scanned the room and made eye contact with as many as he could, "that wasn't so clear up here in Maine."

He didn't enjoy reliving that any more than they did or admitting how close they had come to having their settlement wiped off the map. Their militia had been comprised of the very men in this room, which meant that each one of them knew firsthand how close they had come to annihilation on more than one occasion.

Except Cook, who had scampered off south.

The men grew sullen and crowded closer.

Daniel forced himself not to take a step back. He gave Jacob a deliberate look. His friend should be helping him here, but Jacob merely pursed his lips thoughtfully as he gazed at the crowd pushing forward. Aldrich smiled.

That was all Cook needed to see. "We won the war, and Penobscot didn't observe the treaty. They attacked us unprovoked."

Were their memories that selective? "They never agreed to the first proposed treaty, which meant that the war didn't end for them. Of course, they continued the raids. They were winning, and we tried to pretend they lost and treat them accordingly. We would have done the same in their position. Any nation that wasn't full of cowards would have."

He could hear the pitch of his own voice rise as he spoke. Was it his imagination, or had Aldrich and Jacob stepped back, letting the unhappy crowd focus on him?

"They did the Devil's work, and we are not obligated to pay the Devil."

Others murmured agreement with Cook.

"You cannot simply claim anything you don't like is the Devil's work. Did it occur to you we might be facing a trial of our faith?" He looked out at the crowd. "And that we are suffering the indignity of the quitrent because we failed it?"

The skin all over Daniel's body suddenly pebbled as if from cold. They didn't care about a single word he had said. Even Reverend Maitland scowled, furious that he might suggest such a thing despite having called multiple fast days during the raids with exactly that justification.

Daniel looked from the crowd to the other selectmen. Not a single face gave a sign that his words had penetrated their minds or their hearts.

He searched for Matthias in what felt more like a mob now.

He wasn't there.

Matthias had known this might happen, but Daniel had been idealistic enough to think his brother-in-law was wrong.

His shoulders sagged. He wasn't going to get through to any of them right now.

He turned back to Jacob and Aldrich. "We should move on and address today's agenda."

Mr. Aldrich stepped toward him and spoke so that the entire crowd could hear him. "Because of your recent actions, I am afraid you are suspended from conducting selectmen business until we can assess the damage your actions have done and assess an appropriate penalty."

Jacob gave him a small shrug as if to say there was nothing he could do about it.

Following the law had gotten him suspended from selectman business. He remained silent for a moment to make sense of it, but he couldn't. He would have to figure that out later.

"Very well, then let me move on to warden business—"

Aldrich held up his hand to cut him off. "You are compromised in that as well. Your own wife stands accused, and you yourself appear to have been doing the Devil's work. I am afraid we have to ask you to leave."

Daniel's jaw dropped to his chest.

Cook whispered loud enough to be sure everyone heard him. "As if the two aren't connected."

At that, the crowd inched closer.

Jacob moved out from behind Aldrich. He leaned in and spoke so that only Daniel could hear. "I think it is best you go. I will try to sort this out." Louder, so the crowd could hear, he said, "I will escort you to the door, but please do not linger there."

He took Daniel by the arm and started pushing his way through the milling crowd, dragging Daniel in his wake.

Daniel stared at the back of Jacob's head.

A splat of spittle smacked into the back of his neck, but he didn't turn to see who had launched it.

He could hear his own pulse in his ears as it banged out his frustration at the lack of reason he had just experienced. The Devil had won if they would not listen to reason, and worse, he had no idea how to defend Ruth or himself against this madness.

The crowd pressed closer, and the voices of what seemed to be every single man in the room got louder and louder.

His skin prickled, and his nerves were on high alert, but he kept staring straight ahead and didn't engage them. He refused to dignify their wild ideas with a reaction.

"Goody Francis will have found evidence on her by now." Cook's voice rose above the rest.

His feet and legs lost their coordination for an instant, and his step stuttered. Goody Francis, the midwife, had legal standing in witchcraft cases. They wouldn't send her to examine Ruth without his knowledge.

Would they?

His heart pounded against the bars of his ribs like a caged bear, and his throat got tight and constricted his breath. He should never have left Ruth sleeping this morning without discussing possible actions, and now it might be too late.

Ruth set her basket of onions down near the hearth so she could work in its warmth. The corn might be in, but she still had weeks of work preparing the produce of her garden for winter, and winter was already sneaking up on them.

She laid out fifteen onions on the floor along the front of the hearth, then pulled up her stool, grabbed three onions, and sat. With those three partially dried onions, she began braiding the greens. She took a fourth onion and wove it in with the first strand, a fifth onion and wove it in with the second strand. As she reached for a sixth onion, there was a loud bang at the door.

Her heart jumped, but she held on to the onions so she didn't have to start over.

She stood and took a deep breath to steady herself. Then she walked to the door. She didn't remove the bar.

"Who's there?"

"T'is Goody Francis."

Perhaps the woman needed some ingredients for a treatment that she did not have on hand. She didn't dare hope that the woman was coming to ask for advice on a patient. But even asking to share medicine was a giant step in the right direction.

She un-barred the door, then undid the latch and opened the door wide.

Her breath caught. There was Goody Francis, but she was not alone. Two women from the far side of the settlement flanked her, lips tight in lines so straight they could have connected the three women without a kink. And behind them, face equally grim, stood the constable.

Ruth's stomach lurched, but she kept her breakfast down.

Goody Francis pushed past her into the house before Ruth could get a word out. Her jaws were clenched too tight against the threatened rebellion of her stomach.

The other women followed, and the constable brought up the rear, closed the door behind himself, and then stood sentry in front of it, barring any exit.

"What—" was all Ruth could get out before Goody Francis took over.

"We are here to examine you for your trial."

Ruth felt her eyes go wide. She looked to the constable, who gave a curt nod.

She felt as though she were a spectator of the spectacle, observing even herself. Her worst nightmare, since she was a young girl, was witnessing her mother being searched for witch's marks, and her time had now arrived and she should be shrieking in fury. But the moment wouldn't register as real. She kept observing, as if floating above the scene while it played out.

Goody Francis approached her, and her legs backed her toward the hearth.

"Stand still." The midwife's voice was colder than anything she had ever heard. Her feet stopped moving. "Why do you do the Devil's work? What made you sign your name in his book?"

That brought her back to the moment, and her floating self slammed back into her physical self with a force that made her rock on her feet.

"I do not do the Devil's work, nor have signed his book." The absurdity of the Devil having a book to sign hit as it hadn't ever before.

The other women stood to either side of her, with Goody Francis in front and the hearth to her back.

They could hem her in, but she would not cower before their nonsense.

"What is your familiar? The cat? The chickens?"

They thought she would send chickens after someone? Of all animals, chickens? But the glint in Goody Francis' eye stopped her from laughing in their faces. They glinted with hunger. It was the only word that could describe it. And it turned her laughter into icy tremors from her head to toes. How dare they.

"Never mind, we shall see for ourselves."

The other two women each grabbed one of her arms before their intent registered. The onions dropped from her fist. She tried to yank her arms free, but the constable stepped forward to back them up, so she stopped.

Goody Francis led the way as they dragged her toward the bedroom.

Her chest constricted and her throat closed up, and she could barely draw breath. Her head felt light as they pushed her through the door and closed it. No, no, no. This could not be happening.

Her brain registered that the constable was still in the main room, on the other side of the door, so at least he would not witness her humiliation.

The women began plucking at her clothing, untying tapes and undoing buttons as one six-handed demon.

The cold air hit her skin as they pulled her clothing off her body, but the shivers that wracked her body were not from the cold.

Within moments, she stood naked before them. Goody Francis began inspecting her skin as the women held her arms away from her body. The older woman clucked her tongue as she searched for witch's marks and anywhere she might suckle her familiars.

Silent tears streamed down Ruth's face, but there was no way she could allow a sound to escape. She would not give these women the satisfaction.

Goody Francis stared at her breasts and hissed. "You are breeding."

The other women gasped, and their grips loosened, as if they didn't want to touch her.

Goody Francis took Ruth's jaw in her hand and forced her to look her in the eye. "You have had carnal relations with the Devil."

Ruth's entire body burned. "This child is my husband's." If her mouth weren't dry as the desert in Canaan, she would have spat in Goody Francis' face for such an insult. Damn the consequences.

"Look, Goody Francis," squealed one of the women from behind her.

Goody Francis grabbed her arm and wrenched her around so she could see Ruth's back. The third woman gasped, and Goody Francis hummed, the sound of a satisfied cat.

Ruth twisted her neck to look over her shoulder and see what they were so excited by.

Someone poked at a raised patch of skin on her shoulder blade. "A teat for nursing her familiar. There it is."

All three women stared at her shoulder, and there wasn't a thing she could say that would make them interpret that patch of skin in any other way. But that wouldn't stop her from trying.

"That mark has been there since I was shoved into a fence by my brother as a child." Fury surged through her veins.

"That is a witch's mark, and Satan cannot help you talk your way out of it."

She tried to yank her arms free of the women, but they grabbed her and held her with her arms outstretched to each side and leaned their full weight against each other, stretching her tight like a rope between them. Her head spun. It was not a witch's mark, but they wouldn't hear logic.

She struggled and pulled to no avail and almost didn't register the shouting in the main room.

The door to the bedroom flew open and slammed against the wall. The women yelped with surprise as Daniel appeared in front of them, eyes blazing and looking ready to tear them limb from limb.

She could do nothing but stand there, heat radiating shame over her entire body. The constable stood behind Daniel, his nose bleeding, his eyes gawking. At her.

She felt her whole being shrink in front of this expanded audience. It had been awful enough when it was just the women, but now the constable, and somehow Daniel was the worst. She couldn't bear him seeing her so humiliated.

A hole hollowed out in her gut. This must have been what her mother felt when her children witnessed her search. She had never recovered, even after she had been acquitted.

Daniel stormed into the room, grabbed a blanket from the bed and threw it around her, then he turned to the women and the constable. "How dare you do this without my knowledge?"

Ruth shuddered under his arm. If the midwife called it a witch's mark, no court would disbelieve her. They would sentence her to hang.

Goody Francis squared her shoulders but took a step back. "We are doing the court's business at the court's request." The constable gave a nod to confirm her story but was apparently mute today, as he had yet to utter a single word. Maybe he, at least, was ashamed of their errand.

"You are done, and you may go now." Daniel's voice was so cold it would have frozen the sun.

Goody Francis seemed to have recovered herself. "You have no authority over the court's business in this."

Daniel's voice was deadly flat when he replied. "This is my house and my wife, and I have complete authority over both. You will leave this house immediately, or the Devil will take you where you do not wish to go."

They stared at him, wide-eyed.

"Now." He stomped his foot at them, and they scattered like rats. He didn't bother to follow them out and bar the door. He gathered her into his arms, and she melted against him, trying to disappear into his embrace.

After a moment, he set her out at arm's length and looked at her. "Did they hurt you?"

She shivered, and her soul folded in on itself.

20

She shivered so violently he thought for a moment she might come apart. And she hadn't answered his question.

He pushed her just far enough from him that he could see her face. His blood turned cold, and his chest constricted. "What did they do to you?"

Her face was pale as fresh snow, and her eyes were glazed like ice. She shook her head but said nothing.

His own limbs began trembling to match hers. "Please, Ruth, tell me what they did. I can't help if I don't know what happened."

At that, her eyes snapped into focus and bore into his. "What exactly do you think you can do?" Her tone was almost accusing.

He rubbed his thumbs on her shoulders where he held her, and he willed her to listen to him. Really listen and let him help. "I can make sure they followed legal protocols, and I create an argument against them. They can't just accuse innocent people of witchcraft."

She shook her head like he was babbling nonsense.

"They can't. And we can sue for slander."

A laugh burst out of her so violently he flinched. He searched her face. Please let her not be possessed. He gathered her back into his arms and held her tight as if that might fend off any specters.

Now, it was her turn to push him away, with her hands on his shoulders. "Listen to yourself." Her laughter had gone, and she was lucid, but she was still too pale. "You think logic and law can protect me."

It could, if only she would tell him what had happened so that he could piece together a defense, or an offense, if necessary.

She moved one hand to his cheek and stroked her thumb across it like he was the one in distress.

He placed his hand over hers and turned his lips to kiss her palm. "Tell me what happened."

Her face stilled, and she grew paler. His heart was pounding. She was the one who knew what to do when someone fainted or was ill, not him. But he had to do something.

He turned her toward the bed, and she just stood. So he picked her up and carried her to it, then sat her down. He pulled another blanket around her.

His breathing got short and shallow at the thought of them stripping her naked. The only thing that kept him from further violence when he arrived home was the fact that the constable was in the outer room. It was only the midwife and her cronies who had stripped her naked.

"Please, Ruth. Please tell me what happened." His voice hitched, and he cleared his throat.

She took a deep breath and then another. After the third, she spoke. "They searched me for witch's marks and for strange teats I might use to suckle my familiar."

Her body was perfect. It was heaven on earth.

There, he admitted it, at least to himself. She was his wife. He was allowed to take pleasure in her body. In her.

"They found a mark."

His head snapped up. "What mark?"

She twisted her body and pushed the blanket down to reveal the back of her shoulder to him.

"What mark, Ruth? I just see a scar."

She pulled the blanket back up around her. "You see the scar from when Matthias shoved me into a fence as a child. Goody Francis sees a witch's mark."

"But it's a scar." They couldn't just claim any mark was a witch's mark.

She pulled her feet up under her, so they were covered by the blanket, too. She must be frozen. "What is the legal definition of a witch's mark?"

He opened his mouth, then he closed it.

She shook her head. "Exactly."

"Midwives can't just go around calling scars witch's marks." That would lead to chaos.

None of this made sense, and every time he tried to stamp out one lie or ill deed, two more sprung up in its place.

He turned and paced the room, running his fingers through his hair. There had to be something he could do to keep this from getting out of control. He could stop this. He had to stop this.

Ruth watched him from where she sat on the bed. She was pale and cold. He might not be able to do anything about how pale she was, but the cold, at least, he could do something about.

He went to the side of the bed, stripping his clothes off as he went, letting them stay where they fell on the floor. Then he climbed onto the bed, took the blankets from her, and curled both himself and the blankets around her body as they lay down. He rubbed his hands over her arms, trying to warm them, and pressed his belly and chest up against her back. She was so tiny he could wrap himself all the way around her, cocooning her in his embrace.

"I am so sorry." The words weren't even a start, but he had to say them. He should not have let himself get distracted from his duties as warden. He should have found the Devil's minions in their midst by now instead of letting the pleasures of married life lure his focus away. His duty to her was to protect her, and he should never have let himself lose sight of that.

She needed him now, and he would do everything in his power to make it better.

He tucked her more tightly against his chest and kissed her beautiful hair.

It still smelled of roses.

She turned in his arms and pressed her lips against his, kissing him until he couldn't draw breath. He tried to pull back. His intent was to soothe her, not ravish her, but she pulled his head back to hers and wouldn't let him go.

His cock instantly responded because it couldn't resist her any more than he could.

She rolled him on top of her and wrapped her legs so tightly around his waist he couldn't have escaped if he tried, not that he had any will to. With the strength of her legs and arms, she slammed him against her with such force that she rammed his cock into her, and his bollocks swung against her arse. Together, they writhed and joined and slapped their bodies together until each had worked up a slick layer of sweat.

Her nails raked his back, and that sent raucous sensations down his spine to his balls.

He reached for her breast with one hand and massaged it. She leaned into the pressure of his hand, groaning.

She tilted her head back and kissed the side of his neck. Their frantic thrusting scraped her teeth against his skin, and an inhuman growl escaped his throat. She clamped her teeth down harder, and he shot his seed so deeply into her it had to have reached her heart. His cock kept pulsing, and he kept thrusting and massaging her breast, growling in her ear until she came apart in his arms, screaming his name.

Her voice echoed through the room as their bodies stilled.

He rested his weight to the side so he could keep their connection without crushing her. He brushed his lips over hers, over her cheeks, her eyelids, her throat.

Her eyes opened, and for the first time since he had arrived home today, they were peaceful. She reached her lips up to his and kissed him so lightly it might have been a bird's wing brushing over his lips.

He shifted to his side and gathered her in his arms, turning her so her back was to his front, and he could fold himself around her again. No one would get to her through him.

She snuggled her back and arse against him, making his cock twitch to life again. Then she took his hand and kissed his palm. "You can't logic our way out of this, Daniel."

His breath slowed. He could, and he would.

He had to.

She kissed his wrist. "You have no official standing on this now. I am afraid because of me, you get to find out how little power logic has when you are being hunted."

She wasn't tense. Her breathing was slow and level like she was resigned to her fate.

He rolled her to face him. "Jacob is still part of the process and can be a voice of reason."

Her delicate brows lowered. "You have more faith in the fairness of the system than perhaps you aught." She took his face in her hands and forced him to look at her, as if he could look anywhere else. "You need to see the dangers clearly, for both our sakes."

He kissed her and ran his hand over her hair, the soft strands soothing him as much as he hoped he was soothing her. "I see them, and I will fight them to the—"

She slammed her hand over his mouth as her eyes got glassy. "It's a capital crime."

A tremor shook through her body, and his own body picked it up and amplified it.

The constable led Ruth by the arm to the door of the meeting house where her trial would be held. He showed no more compassion than he had the last time. It was a job that must eat a man's soul.

She paused to take a deep breath and say a quick prayer at the doorway, but he yanked her forward into the building and almost off her feet. She regained her balance just as every eye in the building turned her way. Her shoulders squared.

She would not cower.

Chin high, she walked steadily toward the dais. Jacob and Mr. Aldrich sat there flanking the magistrate from Wells, whose bewigged head swiveled as his narrowed eyes tracked her progress. He was a slight man but held himself with an air of self-importance.

Her heart pounded at the sight of him. This wasn't an indictment. It was a trial. If this stranger from miles away found her guilty, she would hang from the oak in the meetinghouse yard.

Her eyes sought Daniel. He was there, in the front row, eyes on her. She tried to give him a little smile, but she could barely lift the corner of her mouth.

The magistrate stood as she approached the bench. "Goodwife Kendrick?"

"Yes, your honor." Her voice was loud in the quiet room but blessedly steady.

"You are hereby charged with witchcraft. How do you plead?"

"Not guilty." Her voice boomed from the rafters. No one would mistake her answer.

The man let the echoes subside before continuing. He appeared almost bored.

This was her life. How dare he be bored?

Her shoulders pulled back a little further, and her chin jutted forward.

Daniel's eyes widened in alarm, and she forced her shoulders and chin to relax. He gave her the tiniest smile and nod.

He was a good man, and he tried to make everything better, but this trial would not bring order. He had no idea.

She was a fool to think he could protect her. No one could.

"Goodwife Kendrick." The magistrate's voice pulled her out of her own head. "Goodman Smith claims you sent your specter to push him from his loft. Why did you do that?"

She shivered. This was how it had started for her mother. But her mother hadn't been convicted. Not that it didn't kill her, just the same.

The minister's mouser yowled from the back of the meetinghouse behind the dais. No one paid it any mind.

"I did not push him, and I don't have a specter to send."

A buzz of whispers rose at her denial and then fell with a stern look from the magistrate.

He turned back to her and leaned forward. She fought the urge to lean back in response.

"How many times has Goodman Smith climbed down from his loft?" he asked.

"Countless times, I should think."

"And yet you contend that in such a familiar routine, he simply slipped one day?" His tone made it clear he thought that improbable.

"I wasn't there, so I cannot say."

The line of questions dragged on until the magistrate questioned Goodman Smith himself about the day.

"Did she appear quickly to heal you?" the magistrate asked.

"Yes, and she could only have known so quick if she caused it."

She wanted to throw up her hands at the absurdity of it. "His son came running to get me. Was I supposed to let him suffer just to avoid drawing suspicion?"

"Silence." The magistrate's voice boomed, and he glared at her from the dais. He might as well have been a minister preaching hellfire, convinced she was headed for damnation.

At least a few of the murmurings from the crowd noted her point. She looked around the packed meeting house at all the male faces weighing her words.

She glanced at Daniel, and he gave her a smile. The weight on her shoulders lifted just a little.

She looked back at the magistrate.

He turned to Goodman Smith. "Did she heal you well, or did she only partially heal you?"

Smith glanced at Cook, then down at his shoes, then back at the magistrate. "She healed me good." He paused, and then his chin lifted. "But it still hurts when it rains."

Someone in the crowd laughed, then covered it with a cough. The magistrate glared at the gallery but apparently didn't catch who it was.

He turned back to Smith and dismissed him. Then he called Cook, and her heart sank. Cook strutted to the front of the room and smiled at the magistrate, then turned and smiled, or perhaps smirked, at the crowd. He had obviously washed for the occasion, but the stench of hogs still followed him.

The magistrate turned to her, and her stomach joined her heart in sinking. The air in the room almost vibrated with excitement.

"This man, Goodman Cook, states that you had your familiars assault him, and then you afflicted his horse, causing a fire."

Her jaw went slack. Daniel had cleared her in the chicken fiasco, but it was back. "He scared Goody Carter's chickens, and I retrieved one from his hound's jaws. I didn't set the chickens on him. They are chickens. They frighten easily."

Again, a few snickers rippled through the audience until the magistrate cut them short with a glare. He shifted in his seat. For the first time, he seemed a little unsure. She shot a quick look at Daniel, who was studying the magistrate, apparently willing him to recognize that his discomfort was his conscience, trying to point out the absurdity of the case.

A little color rose in the magistrate's cheeks. Surely, he had too much professorial pride to sentence someone to hang on the evidence of panicked chickens. She almost dared to hope.

The magistrate then straightened in his seat. "Tell us, Goodman Cook, how she afflicted your horse."

She had been nowhere near Cook's farm or his horse until they went to help put the fire out. Daniel had rescued his horse, and she had treated its burns. He couldn't connect her to that any more closely than any other person in the settlement who came to help.

Her pulse picked up. If Cook would just say something foolish, it might turn the mood of the gallery and the magistrate that one last step to her side.

Her body inclined forward as she held her breath, waiting for Cook to trip into his own trap.

He cleared his throat as if he was readying himself to address Parliament. "She afflicted my horse with the colic, and when it did not pass, I got an old pipe, filled it with tobacco, lit it, and placed it in its fundament, which all know is a tried way to remedy it."

Daniel gaped, baffled, as did many of the men in the gallery. Sticking a lit pipe in a horse's arse was a foolish way to attempt to cure colic.

Cook gazed around the room and waited, letting the tension build. "Then a great blue flame shot from its fundament, singing the beast and setting my barn alight in the fires of hell."

A collective gasp sucked all the air from the room. Horrified faces turned her way. Cook smirked, and the magistrate gazed at her triumphantly. "Why did you cause a great flame to shoot from the horse's fundament and burn Goodman Cook's barn?"

She stared at him. "I cannot account for it. I do not know how such a thing could even happen." Daniel had found the pipe tangled in the horse's tail, and they had assumed he had been foolishly smoking his pipe in the barn. When the horse swished its tail, it knocked the pipe, and some ashes fell to the straw and caused the fire.

Goodman Smith cleared his throat. "I witnessed this, your honor." The memory of it had turned Smith pale. And with good reason. Who other than the Devil or his minions could cause such a horror?

The minister's gray striped mouser shot across the front of the dais with a mouse in its jaws.

Ruth trembled as the gallery stared at her with accusing eyes again.

"Goodwife Francis, what say you about your search of the accused?"

Panic rose and closed off Ruth's throat as she turned to look at the only other woman in the room.

Goody Francis' eyes gleamed. She appeared to enjoy her moment as much as Cook had. "She bears the Devil's mark on her shoulder."

"That is not true." The words were out of Ruth's mouth before she even thought to speak. "That is a scar from being pushed into a fence as a child."

Her eyes searched the crowd to find Matthias to confirm it. She peered to the back, where he tended to stand, but she couldn't find him.

Her brother wasn't there.

Goody Francis dismissed her explanation as if shooing a fly. "Tis the Devil's mark on her shoulder and the Devil's child in her belly."

All eyes turned to Ruth again, and she didn't dare to breathe as her hands went protectively to her belly. She searched for Daniel.

His face was ashen.

She had been interrupted by Mr. Aldrich and his mob banging on their door when she had been about to tell him. After that, she had been so absorbed in her fear of being hanged she had forgotten to tell him. What sort of unnatural woman did that?

Guilt weighed her gut down. This was not how Daniel should have found out.

"The child is my husband's," she said as her voice shook.

Goody Francis stared at Daniel, and a slow smile spread across her face. She pointed at his neck.

There were Ruth's own teeth marks on his flesh.

The midwife turned to the magistrate, still pointing at Daniel. "And he, too, bears the Devil's mark. As I said, she carries the Devil's child."

21

The next day, Daniel marched into the meetinghouse ahead of the constable. This was a farce, and everyone bloody well knew it. He was no more a witch than the magistrate was.

Jacob and Mr. Aldrich flanked the magistrate again, which was reassuring. They knew him.

He steadied himself with a breath. He could forgive the magistrate being swayed by the evidence when he didn't know any of the people involved. The truth would come out, as it always did.

He scanned the room. Every man in the town had gathered, and the only woman present was Goody Francis. It was harder to forgive her.

His face grew warm, thinking about the entire town seeing Ruth's mark on his neck. It was not for their consumption.

With one last glance around the meetinghouse, it sank in that Ruth was not there. She was being held in the gaol. He hadn't been allowed to talk with her since the morning before her trial started.

His chest tightened for the hundredth time.

She was with child.

"Goodman Kendrick." The magistrate wasn't going to let him wallow in his thoughts. "You are charged with witchcraft. How do you plead?"

That he had to state the obvious felt like an insult. "Not guilty."

Three pairs of eyes watched him from the dais. Two of them belonged to friends. This wouldn't last long. He ignored the many pairs of eyes watching him from behind.

"You are the local horse-master." It wasn't a question, so he said nothing, just gave a small nod of acknowledgment. "Why did you afflict Mr. Aldrich's horse and Goodman Cook's horse?"

His eyes shot to Aldrich, who watched him. "I afflicted neither horse. I tried to help with both and was injured helping Mr. Aldrich's stud."

He had been in agony for days after getting kicked when the stallion had gotten itself cast, and this was the thanks he got.

"How do you account for the flame shooting forth from Goodman Cook's horse?"

That he could not do. He had never heard of such a thing. "I cannot except to note that a lit pipe in a barn is an invitation to disaster."

The magistrate leaned in. "You are accusing Goodman Cook of inviting you to do your devilment?"

"No. I have done no devilment. I merely note what everyone already knows, which is that any tinder in a barn can cause a fire with so much flammable material, and he tempted fate by entering the barn with a lit pipe."

The magistrate said something to Jacob, and Jacob duly took notes. Jacob was now his only ally on the bench, but the truth was also on his side.

The magistrate turned back to Daniel. Everyone in the meetinghouse leaned in toward him. The air grew heavy, and his skin tingled.

"Why have you conspired with the Devil's minions to dispossess your neighbors of their corn?"

"What?" He couldn't stop the question. He must have misunderstood what the magistrate said.

"Did you not understand the question?"

He understood the words, but together they made no sense. "The Penobscot negotiated a treaty with Boston after the war, and we are bound by it to give them a bushel of corn per household per year. They won the war. I do not see how that makes them the Devil's minions."

The crowd leaned in closer. The pressure of their presence was palpable on his skin.

The magistrate conferred with Jacob again, and then with Aldrich. Then he turned back to Daniel. "And did you not do the Devil's work by helping them win the war?"

He stared back. That made no sense. He had lost his father as a result of that war. Jacob had lost a brother, and Ruth, awkward as it was to remember, had lost a husband. They had all lost family and neighbors.

The magistrate was waiting for a reply. "I do not understand," was all he could think to say.

Jacob spoke directly to him for the first time. "You signed a compact with the Devil to interfere with our defense. You let your father be mortally injured so that you could have his land. You let my brother be mortally injured. You let countless men be killed and wounded in the woods that day, and you pressed the Penobscot case to our corn and will not rest until we are ruined and driven from Maine." He stood and pointed at Daniel. "You are the Devil's minion, if not the Devil himself."

Everyone in the meetinghouse gasped, sucking the air from the building.

Daniel stared. His breathing seemed to echo in his ears, and his head grew light, like it had become detached.

Jacob still stood, eyes aflame. He was a man possessed. That was the only plausible explanation for the turn this had taken.

Jacob was saying that Daniel had intentionally led his company into disaster the day Esau was wounded.

Time stood still for a moment.

Then reality crashed in again as the magistrate stood. "Why did you lead your men to destruction that day?"

"The Penobscot weren't even there." That was the absurdity of it. Jacob had cried the alarm, the militia had assembled, and in the confusion, they had gotten separated, and one detachment of their own men had fired on the rest in the woods. The Penobscot had been nowhere near.

Their own fear had sewn chaos, and Daniel had lost control of the men. According to Matthias, Jacob himself had been part of the cause of chaos. Perhaps this was Daniel's punishment for his failure.

But it wasn't witchcraft.

"You are still conspiring to use the corn of your starving neighbors to satisfy Satan."

"I have obeyed the terms of the treaty." How had he been so blind to the animosity of his neighbors to obeying the law?

Jacob conferred with the magistrate, who nodded. Jacob addressed Daniel. "Did your wife not bewitch you and cause you to do these things?"

Every muscle in his body wanted to lunge for Jacob's throat. He quivered with the effort of restraining himself. "She did not."

Jacob tilted his head like an inquisitive dog. "Are you sure?"

The men in the meetinghouse all seemed to press in.

What the hell was he driving at? "Of course."

"How has your sleep been since you married?"

Much better. He hadn't had night visitations in months. "What does that have to do with anything?"

"You were all too eager to marry her. Had she already offered you a deal? Had she offered to stop her coven from haunting your nights in favor of getting us to turn over our corn?"

"No."

Jacob was spewing such slander Daniel would have no choice but to sue.

Jacob seemed to revel in his moment. "How well do you really know her, Daniel? She didn't even tell you she was with child. Why might that have been?"

She had to have had her reasons.

"Can you swear on the Bible that there is no chance she could have witched you?"

That brought him up short. Had he been on the bench, he would have asked the same question. Only now did he realize how impossible it was to answer. Of course, he couldn't swear to it. He didn't live in her head.

"As I thought," said Jacob, waving his hand triumphantly to the assembled crowd.

"She did not!"

All eyes turned toward him. His outburst sounded defensive even to his own ears. But how else could it sound? He was trying to defend himself.

This was his fault. He had let his feelings for Ruth cloud his mind from his duty. He should have seen the lawlessness brewing and stopped it, but she had bewitched him. Not with witchcraft, but just by making him fall in love with her. Because he did love her. And that created chaos in his mind, and it could cost her her life if he didn't fix it.

He raised his hand to gain the attention of the room.

"I have done no witchcraft. You have no legal evidence against me." The crowd watched intently. "If you don't want to pay the corn, then you must take that up with Boston. But you cannot blame me."

Jacob opened his mouth to interrupt, so Daniel didn't give him a chance.

"I have served this settlement, and I deserve a fair hearing." As did Ruth. "I ask to be taken to Boston so that those who made the treaty can decide the legality of my case."

That they could not deny him. Order would prevail.

The constable brought Ruth back to the meetinghouse. A building that had once brought her peace and solace now brought her anything but.

Her back ached from spending the night on a palette on the floor in the gaol, which was just a back closet in the constable's house, but she resisted rubbing the stiffness out in front of the assembled men of the settlement.

Daniel sat to one side of the dais under the watchful eye of Jacob. No one would tell her what had happened at Daniel's trial yesterday, but he and Jacob were each shooting dagger-like glares at the other.

Her stomach dropped. That did not bode well for Jacob speaking on their behalf.

The constable directed her to the front of the room, but on the opposite side of it from Daniel. Her stomach fell another notch. They were apparently deemed a threat if they sat together to conspire. She almost laughed. They were in the meeting house. Even if they were witches, they couldn't harm anyone in the meetinghouse.

Of course, experience showed that this was more about theater than reality. It always was, even though Daniel never recognized it.

Her gaze rested on his face, and she felt the first crumb of peace since she had been hauled off to the gaol.

He looked handsome sitting there, back straight and confident. He gave her a reassuring smile.

Perhaps she should have more faith in his ability to make this right. This was his arena, after all. Goody Carter always told her she needed to have more faith in others.

But hope was a dangerous thing.

She turned to face the magistrate.

He stood and cleared his throat. "These are very troubling times." He gazed out at a sea of nodding heads. "I am called back to Wells and must wrap this case up."

So, despite the troubling times, he didn't feel the need to inconvenience himself by lingering.

Daniel gave a brief gesture with his hands to be calm. Or to wait. She couldn't know for certain from across the room and didn't have any choice, at least in the case of waiting.

The magistrate turned to Daniel. "We deny your request to be heard in Boston."

Daniel's mouth dropped open, thunderstruck. The corner of Jacob's mouth turned up, satisfied. Her gaze bounced from one to the other and back again. Daniel must have thought he could talk logic to the government in Boston, where they would be more inclined to listen dispassionately.

He was about to find out how little power logic had among those caught up in the passion of a witch hunt. She had wanted nothing more than for him to understand that when he was the one doing the hunting, but not like this.

He didn't even look her way. He just gaped at the magistrate.

Her heart ached for him.

She looked at the magistrate, who appeared unmoved.

"In the case against Goodwife Kendrick, she is charged with injuring Goodman Smith, though we find no hard evidence of this."

The audience made a collective inhale of breath.

Ruth blinked. She looked at Daniel, who looked back at her. He appeared to be holding his breath.

The magistrate went on. "She is also charged with tormenting Goodman Cook and his hound by setting familiars upon them, and on this, too, we cannot find enough evidence to convict."

Cook tried to stand, but Jacob was close enough to him to shove him back into his seat. Perhaps he wasn't against them after all.

The crowd began to murmur behind her.

A little ember of hope became a slender flame in her chest.

The magistrate raised one finger to command attention. "But we cannot controvert Goodwife Francis' testimony about the witch's mark on Goodwife Kendrick."

Her hope flickered.

"And Goodwife Kendrick has not even raised a defense about afflicting Goodman Cook's horse and causing a blue flame to shoot from its fundament and burn his barn. Both Goodman Smith and Goodman Cook testify to her being in league with the Devil to harm the horse and Goodman Cook."

Her eyes stung. There was no defense against such an other-worldly happening, except she hadn't caused it. But she couldn't prove a negative.

She looked to the rafters of the building, blinking. Whatever else might happen, she would not give them the satisfaction of seeing her cry.

She didn't dare look Daniel's way. What a fool to think he might be able to get her out of this. She knew better, but he had convinced her to put her faith in him.

"We find her guilty of this."

Her shoulders sagged. Perhaps the court would have mercy and just remand her to someone's care and discipline. As if that was mercy.

A wave of grief rolled over her, not for herself, but for her mother. How had she stood so strong when it was her trial? Her mother had not been a tender woman, but she wanted her here now more than anything she could imagine.

"And as for Goodman Kendrick," the magistrate was wasting no time.

Daniel's mouth was a straight line, grim but resolute, as all eyes turned on him. He stared at the magistrate, almost daring him to violate logic and law. Dear Daniel, who believed that law was black and white, and that it could not help but find truth.

She had to look away.

"He is charged with conspiring with the Devil to deprive this settlement of sustenance, and apart from claiming it was not witchcraft, he has admitted so much, and with the testimony against him from multiple witnesses of good report, including a selectman of the town, and the added evidence of his Devil's mark, we find him guilty."

Her vision grew blotchy, and the dais wavered. She grabbed hold of the constable's arm to avoid falling. She would be damned to hell before she would faint in front of this town. And, of course, they thought she just had been.

Perhaps they were right.

She risked a look at Daniel. His face was red with rage, but he kept looking her way, and his brows cranked down with worry. He had never faced a situation he could not control with logic and rules.

Once again, she had to look away.

"I regret that it is so, but so it is."

The magistrate was so pompous she might vomit.

"I sentence them both to hang until dead a week from today."

Her head snapped up.

A sudden release of energy flowed throughout the meetinghouse from the crowd.

Daniel's mouth dropped open, and it was plain that he hadn't believed this outcome was possible. It had literally not occurred to him.

Oh dear heaven, her heart hurt. She swayed against the constable, who held her upright. The odd thought that she should thank him later popped into her head.

A throat cleared from far behind her. It cleared again.

"What is it?" The magistrate wanted to be on his way.

"You honor." It was Matthias' voice. She craned her neck around to see him. It took a moment to find him, but he was there, at the very back of the crowd. His voice was tight, and he was sweating in the cold of January. "Should she not have a reprieve for the belly?"

Her hand covered her faintly rounded belly. Her eyes shot to Daniel. He stared at the magistrate, not breathing as he awaited the man's answer.

"Yes, yes." The magistrate sounded annoyed.

Her head grew light again. Reprieve until her baby was born. Surely, she could figure out something by then or appeal her case.

But Daniel was still to hang.

Her fingertips went numb and then began to tingle. Those two things shouldn't be possible at the same time.

"I will take responsibility for her until the baby is born." Matthias' voice quavered as he spoke, and it was so high and tight it was almost unrecognizable as his. She turned to look at him. He was pale green and appeared on the verge of vomiting. She whipped her head back to the magistrate.

"And you are?"

Jacob cut in. "He is her brother and therefore not to be trusted. The whole family is suspect. If she needs a guardian until she hangs, I will make the sacrifice and do it."

Daniel inclined forward, clearly poised to lunge for him and tear his flesh from his bones, and she was tempted to join him. She never trusted Jacob and always felt guilty for it. No more.

It would be better to hang with Daniel than to live under Jacob's thumb.

Her belly fluttered.

Oh heavens, was she quickening? She put her hand to her belly, and there was movement. Her baby. Hers and Daniel's. Her eyes sought his, and he was staring at her hand, then he looked up to her face. He was blurring through her tears, but she gave him a nod. Hopefully, he would read it right. She would do whatever she needed to do to protect their child.

"Very well," the magistrate gestured to Jacob, "you are her guardian until such a time as she is delivered of her child and hangs. The child shall be yours to raise as you see fit or put to the charge of the town."

The magistrate gathered his papers and stuffed them into his satchel, and the men of the settlement began to shuffle their feet and angle toward the door now the show was over.

Apparently, she was no longer the greater threat, and the constable went to grab Daniel's arm. Without ceremony or words, he hauled Daniel through the crowd and off, presumably, to the gaol.

Oh lord, would they let her see him again? Talk to him? They had to. The bread she broke her fast with threatened to spill from her guts.

Her heart was breaking into a thousand pieces.

She had been a fool to rely on anyone, and she would not make that mistake again as she figured out how to provide for their child. She would do it.

Jacob took hold of her arm, and she tried to wrench it free.

"Think again, sister. You are coming home with me."

The glint in his eye was demonic.

Her blood ran cold.

22

The gaol was dark, with the window shuttered and barred. Slivers of light crept in around the cracks in the shutter, but when it was full day outside, it was, at best, dusk inside.

Daniel chewed his bread and cheese. The constable's wife was an excellent cook, at least, and the bread was fresh and soft.

Of course, he had to pay for it. And for his lodging while he was locked up, and any debt from his incarceration would be passed on to Ruth and then to their child. Their child, whom the court had effectively given to Jacob to keep in perpetual service.

His heart labored to do its job. They were going to have a child.

And she hadn't told him.

But he had been so sure he could keep them safe, and he had been so very wrong that he wouldn't have told himself either. What was the point? He wouldn't be there to support them. She had figured that out long before he did.

He swallowed his last bite of bread, but it got stuck at the growing lump in his throat, and he coughed until he could get it to go down.

He had been so sure that he would be a good warden, a good selectman, and a good husband. Because he knew the rules. But none of it mattered. The rules were a fiction.

He let his head fall into his hands.

He had failed.

Wood sliding against wood. The constable must be sliding the bar from the outside of his door.

He raised his head, which weighed more than it used to.

The door opened, and he raised his arm to shield his eyes from the sudden increase in light.

The constable set down a jar of water. Then he gestured to the chamber pot. The man would not let Daniel be between him and the door.

Daniel almost laughed.

"I'm innocent." He handed the constable the chamber pot to empty.

The constable just grunted at him, took the chamber pot, and left, closing the door behind him.

In the renewed darkness, the bar sliding into its brackets to block the door was louder than it ought to have been.

His eyes took a moment to adjust to the return of darkness.

It wasn't the constable's place to judge people, and he was just doing his duty. Following the rules and keeping order.

Rules and order.

Were they divine?

He paced the small cell. He had been so focused on rooting out witchcraft, but perhaps witchcraft had never been the issue.

Ruth had tried to tell him.

His feet stopped. He couldn't make them move forward, and he squatted down and curled into a ball. His arms covered his head as if they could somehow protect him from realizing he was partly responsible for distracting the town's focus from the real trouble.

He grasped his hair in his fists and pulled. He was so stupid. The war had gone poorly for them, and he and everyone else had grasped at reasons outside themselves for their suffering. They had been so high and mighty, and they had gotten land greed and tried to take everything. And they had paid for it.

He groaned, and the sound echoed off the empty walls with no one to hear it. He pounded his fists against his skull. The arrogance. He had been perfectly willing to believe that Goody Carter had witched Cook's hogs even though Cook was a sanctimonious horse's arse. They had all been deprived, and they all felt they deserved retribution.

His heart pounded, and the sound echoed in his head. Everything echoed and came back to him tenfold.

He had been willing to take their collective frustration out on a defenseless widow just so that they would have an answer. Someone to punish for their pain. He almost laughed. Goody Carter had proven she was not so defenseless, thank goodness. She was wily. And she was a good friend to Ruth.

The still air pressed in on him, making it hard to breathe.

He stood and paced again, kicking the thin blanket that made his sleeping palette.

Ruth showed him what an unfair situation they created by making a defense against witchcraft impossible.

His face grew hot with shame. He had been a major driver of this horror in the settlement.

Arrogance, arrogance, and more arrogance.

He had reaped what he had sewn when the town turned on him for trying to uphold the treaty. They followed his exact line of thinking. When you have to give something up, blame others and punish them. Channel all of your frustration onto someone else.

He flopped onto the disarrayed blanket so hard the floor shook, causing yet another echo. The sound mocked him. He laid the trap for others and had been caught in it himself because he was blinded by his own sense of virtue. What an arse he was.

He breathed hard in the dark room and let the air move through his body, clearing out the stale corners.

Enough wallowing. He had to do something to fix some of his mess.

He had to save Ruth and their child. He stood and paced again. Then he stopped. His face inches from the wall. He tapped it with his fingers as he thought.

She could run.

Why had that never occurred to him before?

He almost smacked his forehead but started pacing again, his feet unable to stay still.

He would hang in a matter of days, but she had been granted a reprieve for the belly, and that meant she had time. For once, he could not let her down.

He went to the door and banged on it. Then he resumed pacing. He needed to talk with her. Convince her to go.

He banged on the door again. The constable had to hear him, and he had to help him. If the constable could bring Ruth to him, he could convince her to flee.

But he had to figure out a plan so she would have resources. She couldn't just fly into the wilderness, pregnant and alone. She would have nothing to eat, no shelter, no protection.

He pounded his fists against his forehead. *Think.*

She could arm herself, thanks to powder and shot stores in the garrison house.

But it was winter. She would be freezing.

If only Matthias could hide her until she gave birth, but even if he was willing, that would never work. They would be found out.

His feet traced the circumference of the room. He pounded again on the door. "Constable!"

Could she shoot? Well enough to hunt? He had never asked. He had always assumed the order of things was that he would do the hunting and she wouldn't need to. What a foolish notion of order.

She had no relatives that he knew of in Massachusetts other than Matthias, here in Maine. And her sentence would be law anywhere under the Massachusetts jurisdiction, so neither Maine nor Massachusetts would do, anyway. She might be able to make it to New York, but he knew no one there.

At last, the bar slid against the door.

He lunged for the door as the constable opened it, and then he yelped in pain. He forgot to shield his eyes, and the light burned them.

The constable was ready, expecting to be rushed.

Daniel flapped his hand at the man. "I am not trying to escape, man, but I need to see my wife." He squinted, trying to make eye contact. The constable was married. He could hear the man's large family bustling on the other side of the door.

He softened his tone. "Please. I have only days before I hang. I need to see my wife."

The constable was unmoved. "She is under house arrest until she can be hanged. She cannot come."

"Have some compassion. May I not pray with her and say goodbye before my sentence?" His voice hitched, and it wasn't theater. Apart from plotting her escape, he would be saying goodbye. His chest constricted as he tried to push that thought away.

"That is not permitted."

The man ripped Daniel's guts out with his words.

Fucking rules and order. This was all it brought them.

"Please." He tried one last time.

The constable shifted his weight and hesitated. Daniel looked into his eyes, willing him to exercise the compassion that he wanted to.

"I'm sorry, Goodman Kendrick. The law says no."

He turned and went, barring the door against pity.

Daniel almost collapsed.

But he had wallowed in self-pity long enough and refused to do it any longer. He had to make this right.

"She is with child, and a man should not have to tend to her." Goody Carter's voice chirped from the other side of the door.

Ruth stood from the stool she had been sitting on in the tiny back storage room of Jacob's house. He was taking her house arrest seriously, and she had not left this tiny room since her sentencing. He hadn't even pretended to a familial care.

"When was the last time she was permitted to empty her chamber pot?"

The stench filled the room. He seemed to think once a day was sufficient.

He had never been pregnant.

Goody Carter was a godsend. "Fear not, Goodman Turner. I shall take care of her womanly and inconvenient needs."

The door opened, and Goody Carter slipped in and closed the door behind her. Ruth threw her arms around the woman and sobbed. She had never cried so much in her life. But if being sentenced to death and her husband to hang first wasn't something to cry about, nothing was.

Goody Carter stroked her hair and patted her back and didn't tell her to stop weeping.

They stood like that for many minutes. At last, Ruth pushed herself up straight and wiped her eyes. She had to be strong.

"I need to save my baby. I can't let it grow up under Jacob's foot." She looked at the older woman, who nodded her assent. "I have to run away."

"I know you do. First, you need to eat some good food." She handed her two boiled eggs, then she turned to the stool and pushed Ruth toward it. "Sit."

Ruth sat, and Goody Carter stood next to her. That wasn't right. "Here," she stood, "you sit. I can stand."

"Nonsense. You are the one with child. You need to sit."

She didn't have the energy to argue. She sat. How would she ever have the energy to escape and make a new life for herself and her baby?

She would find the energy. There was no other option.

"I have to leave Massachusetts, or they will just hang me if they find me." That meant a long journey, which meant she had to start soon. "I can't wait until the worst of winter passes, or I will be too ponderous to escape." Her voice sounded flat to her own ears.

Goody Carter moved behind her and started to take the pins out of Ruth's hair until it fell loose. Then she combed it out.

No one had done that for her since her mother died. Tears welled up in her eyes, and she let her friend take care of her for a moment. She had been taking care of herself for so long, and now she had a baby coming whom she had to take care of. She was used to caring for others in the short term as she healed them, but this would be an entirely different level of care. Everything she did with her life from hereon in had to include the care of this vulnerable new person she carried.

She set the eggs down, and her hands went to her belly. Time to focus.

Goody Carter wound her hair back into a knot and pinned it. "I have a cousin in New York," she said around the pins in her mouth. "She will help."

That offer was tempting. But she would be at the mercy of this cousin, and she did not know if she could count on her. The only person she had ever been able to count on was herself.

Tears welled up again. "No, I can't let you put yourself in jeopardy like that. I couldn't bear it if they found out and came for you."

"I'm old. There isn't much they can do to me that time will not do soon, anyway."

Ruth spun toward her. "Don't say that." She would never even know if they came for Goody Carter. That thought stole her breath.

Goody Carter didn't push. She just turned Ruth back around to face away from her. "You can support yourself doctoring folks, but people need to know you first, and you can't make a reputation for yourself until after this baby is born." She was stroking Ruth's shoulders from behind, pushing on the tightest muscles.

The pressure from her hands was soothing. She wanted to just lean into it.

But she had to figure this out. Two lives were at stake.

"I think Rhode Island will be the most open to my services." Everyone spoke of Rhode Island like it was Satan's front room, but Rhode Island was safe for Quakers and other dissenters, so it would be safe for a doctoress.

"How will you survive until the child is born? Who will tend you?"

She could manage everything except that by herself. No matter how she calculated it, she could find no simple answer. Only one painful one. "I can put myself out to service." It would mean losing what remained of her autonomy, but for her child, she would do it. At least she would have more say over her life than she would if she was hanged.

"Sweet child." Goody Carter came around in front of her and knelt down. "People will be very reluctant to hire on a woman who is breeding, especially one who shows up with no husband. They will fear you are loose."

Her back straightened, and she lifted her chin. "I am no such thing."

"Of course not, dear, but what will you tell them? That you are a fugitive from the law? That won't help your cause."

"I won't lie. I will just tell them I am a widow. We have been through years of war. How can they question that?"

And by then, it would be true.

Oh God.

Tears spilled from her eyes, and she doubled over and wept. Her breath came in painful rasps, and the sound of her wails filled the tiny room. Her entire body shook from head to foot, and her limbs wouldn't function.

Time faded, and her head swam. Each sob drained her of air, and she could barely suck in more before the next sob choked her further. Her vision was blotchy, and the room lost its firm outlines.

She was going to die. Right there.

But she couldn't die without saying goodbye to Daniel. She loved him.

The reality of that smacked her right between the eyes. She loved him, and she didn't want to live without him.

But she had to.

She gulped in a breath. And then another. She had to live and raise their baby. And she had to do it far from here.

But she had to see him.

"I need your help."

Goody Carter's eyes widened with shock. She might just as well have slapped her across the face with a dead fish. "You will let me help?" The woman gave her a wink and chuckled.

A little snort of air escaped Ruth's nose. "Yes, I know." Then her smile faded. "I need to see him before I go. I don't know how to do it without making them double their guard."

A devilish gleam sparked in Goody Cater's eye. "I finally have a chance to repay your kindnesses, and now you will get to see the heights of my genius." She winked at her.

"The constable's wife owes me for some coneflower, and I think she will help us."

Ruth leaned in toward her. "Are you sure? Won't she be afraid people will talk if the constable's wife was found out to have helped a prisoner?"

Goody Carter gave a wry snort. "I know things she would much prefer not to have the town know. Helping a pregnant wife talk with her condemned husband before he hangs is nothing."

Both of their smiles faded. Daniel was scheduled to die in just four days.

Drawing breath took all of her strength.

Someone pounded on the door.

Her nerves were too spent to even flinch.

Goody Carter raised her voice to be heard through the door. "I am almost done tending to her. Be careful to stand back. My hands are none too steady these days, and I don't want to drop the chamber pot."

She turned back to Ruth. "You be strong and leave this to me."

Ruth tried to stand, but Good Carter pushed her back down onto the stool. Any other day, she could have out-muscled the older woman, but she was wrung out and fell back onto the stool like a sack of corn.

Goody Carter picked up the over-full chamber pot. "You just be ready. It may take a day or two, but I will get you in to see Daniel and back here before that big mule knows you are gone."

She stepped to the door. "Would you be so kind, Goodman Turner, as to open the door? I need both hands." She turned and winked at Ruth and said in a voice that wouldn't carry through the door, "I'll try not to let it slosh too much for Goody Turner's sake."

The door opened wide, and Jacob stood well back to be clear of Goody Carter's path.

"Thank you so kindly, Goodman Turner. I will come back to tend her tomorrow so that you and your family are not burdened by this dirty work."

She disappeared into the house, and the door slammed shut.

Goody Carter was good to her word. She would get her in to see Daniel somehow.

And then Ruth would have to figure out how to say goodbye.

23

Daniel ran his fingertips over the surface of the wall, feeling the notches in the wood. No doubt some were carved intentionally, but some had to be from frustrated inmates hurling objects against it.

He had already hurled his blankets at it and was itching for something more solid and satisfying to send flying.

Time lost its shape and consistency at an alarming rate when you were confined in a small, dark room with only your thoughts for company.

And Ruth had been confined in this very room awaiting her trial.

He doubled over to catch his breath, which flew out of him as if someone had kicked him in the gut. How could they have treated her like that? How could he have been part of that system for so long?

At least she was in Jacob's household for now.

That had to be better. He couldn't bear for it to be otherwise.

He straightened with a groan.

All along, he had thought Jacob was their friend. And he *had* been Ruth's brother-in-law. And after biding his time so patiently, he turned on them with the speed of a copperhead.

Perhaps he had gotten caught up in the hysteria and repented now. As long as that led to him treating Ruth well, he would forgive the man. Anything for Ruth to be relieved of some of the misery he could not save her from. Had helped bring down upon her, if he was being honest.

A noise beyond the door sounded loud in the room's silence. Loud enough, thank heavens, to drown out his thoughts for a moment.

The constable was shite for company, but if he didn't hear another human voice soon, the demons in his head might win the day.

Not that there was anything they could do to him that wouldn't be ended in a few day's time.

He focused on the sounds from the room beyond the door. Anything to keep his mind from the dark places it wanted to go.

The door latch clicked, and the metallic sound made him flinch because it contrasted so sharply with the smooth murmurs of speech he had been hearing.

He wiped his palms against his trousers and readied himself to shield his eyes.

A sliver of light burst through the small crack between the door and its frame as the door opened just enough for someone small to slip in, and then it closed.

But the constable's children were only a few years old, and their parents would never have let them near the gaol.

"Daniel?"

Daniel fisted his hands in his hair. He was going mad. It sounded like Ruth's voice.

Whoever it was mocking him stood in the silence as their eyes adjusted.

Daniel didn't trust his voice. He didn't want to take his fury out on a small child when it was his own mind playing tricks on him. It wasn't the child's fault. He couldn't let the demons win.

Then, there was a little cry, and the small body hurled itself into his arms.

He almost screamed in agony. The body even felt like Ruth's.

The faint smell of roses wafted up his nose and registered in his brain.

He grabbed her by the shoulders and pushed her away just enough to stare into her face in the dim light. "Please tell me you aren't a trick of my brain."

"I'm not, I'm here." It was Ruth's voice.

He grabbed her so tight she grunted as he forced the air out of her lungs, but her arms wrapped just as tightly around him.

They clung to each other for what could have been seconds or hours. The feel of her body against his brought a peace that he wouldn't have ever again.

He forced his arms to loosen, and he gave her a kiss. Time was not their friend.

"Did Jacob bring you?"

Her body tensed in his arms. "He has kept me locked in his back room."

His vision went red, even in the dark of the room. "The bloody bastard." What an idiot he was to have thought maybe Jacob would find a way to appeal her sentence.

Or at least protect their child. But their child would be under Jacob's control, to do with as pleased.

Jacob repenting and protecting Ruth and their child was the only thing that gave him any hope over the last few days. And that was not going to happen.

His breathing slowed, and something deep inside him shifted. It was as if the rules they lived by no longer made sense or even applied.

"How did you get here?"

"Goody Carter helped me come, but the constable's wife isn't happy."

That meant time was even less their friend. And he was going to wring everything out of it he could.

He took her by the shoulders. He could see her face in the gloom now that his eyes had readjusted after the slash of light when she came in. "You have to escape. You have to stay alive." He spoke in low tones so the constable's wife outside the door could not hear. All his life he had followed the rules, but nothing could be clearer to him right now than the truth of those words.

She gave a quick inhale. "I know." But her voice was small as she spoke. Like she was reluctant.

He took her face in his hands and ran his thumbs over her cheeks. "I am so sorry." He pressed his forehead against hers. "I have failed you so catastrophically. But only I should pay for that. Not you." He kissed her. "And not our child."

She took a few deep breaths, and her shoulders drew back as she straightened and stood taller. "I will go to Rhode Island. I can support the baby by doctoring. They are not as closed-minded about such things there."

That was his Ruth.

"Can Goody Carter gather provisions for you?" His whisper sounded loud in his own ears.

Ruth started, then grabbed his hand and placed it on her belly, which was convulsing. "Are you alright?" She couldn't miscarry. She couldn't. That life was too important. And it was what granted the time to save hers. Panic rose in his throat, and he tried to bring her to his palette to lie down.

She rooted her feet to the ground. "That's the baby. Kicking."

His breath stopped. He pressed his hand against her belly again.

The baby kicked him squarely in the palm of his hand.

A sob broke from his throat before he could stop it. This precious little person was his flesh and blood. At least something of him would live on.

He bent and pressed his cheek to her belly. The baby kicked him in the eye. It was a fighter, thank goodness.

He had to get Ruth to safety. Protect both her and the baby. Someday, their child could carry on his failed duty and protect her in her old age. Because she would live to ripe old age. She had to.

He straightened and held her face in his hands again. "Matthias and Goody Carter are the first people Jacob will haul into court when you go. He will tear their houses apart to find you. Go to the Penobscot."

They respected her and valued her doctoring. Please let the corn be enough for them to think well enough of him to be willing to take the risk.

She was silent.

"Stay with them until you can escape. With great good luck, you can stay with them until you are delivered of the baby."

"Yes." She kissed him. "Jacob would be too concerned they would force him to pay his bushel of corn to go near the Penobscot."

He traced her face with his fingers. Its outlines were forever engraved on his heart, but if he didn't feel them, imagine he could see them clearly, then his heart would crack open. This might be his last opportunity.

Her sob filled the room as she wrapped her arms around him and grabbed him to her. She drenched his chest with tears, and he pressed his face to the top of her head, his own tears soaking her hair.

"I don't want to leave you." Her voice was muffled and broken.

No one had ever particularly cared whether they left him. And somehow, despite his failing her so spectacularly, she did.

"Go." He tilted her head back and pressed his forehead against hers. "Live. I can bear being punished for my failures, but you hanging for my sins would be a thousandfold worse than my own death." He kissed her. "Ruth, promise me you will survive. Go before I hang so that I can at least go to the gallows knowing you are safely away from here."

The door swung open, and they both started, even though they had been whispering and couldn't have been overheard.

"You have to go. My husband is coming, and I cannot risk you being seen." The constable's wife sounded near panic.

He clung to Ruth, kissing her.

"Now," the woman hissed. She must have grabbed Ruth's arm because Ruth was yanked from his embrace, and before his eyes had had time to adjust to the light, the door slammed, and the bar banged into its brackets, and he was plunged into darkness such as he had never experienced.

Ruth ran to the edge of the woods nearest the constable's house. Her legs weren't steady, but she plunged into the security of the trees and undergrowth. She kept running.

Branches tugged at her skirts, and tears blurred her vision, but her legs kept pushing her deeper into the trees. Her lungs burned. Whether from running or sobbing, there was no way to know.

Her skirt caught fast to a thorn bush, and she was forced to stop to work it free. Her fingers felt a tear in the fabric that her eyes were still too blurred to make out clearly. She worked the fabric with numb fingers, but it wouldn't give. She was shackled to the bush.

Her heart pounded harder than when she was running, and she yanked with all her strength. The fabric ripped, and she stared at the large hole in her skirt. She could never mend that.

Her knees buckled, and she sank to the ground. She couldn't mend anything. Everything was rent beyond repair. Her head fell into her hands, but no tears came. They were used up. She was used up.

She breathed into her hands. Daniel's scent was there. Pine and lye soap.

Her nose savored that small comfort. But she couldn't afford to linger.

She tucked her feet underneath herself and forced her legs to lever her up off the frozen ground.

The wind howled in the bare branches of the trees, and she shivered. She pulled the cloak Goody Carter had brought her more tightly around herself.

The sun, blurred by a blanket of gray, wasn't yet overhead. The selectmen's meeting, she knew from experience, would go on for hours yet.

It was time to find Marie before they missed her at Jacob's house.

She pushed further through the trees until she came to the trail, where she could make better time.

Around the first bend, she pulled up short. There were three men and Marie heading toward the town.

Marie rushed to her side. "What has happened to you?" The Penobscot woman wrapped an arm around her.

A laugh burst from Ruth's lips. What hadn't happened? The absurdity of it was more than she could bear.

Marie pulled her further from the men. She pulled something from Ruth's hair and ran her eyes over Ruth's body. "You are with child."

Everyone could tell that at a glance, and she hadn't even been certain herself until a few weeks ago. She was the least natural woman alive.

"We will take you back to the town."

Ruth's gaze snapped back to Marie. "No." She paused. Then she stepped off the cliff. "I need your help."

Marie searched her face, looking for signs of madness, no doubt. They shouldn't be hard to find.

Ruth's limbs trembled. Asking for Marie's help felt like handing her life over. But she had to. There was no way she could do this alone. She could not, would not, risk her baby.

She took a deep breath and then let the words fly. "My husband and I have both been convicted of witchcraft. My husband will hang in a few days, and I have to escape before the baby arrives, and I hang, too."

One of Marie's eyebrows rose, but that was her only reaction.

"You are the only people we trust to help." She studied Marie's face for any further reaction.

The woman just returned her gaze.

Ruth's hope ebbed.

"I am sorry." Her shoulders drooped. "I shouldn't have asked. I will find a way without dragging you into my troubles." The Penobscot had enough tension with the settlement without being asked to harbor a fugitive from justice.

"You can't."

Oh yes, she could. Her head came up. Then she stopped. Marie was calling over one of the men.

She had overstepped. She should go.

But she was exhausted, and thinking she could outrun the men was foolish.

Marie and the older man spoke in their language. The man scowled. He shook his head and gestured toward the town. Marie's voice grew more animated, and she gestured toward the other men and then back at Ruth.

Then she turned back to Ruth.

"I cannot promise what my people will do for you. That has to go to the Sagamore. But my mother was born a Narragansett, and I have a cousin who will shelter you."

A Narragansett. They had been a reluctant but significant part of the war and had not fared well. This was hopeless. "They are starving. I would just speed that process."

Marie rolled her eyes. "You are in a far more precarious position than they are. And they could use your skills to help them survive the winter. Too many Narragansett healers died during the war."

If she could help, that would change everything.

Almost everything.

A tear spilled over her lashes. Daniel would still hang. She would be doing this without him. She couldn't. She didn't want to.

She wouldn't.

The cold air seared that realization into her lungs with each breath.

She turned to Marie. "I can't go without Daniel."

Marie's eyes went wide.

"You have been so kind. But I cannot go without him."

Marie narrowed her eyes. "Is this what he wants?"

"No. He wants me to be safe. The baby to be safe." She looked into Marie's eyes, trying to plumb her soul. "But how can I let him die while I run away?"

Tears began flowing down her face, freezing on her cheeks, but she had never been so certain of anything in her life. And if Marie couldn't help. She would find another way.

They would live or die together.

Her mind started working through ideas that wouldn't come before but now offered themselves.

"If we both come to you, will you ask the Sagamore if we can stay? Just until we can avoid detection and then head south to Rhode Island?"

Marie's brows wrinkled together like she was trying to parse out a foreign language.

"If you can't, I understand. We can head for the shore and try to find passage with fishermen."

The men had all come closer and were listening. They started talking among themselves, and Marie turned to listen.

Then she turned back. "Did the man Cook cause this?"

"He accused us both." That didn't seem relevant.

The men started talking again. They appeared to be arguing. Then, one said something that put an end to the gesticulating, and they appeared to be in reluctant agreement.

The men didn't seem interested in telling her what they had decided, but Marie turned back to her. "We cannot do something that will put our entire village in the way of danger without the Sagamore's consent."

Very well, she would find another way. "I understand." She turned to head back to town.

Marie tugged at her cloak. "We will ask him. You helped his family. He might say yes."

Her heart leapt. Relying on 'mights' and 'maybes' from others sent her stomach spiraling, but saving Daniel was worth the risk.

"We will send word." Marie started to turn away, then turned back. "How are you free when you are to die? How can we find you?"

"Goody Carter helped me slip out to see Daniel. I have to get back before I am discovered." Ruth glanced at the sky. The sun was now past its peak. "I am being held at my brother-in-law's house, but you can get word to me by Goody Carter. She is the only person he allows in."

Her chest tightened at the thought of putting Goody Carter at risk. She turned back to Marie. "No, I can't...." But she could. Maybe not for herself, but for Daniel, she would risk all. "Yes, send word by Goody Carter."

"We will help you back before you are missed."

"No, I can make it."

Marie tut-tutted her like she was a child.

"It wasn't a question."

Ruth's mouth opened to reply, but the men started scouting ahead, and Marie took her arm and led her down the path toward the town. They got to the woods nearest Jacob's house with nothing to waylay them.

Marie turned to her. "I do not know the Sagamore's mood. I cannot say what he will decide. But we will send word."

Ruth nodded and turned away. Then, her gratitude for the hope Marie brought made her turn back and fling her arms around the other woman. No one had ever offered to risk anything for her.

Marie extricated herself from Ruth's embrace, and her cheeks were flushed, no doubt with embarrassment over Ruth's unseemly display. "We will try." Marie stepped back, and they retreated further into the woods.

24

Daniel sat on his palette in the dark room. The room stank of piss from the chamber pot and of sweat. They hadn't given him enough to eat to add shite to that mix today.

He rubbed his hands over his face. It was damp with fruitless tears. Ruth was the most resourceful person he had ever known. She would get herself to the Penobscot and then to Rhode Island. She would.

He banged his forehead against his fists. There had to be some way he could get her resources, but his land would be forfeit since he was a convicted witch. And it would go to Jacob. At least Ruth's plot would, since it had been his brother's, and Jacob was officially an aggrieved party in the case.

There was no point in wasting energy on Jacob. He spat anyway.

Voices sounded outside the door.

He jumped to his feet.

The door latch clicked, and he readied his arm to block the light.

The door opened wide, and he threw his arm over his eyes.

"Just knock when you are done." It was the constable's voice. Who was he leaving in the cell?

Daniel squinted at his visitor. "Matthias?"

"Yes," Matthias said, then he paused. "Sorry, I didn't come sooner."

"I'm allowed visitors?" Only Ruth had been to visit, and that had been thoroughly illegal.

Matthias shifted from one foot to the other and fussed with his hat in his hands. "I just wanted to say I'm sorry that I didn't speak up for you two in your trials. I know they wouldn't have listened to me, and it might have made things worse instead of better, but it feels wrong." He still wasn't looking at Daniel.

Matthias was right, but it didn't matter. Pouring over what-ifs took time, and that was something thing he didn't have. "I need your help."

Matthias stared at him, his forehead puckered in confusion.

Daniel leaned close and whispered. "Ruth needs to escape."

Matthias' jaw dropped, and no words came out of his open mouth.

"And she needs to go soon, before she is any heavier with child or the winter gets worse."

Now Mathias' mouth was opening and closing like he kept trying to say something. Judging by his wide eyes and arms shoved toward Daniel, he was trying to find words to protest.

"She needs resources."

"She has been sentenced." Matthias stared at him now. "You tried to have her sentenced just last summer."

"Yes, I know this is my fault." His chest hurt just thinking about it. "But she doesn't deserve to hang for my mistakes."

Matthias was scratching his neck like it would help him somehow make sense of this. There was no sense to be made. But there were things to do and little time to do them.

"I know she can't go to you or to Goody Carter. They would just haul you all into court and still hang her."

Matthias relaxed just a fraction. "I can't take her in."

"I just said that. I told her to go the Penobscot."

Now Matthias rubbed his hands through his hair until it stuck out in all directions. "But how did you talk with her?"

"She was—" But there wasn't time to explain. "Can you get in to see her?"

"I don't know."

He hadn't even tried to go see his sister. Punching him would be so satisfying right now, but no time. "You need to go see her and figure out how to help her get to the Penobscot village without being tracked."

"She can't go on the run from the law. She is a convicted witch." Matthias' whisper choked on the final word.

Daniel threw his hands in the air. "Do you honestly think your sister is a witch?"

Matthias groaned. "I thought I could protect her by getting her married to you so that you could keep her in line." He stared hard at Daniel.

They both knew that was Daniel's duty as her husband. A duty he had spectacularly and publicly failed to perform.

Not that anyone ever could have. "Have you even met your sister?"

Matthias looked at him hard, then snorted out a laugh. Matthias never laughed. "Fair point, I suppose." Matthias's laughter died out, and he sighed. "But it would have been worse if she had become Jacob's ward."

"Worse? She is sentenced to hang." There was no worse.

"She would have been sentenced to hang for murder within a week if Jacob was her guardian, and she wouldn't have been pregnant to give her a few extra months." Matthias looked Daniel in the eye. "At least you managed to figure out that part."

"Fuck you."

Matthias gave a wan smile. "Jacob is already planning what he will do with Ruth's land."

Daniel's head snapped up. He could get resources to Ruth. "She doesn't have any land. I do. But I don't have any land because I sold it to you right before our trial."

"No, you didn't."

Daniel stared hard at Matthias. "Yes. I did. I sold you the garrison house, its farm, and the land Ruth brought that was her first husband's."

"Was I drinking?" Matthias didn't drink.

He grabbed Matthias by the shoulders. "Look, anything I own is forfeit because of my conviction, and Ruth can't inherit it anyway because of hers. No way in hell am I letting Jacob take that land."

Matthias leaned away from Daniel as far as he could get without yanking out of Daniel's grip. "You know that is all he has wanted since before Ruth married his brother?"

Daniel pasted on a big smile. "You can be magnanimous and sell it to him for a fair price if you like." He tightened his grip on Matthias' shoulders. "Just get the money to her so she can survive."

Matthias recoiled like Daniel had handed him a decayed squirrel corpse. "How would I do that?"

Don't hit him. "Go see her. She will figure it out." Clearly, Ruth had inherited the family's entire quota of ingenuity.

Even in the dim light, Matthias was paler.

"Don't tell me you aren't willing to go visit your sister. Do not tell me that if you want to leave this room alive."

Matthias flung Daniel's hands off his shoulders like they were flies. "You couldn't kill me if you tried." He was still pale. "Her, I'm less sure of."

She could, but she wouldn't. "She loves you. Despite your being a giant arse."

"She has to. I'm her brother." Matthias paused. "The crazy thing is she loves you, too."

They looked at each other for a long moment. Neither spoke.

Matthias raised his arms in surrender. "Who witnessed you selling me your property?"

Shite. "Goody Carter?"

Matthias lowered his eyebrows, then closed his eyes entirely. "Maybe if Anne was there too...." He shook his head, and then Daniel's eyes got glassy. Anne could write, so she could write up the documents and they wouldn't be in Matthias' hand. "I'm just trying to keep my family safe and out of trouble."

Who couldn't relate to that? But Ruth and the baby were his family, too. "I'm trying to keep mine alive to have the opportunity to get into trouble."

"I hate you."

Daniel reached his hand out.

Matthias started at it, clearly debating, and then he grasped it, looking like he had just cast his lot with the Devil.

"Thank you." Daniel's voice caught. "She has to escape. She has to."

"What did I pay you for the farms?"

"Not enough, you stingy bastard." He chuckled. It was that or weep. "Just get what you can for her land and get it to her. You have my farm free and clear to do with as you please." He dashed tears from his cheek. "And you have my eternal gratitude."

They stood in silence. The silence grew awkward.

"Please go to her today."

Matthias nodded, but then he hesitated. "I have to protect Anne and the children. But I can try to cause a distraction of some kind. Give her a head start."

A sob of gratitude rose in Daniel's throat. He clamped his jaw shut to keep a second one from escaping. He stared at the ceiling and tried to breathe. After a few long moments, he risked looking at Matthias again. "She will figure it out." They both smiled. "Just give her a fighting chance."

Matthias nodded.

"And for the love of all that is holy, get her some money so that she can set herself up far, far from here and raise our child...." His voice cracked on that last word, and he gave up.

Matthias clapped his hand on Daniel's shoulder and then turned toward the door and raised his voice to a normal register. "I'm ready."

After a moment, the door opened, and Matthias left. The door closed behind him, and Daniel was alone again.

And he was going to die alone. She had to go while they were still focused on him. But she would go, and she would live.

He went to his palette and lay down, exhausted. He had done what he could, and now there was nothing to do but hang.

"Matthias!" Ruth launched herself at her brother and threw her arms around him before Jacob had even closed the door after him.

She let herself hold him tight for a few seconds before pushing him to arm's length and whispering, "I need your help."

He groaned quietly. "I will do what I can." Then he looked at her with his head cocked to the side. "You have never asked me for help in our entire lives. You wait until it could get me arrested to ask?"

She smiled and then stuck her tongue out at him.

He groaned again. "You two are going to be the death of me."

Her head snapped up. "Have you seen Daniel?" Her voice rose in pitch, though she managed to control the volume.

Matthias glanced at the closed door, then leaned in. "Are you really going to escape?"

Her hand went to her belly. "I have to." She willed him to understand. "I can't let my baby be born into service and become an outcast because of something I didn't do."

"It wouldn't be an outcast."

They both knew better. "It was bad enough being the child of someone who was acquitted." She worked hard not to roll her eyes at him. Denial had always been one of his favorite defenses.

His eyes dropped to the floor. "You could try to appeal."

She snorted. "I could try. And when they denied the appeal, it would be too late to escape."

His head drooped. "I told Daniel I can't endanger Anne and the children. I can try to create a distraction when you need it. But that's all."

For Matthias, it was a good start. But it would not be enough. "I am going to need more from you than a distraction."

"If you send word where the Penobscot take you, I can send money. I arranged that with Daniel." He was running his hands through his hair, which looked like it hadn't seen a comb in weeks. "I just have to figure out how to do it without breaking the law."

She put her hand on his giant shoulder. "There is no way to do it without breaking the law. Thank you. We will need it."

His eyes tracked to her belly.

She took a deep breath. Relying on anyone other than herself was making her stomach do flips, and every moment made it more complicated and more likely to fail.

Maybe she should just sneak out and start running. She wouldn't be putting anyone else in danger, and there were fewer people who could ruin everything.

She studied her brother. He only ever wanted to be left alone to live his life. And she was asking him to put his family, everything, in jeopardy for her.

He stuffed his hands in his pockets, pulled out a leather pouch, and shoved it at her. "Take it."

The leather was soft in her hands, well worn, and warm from being in his pocket. It also jingled when she took it.

Her eyes shot to his.

"It isn't much, but it will at least let you buy food on the road." The toe of his shoe traced the edge of the floorboard. "If you send word, I'll try to get more to you when I have it."

Her eyes blurred with tears. "I hate to take this. But thank you. We will need it." She didn't reach for him. He might shrug her off. She gave him a watery smile. "I look forward to the day that my child gets to meet its very kind uncle."

His eyes went wide like the thought frightened him.

She sighed. "Don't worry. We will find a way to do that without putting you or your family in danger of legal trouble."

He blushed. "I want to meet your baby, too. I just—"

"I know." She stepped up to him and put her arms around his colossal form again, hugging him close. He had always tried to protect her in his own awkward and misguided way. Bringing him more stress and fear felt awful. But it had to be done, and who knew how long she had before he had to go, so it had to be done now.

She tilted her head all the way back in order to look into his face as he towered over her. "I can't leave without Daniel."

Relief softened his face for an instant. Then the look was replaced by sheer panic as he realized she didn't mean she wasn't going. "You... what...?"

She held him tight and nodded at him. "I need you to help me get Daniel out so we can escape together."

He pushed her away. "That is not what Daniel said was your plan. He said nothing about escaping himself. He said he wanted to die knowing you were safe." Panic and confusion battled across his face, but somehow, he managed to keep his voice low.

His hands dug into her shoulders, where he held her as he processed what she had said.

"I can't let him die."

"You can't stop it."

"I can't live without him." And that was the truth of the matter. She had never let herself need anybody, but somehow, he had snuck into her heart and anchored himself so firmly there that his removal would kill her. "I don't even want to."

Her body shook from that admission, and the room was blurry from the tears spilling unchecked from her eyes.

"I have never asked anything from you in our entire lives. I ask you this. Please help me get him out so we can flee together."

His face was ashen. "But what if you get caught?"

"I don't know." She shook her head. There was no "if" that she could process other than getting him out and getting away from the town that had consumed their lives and spat them back out, mangled and left for dead. Even better would be if Matthias would join them, but reality cut in at that idea. He would never survive life outside the law. It wasn't who he was, and that she couldn't ask of him. But she needed Daniel. "I need your help."

Matthias swayed on his feet and then turned and found her stool. He sat down hard. "Anne. My children." He looked at her, eyes pleading.

"Matthias. I need your help."

His head dropped and hung from his shoulders like a dead weight. "Do you have a plan?"

She went to him, dropped to her knees, and flung her arms around him yet again. Her arms barely made it around his waist, and her cheek was crushed against his belly. "I love you, big brother."

He looked down at her. "I haven't said I will help."

But he would. Because she had no other option, he had to. Without letting go of her hold on him, she explained she was waiting for word from the Penobscot if they could help her to Rhode Island with Marie's Narragansett cousins.

She looked up at him, and he stared back at her like she had hit him over the head with a rock. "I may need you to go to them so they understand the timing," she said.

"Go to the Penobscot village?"

"You have been there with Daniel. They will recognize you. You paid them their due by the treaty, so the Sagamore will treat you well. They are fairer than our neighbors here."

She tried to keep the bitterness out of her voice, but she was captive in Jacob's house because he had helped convict her of something he knew she didn't do. And he would no doubt be rewarded with her farm for his deceit. Maybe that was the root cause of it. But it didn't matter anymore.

Jacob didn't matter anymore.

Only Daniel and escape mattered, and their baby.

"Maybe a diversion *is* what we need."

"Uh...it is?" Matthias gaped at her like she had sprouted a second head instead of agreeing with his earlier offer.

"I don't suppose you can light the constable's house on fire?"

His mouth gaped in horror. "People could be killed." His head was snapping from side to side. "I will not murder."

"Of course not." The last thing she wanted was for anyone else to be hurt. Too many had been hurt already. "But we need a diversion that will get Daniel out of the gaol."

He patted her head like she was a horse. "That could get Daniel killed if something goes wrong."

She sighed. He was right. "Well, what do you suggest, then?"

He let out a weak laugh. "I'm the one who knows how to stay out of trouble, remember? I have no talent for this."

Fine. He was right. She had the talent for trouble, and it was time to employ it for a good cause. The only cause in her life right now.

25

The constable led Daniel along the slushy path in the snow, through the crowd, to the small platform set up under the oak tree. The tree outside the meetinghouse suddenly seemed a very inappropriate place to hang people.

He kept his eyes on the constable's back, not meeting the gazes of his gathered neighbors.

Ruth should be far away by now. As long as she was safe, he could bear this.

His soul was as numb as his feet when they arrived at the oak. He looked at the rope hanging from a stout branch. The noose at the end of the rope. This would be over soon enough.

There was a stump in front of the platform to serve as a step, and the constable gestured for him to step up. His hands were tied behind his back, and he almost lost his balance when the stump wobbled, but the constable caught his arm and helped him stay upright. The small act of compassion underscored the general lack of compassion the community showed. It would rather kill its own than acknowledge its own role in its problems.

And yes, he had been part of that.

He turned to face the crowd but looked out over their heads. Ruth was out there somewhere. That idea made his heart both heavy and light at the same time. Or perhaps he had gone mad.

The minister stepped onto the platform beside him and began his sermon, extolling Daniel's sins to serve as a warning to others. The energy of the crowd grew more intense as the sermon reached its pitch.

In the distance, Daniel could see the Penobscot boy he had met.

News traveled.

When the minister wrapped up his sermon, Daniel's soul rebelled.

This was shite. They needed to know what they were doing was murder, not justice.

The crowd was silent, and the wind moaned through the naked branches of the trees.

The minister turned to him. "Save your eternal soul and confess."

Daniel's chin rose as he took in a deep breath to speak and be heard by all. "I submit to the law, but I do not confess. I have not committed witchcraft, nor has anyone else." Mentioning Ruth by name would only endanger her. "To show you that this is not justice, I shall do what witches cannot." He then launched into the Lord's prayer, as clear and loud as if he were leading a service on Sunday. "Only the Lord can decide if he forgives you for what you are about to do."

The minister blanched.

The crowd was silent for a moment, and then a murmur rose until it became a loud, indistinct buzz. Neighbors glanced at each other, whispering.

Someone in the back called out. "He can't be a witch. Someone get him down from there."

Daniel stood, breath steady, shoulders relaxed. He would still hang, no matter what doubt he sewed. But maybe someone in the crowd would think twice next time they were going to throw around accusations of witchcraft. That good, at least, might come from this travesty.

His eyes fell on Matthias standing in the front row, holding Daniel's horse. It was Matthias' horse now since he had sold him everything, so there was no reason he shouldn't make use of the horse, but the sight was jarring. And Matthias never stood at the front of any gathering.

Matthias glanced around at the crowd and then rested his eyes on his own shoes, covered in muddy snow.

"He has had his day in court." It was Jacob's voice. His parents should have named him Judas. "The court has decided his fate, and he cannot change the sentence with a last-minute stunt."

Jacob turned to Aldrich, who hesitated. Cook was there, too, and whispered something in Aldrich's ear.

Aldrich spoke. "Yes, he has had his day in court."

The minister stood at the edge of the platform, apparently unsure if he should stay or go.

Daniel looked back to Matthias and then to the person next to him. With everyone in winter cloaks and hoods pulled around their faces against the icy wind, he couldn't see who it was.

Then he could.

He stopped breathing. His heart stopped beating.

His eyes had to be deceiving him.

Between Matthias and Goody Carter stood Ruth. She was here. Not far away and heading to safety, but here in the lion's den.

He glanced at the crowd surrounding her. They didn't show any sign of recognition.

His eyes locked on to hers.

She smiled.

He wanted to scream at her to run. Get away. But drawing attention to her would be fatal. She shouldn't be here even if she had not escaped. She was sentenced to house arrest until she, too, could hang.

Another murmur swept through the crowd, starting at the back and making its way to the front.

Daniel looked to the back of the crowd. Something had to be happening back there to distract the mob.

A group of young Penobscot men had arrived.

"Good," one of them called, "you are assembled so we can speak to you all at once."

Everyone in the crowd began turning to their neighbor and whispering again.

He shouldn't welcome a delay to the inevitable, but a few more moments in Ruth's presence were worth it. His heart was ripping in two because she was not yet to safety, but surely his resourceful, trouble-making wife would find a way to get out.

He looked into her eyes. Willing her to feel the love he felt for her. She smiled at him, and that burst the dam in his chest and spilled tears down his cheeks.

"We are here to collect the corn you owe us."

Daniel's eyes snapped to the Penobscot men. That had been the Sagamore's voice.

"You will go to your homes and bring it here. Now." The Sagamore stood tall, imperious, and the men behind him tensed and pulled their muskets and axes to the ready.

"You cannot be serious." Jacob sounded like he was talking to an out-of-line child.

The Sagamore replied in the same tone. "I assure you, Jacob Turner, I am very serious."

Jacob started at the sound of his own name in the Sagamore's mouth.

Everyone in the crowd turned to the Sagamore. Their financial interests were suddenly more important than Daniel. Even the constable and the minister pushed closer to the Sagamore to see where this surprise would take them.

Daniel's jaw dropped when Matthias strode to the Sagamore and then turned to face the crowd. "The treaty says we owe the Penobscot a bushel of corn per family per year." His voice was tight. "I, for one, do not want to see a return to hostilities...."

A small hand touched Daniel's arm. Ruth was behind him, and after a few seconds, his hands were free.

He turned to her, but she gestured for silence and turned to the horse that was now right next to the platform. She shoved him toward the saddle.

He anchored his feet. He was not leaving.

"Get on so I can get on behind you," she hissed at him, shoving him at the horse.

He clamped his hand on her arm and dragged her behind him as he slid into the saddle. He was not letting her slip away from him.

"How—"

She flailed her hand at him to shut him up, then slid onto the horse's back behind the saddle. "Later. Head for the creek."

Her arms around his waist were warm, and his head spun, but he didn't dare disobey.

He turned the horse's head away from the direction of the Sagamore and the crowd's attention. The snow was well enough trampled here that their tracks wouldn't stand out.

The horse stepped politely along, and Daniel pulled Ruth's arms tighter. Her body merged into the back of his. Her heat rekindled his soul. He risked taking one of her hands and pressing his lips against it, hoping that one action conveyed to her all she meant to him.

She pressed harder against his back.

He looked forward. She seemed to have a plan, and he had to trust she had thought it through. He scanned the trees ahead and headed to the path at the edge of the woods that would take them to the creek.

Matthias had made sure not to leave any loose metal buckles to jingle on the horse, so they silently slipped away from the arguing crowd.

Then someone yelled. He risked a look back. Someone was cursing out the Sagamore. That wouldn't end well for them, nor should it, but it bought Daniel and Ruth more time.

Their slow pace had Daniel's stomach so tight he almost puked, but he didn't dare urge the horse faster because it would draw attention.

Ruth's body was tense against his back. No doubt their pace was killing her, too.

He could make out the path more distinctly now.

Then, a hound barked.

Cook's voice yelled. "Hey, he's getting away!"

He dug his heels into the mare's sides. She lunged forward, and Ruth slipped to one side behind him. He grabbed her arm and hauled her back to center.

The mare's hooves pounded the muddy slush, but his pulse pounded even louder in his own ears.

He steered the mare one-handed toward the path and prayed Aldrich hadn't ridden his stud to the hanging.

Ruth clung to Daniel as she was almost bounced off the horse with every stride the mare took. She pressed her face against his back to protect it as much as she could from the branches whipping by that grabbed at her hair and scratched at her skin.

The horse swerved around a bend in the trail, and she almost bounced off into a tree. Sitting behind the saddle was a terrible idea because it put her at the most unstable part of the horse. If they weren't running for their lives, she would have laughed at the absurdity of it. It was weird how the mind could latch onto a thing like that at a moment like this.

She risked a quick glance back.

A horse was galloping behind them and gaining. Her heart began to beat so hard against her ribs that they might crack.

Jacob.

"Daniel," she called in her husband's ear. "Faster."

He glanced back. "Shite."

Their horse was burdened with the weight of two people and could only stay ahead so long. Daniel urged the mare faster, and the rhythm of its hoof beats barely increased. The horse was already giving everything it had.

"Hold on," Daniel said, then reined the horse off the path suddenly and through a gap in the trees.

Her body slid until only her leg from her knee down was left on the far side of the horse's body. Daniel tried to catch her, steering the horse with one hand. Her arms were locked so tightly around Daniel's waist that she was probably squeezing the air right out of him.

Jacob swung his horse into the woods after them. He was gaining.

Her arms started to quiver from the strain of hanging on. She would not let go. They were too close.

Jacob turned his head for an instant, perhaps to see if he had help behind him. As he turned to face them again, he had straightened in his saddle just a fraction too much and couldn't duck beneath the next branch quickly enough. It caught him across the face and knocked him off his horse.

He landed with a thud, and his horse took the opportunity to turn back and head for home, leaving Jacob cursing in the muddy snow.

Daniel slowed the mare just enough to get Ruth centered on the horse again, headed back for the path, and urged the horse to its greatest speed.

Was someone following Jacob to help, and he had simply outpaced them? There was no way to know without stopping, which Daniel, wisely, was not doing.

No one was in sight, but that didn't mean they weren't on their trail. The sound of the horse's hooves and the gasping breath of both the horse and humans drowned out any sounds their pursuers might have been making and would make it easy to follow them, even without visual contact.

The path began to go downhill, which meant they were nearing the creek. The tilt pushed her up even closer to Daniel. His body's warmth sustained her.

"Hold on." Daniel leaned back into her as the horse tilted forward. Suddenly, its shoulders were far below its rump, pushing Ruth up so she was level with Daniel's head despite their height difference.

For the first time, she could see ahead of them. The horse was descending the steep bank to the icy creek. No one was in sight.

They weren't here.

Daniel pulled the mare to a halt and looked around. "Now what?"

He sounded calm. He didn't know what the plan was, so he didn't know there should be a group of Penobscots here to meet them. Now what, indeed. "Downstream." It was a guess. The Penobscot village was downstream.

Daniel steered the mare into the creek and headed her downstream. The water only came up to the mare's knees, but it slowed them to a walk. She looked over her shoulder again. No pursuers in sight. If they stayed in the creek and could get around the bend before anyone showed up, at least they wouldn't know which way they had gone.

It wasn't much. There were only two possibilities. But it was better than nothing.

The slower speed allowed them to all catch their breath, and the mare's hooves splashed into the water with each step blending into the rushing of the water over rocks.

It was eerily peaceful.

Daniel turned his head and spoke just loud enough for her to hear him over the water. "Are you alright?"

Her arse might never be alright again. "I'm fine, keep going." She squeezed her arms around him, and hopefully that would reassure him. Her body ached everywhere, but it would serve no purpose for him to worry about that. They had to keep going.

Daniel pulled the mare to a stop so suddenly that Ruth's nose slammed into his back. She didn't risk letting go of her grip on Daniel's waist to check if it was bleeding.

The muscles of Daniel's back had gone solid as a stone wall.

She peered around him to see why they had stopped.

In front of them, in the middle of the creek, stood the Penobscot man with the deep scar on his face. He held a hatchet at the ready.

"He is here for us." Which was obvious. Less obvious was whether that was a good thing or a bad thing.

Daniel kept the horse angled so that his own body shielded hers, and while his hands kept the horse from continuing forward, his legs on its sides kept it ready to spring into motion, and it shifted under them. Its sweat from the gallop soaked through Ruth's skirts despite the freezing air.

They stood like that, silently, Daniel and the man with the scar, eyeing each other.

The horse twitched its skin where the hem of Ruth's skirt must have brushed it. It felt like a keg of black power about to explode underneath them.

"Get off." The man gestured at them to hurry.

Daniel sat like a statue. "Forgive my hesitation, but with my wife's life at stake, I have to ask. Why should I trust you?"

It was lovely that he wanted to keep her safe, but he was being stubborn now. She started to swing her leg over the horse, but he stopped her.

The Penobscot man gave a small nod as if in approval. "You are a good man. You pay your debts." He gestured with his chin toward Ruth, leaning awkwardly from behind Daniel. "She has helped my sister and saved the Sagamore's father-in-law." He smiled a wry smile. "We owe *her* a debt of thanks."

Daniel still hesitated.

Ruth swatted him on the arm. "We have to go with him. Now." She swung her leg over the horse's rump, and Daniel grabbed her arm to keep her upright as she dropped into the water.

The ice-cold water shocked her into paralysis for a moment, but then Daniel swung his leg over the mare's neck and dropped down beside her. He turned to the Penobscot man. "Let her ride. She is with child."

The man shook his head. "No." He turned to the northern bank and gave a signal. Another man emerged from the trees. The man handed the reins to him, barked what sounded like orders to him, and the man swung up on the horse and took off.

Daniel's body twitched like he wanted to go after him and get his horse back.

The man held up his hand. "Too easy to track." He looked after the man retreating on horseback. "So he is leaving tracks." The man turned back to them and gestured to them to follow him in the opposite direction from the man who had taken Daniel's horse.

Her heart warmed, even as her fingers and toes froze. The Penobscot were putting themselves at risk for them. And most importantly, she had Daniel by her side. She reached for his hand.

Instead of taking her hand, Daniel wrapped his arm around her waist, supporting her weight as much as he could and pulling her to his side. His body heat warmed her.

Their rescuer set a brisk pace, and she struggled to keep up, but she pushed on and did her best not to slow them.

They were lucky that it hadn't snowed recently. That would be too easy to track. The week-old snow that lay on the ground was already full of tracks that might confuse pursuers.

On the fifteenth day, they came to a river. Ice had accumulated along the bank, but in the main current, it flowed freely.

Their guide headed south along the bank until he came to a bend in the river. Behind a pile of rocks was a small canoe.

Ruth groaned with relief.

Her legs could barely hold her up, and she had more blisters than skin on her feet now.

Daniel turned to her and wrapped his arms around her. "You can finally rest."

She burrowed her face into his chest.

The man with the scar, 'Pierre' as he had told them to call him, gestured for Daniel to join him in moving the canoe to the water.

The two of them lifted it over their heads to carry it the hundred feet to the water.

Pierre. Marie. The French had been far more successful in their diplomacy with the Penobscot than had the English. Which probably just meant they made an effort, which the English had not.

Just then, another man emerged from the woods. He was dressed differently than Pierre and was clearly not Penobscot.

Her heart pounded, and the distance between herself and the man was much less than the distance between herself and Daniel. He was too close. Should she yell to warn Daniel? Stay silent and not draw the man's attention?

The man was eyeing Daniel and Pierre and started to follow them.

"Daniel!"

All three men spun to face her.

She stared at the newcomer, only about twenty feet from her. He was thin, and his long hair was pulled back from his angular face.

Daniel tried to drop the canoe, but Pierre yelled at him.

The man turned to them.

Pierre called out to him.

The man acknowledged him.

She looked from one to the other and to Daniel, who had dropped his end of the canoe and grabbed a rock.

Pierre barked at him. "He is here to take you south."

Daniel froze. Ruth turned from one man to the next.

Pierre set his end of the canoe down and walked up to the new man, bringing Daniel along with him. "He will take you to Marie's cousin. He is Narragansett and knows the country."

Daniel strode to her side and put his arm possessively around her waist.

The new man smiled at them. "I will take you to our town. You will be safe." As if that should be enough for them to place their lives in his hands.

But they had come this far.

Pierre started to head back the way they had come.

"Wait," she called.

He stopped. "You are safe now. And it is good that you are out of our territory. I cannot say that the peace will last if your people don't pay what they owe."

Her chest constricted. "My brother...." He had risked everything to help them. She had to warn him.

"He paid. We will give him warning if he needs to go." And with that, he turned and walked away.

Daniel was sizing up the new man, who wasted no time in going to the canoe and looking it over to be sure it wasn't damaged when Daniel dropped his end.

"I'm sorry," Daniel said as he approached the canoe.

The man waved off his apology. "You were protecting your wife." He finished his inspection of the canoe, apparently satisfied. He turned back to Daniel. "Let us get underway." He gave Daniel a knowing smile. "I would like to return to my wife before she hunts me down."

Somehow, despite the cold and exhaustion, all three of them chuckled.

They maneuvered the canoe into the water, and Daniel steadied it as she climbed in.

She held the paddles as the men climbed in, the Narragansett man in front and Daniel behind her.

"Blankets. Wrap up. You will be too cold just sitting." Their new friend said over his shoulder.

She grabbed two blankets and wrapped them both around her.

Daniel leaned forward and nuzzled her neck. "We made it. We are past Boston." He kissed the soft skin under her ear and then straightened up to paddle.

The sound of the paddles dipping in and out of the water, pushing them further and further from danger, was a lullaby. They had miles to travel yet, but they were safe from pursuit now.

She pulled the blankets more tightly around herself, and the music of the water lulled her to sleep.

26

Narragansett Bay, Providence Colony, June 1680

Ruth lay on the blankets that made up their bed, and she tried to lift her hand to brush a stray strand of hair from her face, but her muscles quivered and protested until she gave up and let her hand fall back to the covers.

She became aware of Daniel's voice drifting from his side of the bed. No matter how hard she concentrated, she couldn't make out the words. Maybe he wasn't speaking in words.

She let her head drop to the side so she could see him. A rush of warmth filled her entire being. There he was, cooing to their tiny daughter, who lay sprawled across his chest. No wonder she hadn't been able to make out the words.

Her eyelids drifted shut, and she listened to them chattering away to each other as she drifted off again.

A voice called from outside the wigwam.

Her eyes snapped open. A month on the run through the woods, followed by months of hiding with Marie's Narragansett cousin, meant that she couldn't ever assume anything was safe, and she still hadn't heard from Matthias.

But they *were* safe. At least for the moment.

She looked at Daniel. He bent over and kissed her forehead, then lay their daughter on Ruth's chest.

"I'll see what it is." He stood from the blankets and stepped out the doorway.

A few seconds after he left, a shadow crossed the door. Her arms tightened around the baby, and she rolled to her side to shield the baby with her body.

Susanna. She exhaled, and her muscles unclenched. Susanna was the daughter of Marie's cousin and, with her mother, had attended Ruth in labor. She came to Ruth's side and ran her hand over the baby's fuzzy head, making exaggerated funny faces at her until she got a wide-eyed reaction from the baby.

No one seemed capable of retaining any dignitary when confronted with that sweet little face.

Susanna giggled, and Ruth had a moment to study her face. It was too gaunt. The war had been far harder on the Narragansett than on the English or the Penobscot, and yet here she was, taking in an English family on the run from the law simply because her mother's cousin asked her to. Both her husband and father had been killed in the war, and she moved in with her mother to give Ruth and Daniel her home so they could have a little privacy when she gave birth. They could never repay her.

Ruth braced one hand on the blanket while clinging to the baby with the other and tried to shove herself into a sitting position. Her guts felt like they had been rearranged, and every muscle screamed in protest.

"Let me," Susanna said, taking the baby onto her lap, and then, with one arm wrapped around the baby, she helped Ruth sit up with her free arm. Then she handed the baby back to Ruth so she could nurse.

"I now have far more compassion for my patients. This hurts."

"It does." Susanna reached for a rolled blanket to wedge around the baby to take some of her weight from Ruth's arm.

It brought immediate relief to the muscles that had been about to cramp. Her eyes drifted shut with relief.

"Be grateful she is tiny," said Susanna.

Susanna's surviving sons were enormous, and Ruth shuddered. A child as large as they must have been at birth would have killed her. Especially in the condition she was in when they arrived. Tears welled up in her eyes, and she had no power to stop them.

Then Daniel poked his head back in the door. He smiled, and her heart went all soft and warm. He came to her side and brushed the tears from her cheeks. He was so good to her. More tears spilled down her cheeks. She was too tired to stop them.

He bent his head toward her and kissed her right in front of Susanna, and that sent heat burning up her neck to her cheeks.

"The sachem just returned from Providence." Daniel was grinning.

Ruth clutched the baby so tightly to her she stopped nursing for a moment to let loose a wail of protest. Ruth forced her grip to loosen, and the baby quieted and resumed nursing. "Does he have news?" He had to have news. What else would make Daniel smile like that?

"Better." Now he was grinning like a boy with a big secret who was about to spill it because he didn't have the self-control to keep it to himself. Except he wasn't spilling it fast enough.

"What?" Only Susanna's presence prevented her from smacking Daniel's arm for keeping her in suspense.

Daniel smiled at Susanna and gave her a brief nod. She got up and went to the door. "He brought guests."

Guests? Did they have to give up their quarters? She tried to sit up straighter without disturbing the baby.

He laughed and gently pushed her back. "Guests for *us*."

She turned to the door as Susanna motioned a small group of people in.

"Matthias!" She almost dropped the baby, who had finished nursing and was starting to doze. She had been waiting so long for news from him, and here he was, standing right in front of her.

She looked behind him. His entire family was here.

"But how?"

Daniel sat down next to her and took the baby into his own arms, patted her on her back, and chuckled when she dribbled spit-up over his shoulder.

"We thought we might like to try out a warmer climate. Couldn't let you enjoy all the lovely weather." Matthias's clothes were filthy, and they all looked like they had been on the road for weeks. "We sold everything and came to see if you needed neighbors."

"What?" He couldn't be serious.

Anne came and took the baby from Daniel and started to rock her in her arms. They had come all this way. To stay.

"We are on the run, Matthias. You realize that?"

Matthias and Daniel exchanged glances. "Not anymore," Daniel said, putting his arm around her and pulling her close.

"Reverend Williams and the town selectmen say you may stay. And us, too."

"But—"

"No buts." Daniel kissed her on the forehead. "Providence colony won't recognize the conviction because they consider it persecution. We aren't running anymore."

But they still had nothing. They couldn't even rent a room, let alone make space for Matthias and his family.

"I need to start charging for doctoring." She turned to Daniel. "Are there people in Providence who will hire us?"

Daniel's smile sagged a bit. "We will find a way."

"You don't have to abandon your baby to run around doctoring people."

She whipped her head around and glared at her brother. He still didn't understand.

"We have to feed her. We can't live off the good will of the Narragansett forever. They are starving themselves, you oaf."

Matthias held up his hands as if in surrender. "That's not what I mean."

She stared at him. Daniel did the same.

They had been living in a safe little bubble, away from reality, but they couldn't stay much longer. They needed to stop living off the charity of others and start fending for themselves.

Matthias began to un-tuck his shirt and pull it up. He had lost his mind.

"What are you doing?" Ruth asked. But Anne didn't seem concerned as she smiled and cooed at the sleepy baby in her arms.

His ribs were wrapped in linen. "Did you break your ribs?" She sat up straight and tried to stand. "Let me look."

"I don't need your doctoring." He flailed a hand in her direction, and Daniel pulled her back into his arms. She wanted to elbow him in the gut and go to her brother, but she could barely raise her arm, and Daniel just pulled her closer while they both stared at Matthias. Maybe her brother really had gone daft.

He unwound the linen, and a bag fell to the dirt floor with a loud clank. He bent to pick it up and then stuffed his shirttails back into the waist of his trousers. His cheeks flushed. Susanna had ducked out the door to give them privacy. Or to get away from Ruth's unstable brother.

It was too much to take in, and she was too tired to make any sense of what was going on.

Matthias took the bag and pulled two additional pouches out of it. Perhaps it was just bags of bags.

He took one bag and handed it to Daniel, who took it. Daniel's brows were pulled so closely together that she almost laughed. He looked as bewildered as she felt.

"The Penobscot suggested it might be a good time to move on. So I sold your farm."

Ruth just stared at him. Daniel opened his mouth, closed it, and opened it again. He looked like a trout. A very handsome trout.

"How?" he finally said.

"Didn't get as much as it was worth, but a man from Boston was certain he would make his fortune with it." Matthias shrugged. "He bought mine, too."

Daniel weighed the bag in his hand and looked at Ruth. Her heart leapt. Could they buy their own land here? Could that even be possible?

Then Matthias took the other, smaller bag and held it in his hand. "I sold your farm to him, too." Matthias grinned. Matthias never grinned. "Jacob isn't happy."

Daniel reached for the bag, but Matthias put it in Ruth's hand.

"It's hers. So she never has to be dependent again."

She stared. Then, she burst into sobs that threatened to rip what was left of her guts into pieces. She tried to breathe but sobbed harder. Daniel stroked her back, and she just cried uglier. She cried until she was rung dry.

She gasped for air and collapsed against Daniel, burying her face in his chest. It wasn't hers, legally. But the gesture undid her. Her brother understood, after all.

Daniel stroked her hair, and she felt his lips kiss the top of her head.

After an awkward eternity, she gathered the strength to lift her head.

Matthias blushed like he wanted to crawl into a hole and hide from her emotional display. Anne, unconcerned, had turned to give them a little privacy.

She looked at Daniel and froze. He had tears on his cheeks. He never cried. She reached up and wiped them away.

"He's right. It's yours. You shouldn't ever have to rely on me or anyone else." His head hung.

But she did rely on him. Not for money—they had had none for months—or even for security. She relied on him. She just relied on him. For everything.

C haos reigned. Daniel tried to stay out of the way at bedtime. The baby had preferred the Narragansett wigwam where she was born and was adjusting slowly to their brand new farm on the bay. And she screeched her displeasure as Ruth tried to put her bed.

But the two of them had developed a ritual dance of sorts, and whenever Daniel tried to help, it disrupted the precarious timing. He was content to let Ruth dictate the evening rhythms in the house.

For all that the Narragansett had made them feel welcome, Daniel was grateful for the privacy here. He was pretty sure Ruth was, too, though Marie's cousin and her family had already visited twice and promised to continue to do so regularly, which they both encouraged with every ounce of their being. It felt good to be able to start repaying their hospitality.

Once they had their first crop, Daniel would find some way to convince them to take at least a few bushels of corn in belated rent for keeping them safe and fed for their first months in Providence Colony. They wouldn't have survived without them.

The wind howled just as loud off the ocean here as it had in Maine, but at least the temperature was a bit more moderate. And their new house was bright and sunny, and with Ruth's touches, it had become downright cozy.

He watched Ruth rock the cradle, and his heart felt soft and warm as she sang the baby to sleep.

He went around the house and made sure the shutters were fastened tight against the wind for the night.

Ruth was still singing, with occasional accompaniment from the baby, so he turned to his tools at the door. He lifted his tool belt and counted the nails he still had in its pocket. He would need to get more tomorrow from the smith in town.

The farm was in good repair for having been abandoned since the last year of the war, but he was earning a little extra money by helping the Nunezes, a family from New York, build a new room onto the house they had just bought. They were going to be bringing their rabbi to the community and wanted him to have some privacy until they were well enough established in their trading business that they could set him up in his own residence.

A year ago, he might have felt uncomfortable with all the diverse beliefs in Providence, but Ruth had taught him better. He counted the remaining nails.

Silence.

Already?

He looked up.

Ruth was looking at him, a little smile curling her lips up at the corners. He walked to her, avoiding the two floorboards that creaked.

He peeked into the cradle. The baby had her arm flung over her forehead like a dramatist, but her mouth hung open, and the tiniest of snores reached his ears. Given a few years, their daughter would be able to out-snore her Uncle Matthias.

Ruth put her hand over his mouth before he could get those words out.

He nodded to let her know he understood her directive. Don't talk and risk waking the baby. She removed her hand and replaced it with her lips. He would not groan. He would not groan.

He groaned.

They both stopped and held their breath.

He tried to make his heart beat more quietly.

A tiny snort and then more tiny snores.

They both exhaled.

She shook her head at him with an exaggerated frown.

He led her to the bed and sat her down. She was too light to make it squeak. This was the part of the evening ritual where he was permitted to participate.

He knelt down in front of her and removed her shoes. Then her stockings. Then her drawers. He got an unholy pleasure in seeing her in her dress without her drawers. And he had no inclination to question that.

He stood her up again and removed her dress and stays. He left her shift on. She would let him know when she was ready for anything further.

She then reached out and sat him down, performing the same ritual on him. As always, he was bared to her entirely when she was done. She had no qualms about gazing on him naked while she was still recovering from childbirth.

God, she was beautiful.

His cock stirred. Crap. He would need at least two hundred more nails, ten additional planks, and some new shingles to cover the section of the roof he had to raise.

His cock stirred again. It refused to be distracted by building supplies.

He pulled back the covers and sat her down, then swung her legs up so that she was lying on the bed. He climbed in next to her and pulled the covers around them both until they were in a snug little cocoon. At least he couldn't see her body now.

She pressed back against him.

And now he could feel the heat of her body pressed along his skin and her luscious arse pushed against his cock. He might die.

He shifted his hips away from her to ease the pressure.

She shifted her arse right back up against him.

"You're trying to kill me." He kept his voice so low he wasn't sure she heard him.

"I thought you deserved a return to marital relations since you have been so patient," she whispered back.

He froze. "Just because my cock was happy to see you does not mean I can't wait until you are more ready." He would never forgive himself if he hurt her.

"Let me rephrase. I'm trying to get you to give me *my* martial rights without having to drag you into court and sue you for them." She wriggled her arse against him.

Lord, help him. "Are you sure?"

She jolted upright in the bed, taking the covers with her, leaving him bare, cock poking up at the ceiling. She grabbed the hem of her shift and, in one move, pulled it up and over her head.

Then she leaned down over him, her face right next to his ear so she didn't wake the little tyrant. "You are kind, but you are a bit dense."

She grabbed his hand and drew it down between her legs, and her slick heat almost burned his fingers.

His brain went blank for a moment.

Then she moved her hips, and his world came back in a rush.

He pulled her shoulders down until their lips met. He pressed hers with his own, still afraid he would hurt her somehow.

She bit him in return, so he ran his hands up her sides and toward her breasts but didn't touch them. The baby was already popping her first tooth, and Daniel didn't want to cause her pain.

"Thank you," she said, her mouth brushing his ear. His pulse throbbed through his entire body, and it felt like his torso jolted off the bed with each slam of his heart. But he didn't know what to do next.

He tugged her ear to his lips. "I don't want to hurt you."

She kissed his ear. "I won't let you." She sat up, a smile on her face that made his stones throb.

She shifted herself until she was poised over his straining cock. He lay still, gazing at her face.

She looked down and grabbed him in her tiny hand.

Two hundred nails, ten planks, shingles.

For an instant, she hesitated, but before he could reach his hand to her, she impaled herself on him, and her heat around him stole every thought from his head except 'don't move'.

He lay rigid. Every muscle in his body screamed to rock hard into her, but she was in control here, and he would not hurt her, even if it killed him, which seemed likely at that instant.

She groaned.

He moved.

He couldn't help it. His hips pushed up against her, and she threw back her head and started moving her body against his, rocking with increasing intensity.

He kept pushing against her as she took her own pleasure, rocking frantically now, breasts swaying with every move.

His spine started to tingle down to his balls, and just then, she let out a loud groan, and he pulled her to him and quieted her with his own lips as she came apart around him. He lost all control then and shot his seed into her as she collapsed down on his chest.

He held her so tight he was probably bruising her, but he couldn't let go. Her body still gave little after-shocks. His heart was going to burst at any moment.

His life was unrecognizable since the end of the war because this woman had turned it upside down. Thank heavens.

She nuzzled his ear. "I've missed you."

They drifted to sleep, and the baby let them lie in peace for almost three hours.

They woke for Ruth to feed her, and after Ruth had tucked the baby back in, she curled against him and lay in his arms until her rhythmic breaths lulled them both back to sleep.

When the sun began to glow with the new day, Ruth fed the baby again. Daniel stroked Ruth's cheek when the baby's contented gurgles quieted, and she smiled at him and said, "I suppose we should be good, productive citizens and get out of bed."

He took the baby from her and lay her down in her cradle, tucking her blanket around her and kissing her new tuft of silky hair.

Then he turned and crawled back into bed with Ruth and pulled her against him, letting the heat from her body warm his soul.

The world could wait.

Did you enjoy this book?

Please help other readers find this book by leaving a review on Amazon or Goodreads, or anywhere else you leave reviews. That is the primary way most readers find books and is an immense help to both readers and authors. Thank you!

To find out about upcoming books, you can sign up for my newsletter at LizzieJenks.com/newsletter/ and learn more about me and my writing at LizzieJenks.com.

Author's Note

As both a historian and a descendant of Puritan New Englanders who lived in the next town over from Salem, the topic of Puritan witchcraft has been part of my life for as long as I can remember. The Salem trials are a powerful illustration of how a mob mentality and stresses from recent wars could trigger accusations. Being a daughter and granddaughter of ministers, I have also seen how hard it is for clergy to rein in the actions of people who misconstrue their message and use it to justify abhorrent things.

There is little evidence that Puritans consciously used witchcraft accusations to control women, but there is extensive evidence that they used it subconsciously for that purpose. Imagine being accused of witchcraft and having to defend yourself against an accusation that you burned down a barn by somehow making a great blue flame emanate from a horse's backside? We know today that farts are flammable, but they didn't know it then. One of the Salem witches was convicted, in part, on exactly that flaming horse fart! Do not place a lit pipe or other incendiary device near a horse's backside. They are flatulent beasts.

I did give Ruth, and even Daniel, sensibilities that are more accessible to modern readers. They are steeped in Puritan beliefs, and certainly some Puritans did not believe in witchcraft, but not believing in witchcraft was legal grounds for suspicion of witchcraft, so it was a pretty dicey defense. There is not much evidence that puritans saw strong-willed widows accused of witchcraft as being persecuted. They thought widows should be protected, but what they meant by that was their sons or a male head of house should control the widow's financial, moral, and legal existence.

We moderns also have a hard time understanding the dread a woman might have of becoming domestic help under the laws and mores of the time. Women in a wilderness setting might have the opportunity for some upward mobility, but legally, they were under the thumb of the male head of house who could do pretty much whatever he wanted to her and had complete control of her fate.

It is also worth noting that men were legally responsible for any acts or financial obligations of the women in their household. That is part of why widows were a "problem". If they had no son, they were in legal limbo. To give a sense of this in action, there is a legal case of a woman who was accused, convicted, and fined for physical abuse to her husband. Her husband was responsible for paying that fine. This was a very rare instance of the man coming out worse for the legal principle, but it illustrates the lack of legal standing or autonomy of Puritan women.

Most Puritans also had very problematic relationships with Native Americans. More often than not, they thought Native Americans were in league with the Devil. Needless to say, this illustrates Puritan religious beliefs and bigotry and not anything about Native Americans. Europeans generally conflated religion and culture and race, so even Native Americans who converted to Christianity were treated as less than and always suspect.

But Native Americans did have political power. The treaty I reference in the book with the Penobscot did exist and came about essentially as I describe it in the story. The treaty called for a peck of corn from each family, not a bushel. But for those who know the difference (four pecks to the bushel), one peck felt like insufficient motivation for a modern reader to believe the obstinate refusal.

In reality, only one English colonist paid the corn owed in the treaty. And when the Penobscot had had enough the English in Maine not abiding by the treaty, they gave that one man early warning and safe passage out of the area as the Penobscot sided with the French in the next war. They exhibited far more fairness and justice than their English neighbors did.

It would be stretching the point to say that many Native Americans and English became friends, but many certainly entered into mutually beneficial relationships. Humans are humans, and just as that makes group affiliations and animosities inevitable, it also means that many are going to overcome those animosities and learn to respect and appreciate one another, as Ruth and Marie did in the story.

And in case anyone was confused by Boston making treaties for Maine, it may be helpful to know Maine was part of Massachusetts at that time, so Boston was its capital, too.

Here are a few of the historical works I consulted while writing this book in case you want to dig further into any of the topics the story covers.

- Hall, David D. *Witch-Hunting in Seventeenth-Century New England: a documentary history, 1638-1693*. 2nd ed. Boston: Northeastern University Press, Boston, 1999.

- Karlsen, Carol F. *The Devil in the Shape of a Woman: witchcraft in colonial New England*. New York: WW Norton & Company, 1998.

- Pulsifer, Jenny Hale. "'Dark Cloud Rising in the East': Indian Sovereignty and the Coming of King William's War in New England," *The New England Quarterly* 80, no. 4 (2007): 588-613. This article can be accessed via JSTOR.

- Romeo, Emily C.K. *The Virtuous and Violent Women of Seventeenth-Century Massachusetts*. Boston: University of Massachusetts Press, 2020.

About the Author

Lizzie Jenks has always loved stories. This led her to spend many years in graduate school, engrossed in the tumultuous realities of American history. It also led her to spend her down-time devouring romance novels about Vikings and Highlanders, but she couldn't find enough romance novels set in the eras she was studying.

American history is too ripe with heart-pounding tales of adventure and passion to let that stand! So she has set out to write the novels she couldn't find and to help her readers discover the delicious secret lives that have been locked away for far too long.

Lizzie writes steamy historical romance about strong women and the men who earn their love.

Connect with Lizzie by signing up for her newsletter at LizzieJenks.com/newsletter/ and on Social Media.

Instagram: @LizzieJenksWriter
Twitter/X: @LizzieJenksBook
Facebook: Lizzie Jenks Author

Made in United States
North Haven, CT
28 April 2024